HILLS OF COTABATO

HILLS OF COTABATO

BY

MARC SCHIFFMAN

Penmorepress.com

CHAPTER 1

Eddie Finn's home in Kigali, Rwanda faced the eastern slope of Nyarugenge Hill, with its steep rolling hills and evergreen patches of farmland. A soft, blue pallor covered the land, and the sun burned away the morning haze, revealing a cloudless day. In the early morning, on a Thursday in April, Finn stood on the tiled terrace. He drank coffee from a ceramic mug, smelled the yellow daylilies and spotted a red-billed fire finch in the branches of a jacaranda tree. The noisy hadada ibis bird that woke him most mornings with its repetitive chirps—which exasperated Jocelyn, the woman who maintained the lodging—was oddly quiet.

"Don't go out into the street today," Jocelyn warned from the doorway.

"Why?" Finn asked.

"With President Juvenal Habyarimana's plane shot from the sky, the presidential guard and the Interahamwe boys have a blood campaign against the Tutsis and all who get in their way. All they want to do is kill. This Hutu regime wants to eradicate the Tutsis. Their machetes are running with Tutsi blood."

"I'll be fine."

"Don't be cavalier, Mr. Finn. If you get in the way of the Interahamwe, they'll hack you to death."

Finn ruminated how Rwanda could be inundated in chaos when nature was serene in this enclave. Each morning, he savored the fragrant banana trees and hibiscus that flourished in the garden. He thought of Marta Davide, who had risen hours earlier, the sensuous fragrance of her skin that no soap and water could displace, nor the memory as she stepped naked out of bed, her stride languid as she walked toward the window to stare out onto the breathless night.

"Do you think the bird is aware of the racket it makes?" Finn asked.

"Indeed, he is. Listen, sir, I'm your friend. Stay here. Better yet, leave Rwanda. All you need to do is listen to the radio. The Interahamwe are on a rampage in Kigali. Save yourself."

"The majority of the American Embassy families have already been evacuated, but I have to stay on. An embassy representative is needed. I'm more worried about you."

Jocelyn stepped up beside Finn, her bare, black Tutsi feet small and courtly, compared to his own. Finn always perceived the voice of reason from Jocelyn, and her companionship gave him pause to analyze with objectivity and not the vitriol that systematically coursed within him and regulated his decision-making process. He had been reading Buddhist scripture lately, and he recalled a passage he had read the other night from The Noble Eightfold Path, which stated that ego did not exist, because nothing can belong to ego, so one can accept the world with its diverse manifestations. As he treasured the flora in the yard, this concept made sense to him. Yet, events in Kigali in recent days had shown him that ego was intertwined with vengeance and avarice. Jocelyn's arm brushed his elbow, and Finn predicted he would feel the gift of serenity that resonated from within her. But she was aloof this morning, oppressed with thoughts she could not contain and that overwhelmed her aura.

"And what of your family in Byumba?" Finn asked. "Have you spoken to them?"

"There's no word."

"Are the Interahamwe at your village?"

"Most likely. I'll be leaving this morning to check on everyone."

Finn emptied his coffee into the grass. "It's too dicey to go there, Jocelyn. I'll always take care of you and your family."

"You silly man. Thank you. But I need to see them."

A grey hue suffused her eyes, and her respiration grew shallow, with the unimaginable only yards away from their Kigali doorstep and spreading hundreds of miles into the countryside.

*****

On his way to the American Embassy the streets were unoccupied, but a palpable electric current haunted the scenery. The blanched houses had the same stark reserve of a French village. He sighted armed military men on rooftops, a UNICEF jeep at a petrol station, a scorched Toyota truck with three corpses near its wheels, and buildings pockmarked by gunfire. He paused at a red light, though there were no cars on the road, and heard screams. They may have been young or old Tutsi Rwandans. A group of women led by armed men were marched to a grocery store and told to sit on a pile of bodies. With clubs, the men belted the dead and dying underneath the women as they pleaded for their lives. After the light changed, and Finn depressed the accelerator, he gazed into his rearview mirror as the men turned their clubs on the women.

Finn parked his Saab on the shoulder of Avenue de la Gendarmerie. In front of Century Movie Theater, with the marquee, *True Romance*, a new checkpoint had been erected, barring Finn's access to the American Embassy. After locking the car door, he readjusted his necktie and hitched his satchel over his shoulder. Halfway toward the barrier, he halted. Four Rwandan UN soldiers were sprawled, bootless, on the pavement. Ears had been severed; yawning slashes had opened their necks, with numerous wounds on their chests. Two faces had been nearly halved, fracturing their skulls.

Finn's shoes stuck to the pavement from the dried blood. He decided to walk around the Rwandan UN soldiers. From the barrier, military men, presumably the presidential guard, watched him with curiosity. They were trim and muscular, and Finn speculated whether his probability of survival would have been stronger if he had stepped over the bodies instead of making this detour, as if claiming a ribbon of bravery. He approached the barrier, his leather shoes clashing against the pavement with each footfall. 'You don't axe a white bureaucrat to death,' Finn thought. 'What's to be gained?' Then he saw the speck of brain matter on the top of his shoe, and he realized human logic had flown, days ago, as he passed a dead child sitting against a mailbox, her intestines resting in her lap like a tiny animal.

A pre-teen girl held a Kalashnikov at waist level. Finn pondered how boys and girls could be molded into killers to mutilate and murder. But he knew in the genome of youth burned the inferno, the toggle switch, which once snapped on, creates a loyal cadre. To dominate them, all one needs is to supply the pinprick of hate, either from class, race or income disparity, and these child followers, believing in the manufactured savior, will kill with the tenet that they follow a pathway to a prosperous life.

At the checkpoint, the man in charge, Solomon, asked for Finn's identification. Finn recalled Solomon from the embassy compound, hired as a technician. He showed Solomon his American Embassy identification card. Two men, on either side of Solomon, scrutinized the perimeter, their automatic weapons swinging on cloth belts. Close to his hip, the pre-teen girl probed the side of Finn's face.

Solomon examined the list on his clipboard. "You should be careful on the streets, Mr. Finn. We're in the nucleus of a coup. In this hysteria, passersby get abducted as we weed out these Tutsis traitors."

"I'll watch myself."

"To be honest, you're on your own outside the embassy walls. As you can see, the streets are lawless."

"Who's on that list?" Finn asked.

"The Tutsis cockroaches that need to be liquidated. Your name isn't here," Solomon said with a gap-toothed smile. He spoke with a seductive cadence that enchanted women, or so Marta Davide, the American Embassy's communication specialist, had once commented.

"Are you going home after your day at the office?" Solomon asked.

"Definitely."

"I suggest you don't leave the embassy. At dusk, the streets will be hazardous, and a decent-looking man like yourself may come face-to-face with a soldier who finds your white face abhorrent."

Solomon pointed at Finn's shoes and spoke in Kinyarwanda with a sarcastic inflection to his collaborators. "*Mugire amahoro*," Solomon said, which Finn interpreted as *Go with God*. The soldiers laughed.

"And is that Tutsi whore still a servant at your residence, Mr. Finn?"

"Miss Jocelyn is the proprietor, Sergeant Solomon."

"I like it when you call me Sergeant. It makes me feel part of your American military club."

For the first time since President Juvenal Habyarimana's plane crash, fear roosted in Finn's heart. Solomon's hand clinched his shoulder muscle, and Finn received a sexual charge from his fingers. His grip was more potent and threatening than the

Kalashnikov lodged against his spine. Finn sighed, and Solomon augmented his clamp on the tendons. Briskly, Finn slammed his forearm up against Solomon's wrist, breaking his hold. Solomon winked his approval.

With a laid-back gait, a presidential guard marched a man in the street, hitting him on his kidneys and buttocks with the flat of his machete, leaving bloody patterns on his clothing. They walked within yards of Finn and Solomon. "I can tell you're a Burundi fan," the guard said. "I'm overjoyed to rid my country of Burundi football fans like you. You should all drown in a stinking cesspool."

Every few seconds the machete walloped the man, causing spittle to dribble from his mouth.

"Your friend Marta is inside the embassy," Solomon said. "She's made of carbon steel. She's Hutu stock." Solomon returned Finn's identification card. "I bet she'd be an effective member of the presidential guard. She's stronger than you. She recognizes evil's stature in the world."

"Do you think it's possible to rid the world of evil?" Finn asked. But given the circumstance, the Tutsis falling under the swings of machetes, his question bordered on lunacy.

"Evil is here to stay," Solomon said in a monotone voice, as if speaking to a novice apostolic. "It will never vanish as long as countries like yours manipulate power."

"I don't share your pessimism, Sergeant."

Solomon wagged his head. "You deserve your rank as an embassy inspector. It suits you."

"And why is that?"

"You think your actions have decisive consequences when all you're doing is cooking up discontent."

"You're way off base."

"Not at all. I've learned domination is cyclical, and right now I'm surfing the swell, and it's moving into your hemisphere—the disintegration of white governments. Don't deny it. We live in a globe of color with the white man dictating to the black man under the camouflage of democracy."

"That's a sinister view of life."

"Perhaps," Solomon said, "but I've seen your type come and go. A civil servant who winds up in his country cowering under a blanket."

"I'm not that whimpering toad," Finn said. "But some day persecution may come to your front door."

Solomon's face took on a glossy sheen from the harsh morning light. "You think you're superior, and this belief is the catalyst which will send you into a hut one morning to meet a happy machete."

"That day is far off."

"Smarten up. Who do you think you are? Superman? No one gets out alive."

Finn glanced at his Saab. His lips were dry, and he felt claustrophobic without a departure stratagem.

"We'll take care of your car," Solomon said. "It'll be here for you after you clock out."

Solomon gestured toward the two soldiers, who allowed Finn to cross the barricade. The girl's automatic weapon butted Finn's spinal column. As he passed a hissing cat, the sweltering climate anchored a glare on the building ahead, causing the warped American Embassy windows to reflect the silvery silhouette of a body swinging from a metal lamppost.

*****

Finn walked the embassy's third-floor hallway as radios broadcasted daily events from almost every office. He listened from one of the doorways. Names of those to be killed were read on air. It disclosed that countless bodies of Tutsis were being thrown into rivers.

"We are sending them to Ethiopia," the journalist stated. "Even Rwandan priests and nuns are required to kill Tutsis, including those who seek refuge in churches. Since the colonization from the late 19th to the mid-20th century, the German and Belgian colonial nobility manufactured a native elite in the Tutsis. Beginning with the first school for Tutsis in 1917, Hutus were denied education, and as a result of this denial of access, the Hutu became slaves to the Tutsi who, according to the colonial legend, were born to rule.

"We Hutus, have been subjugated as slaves to the Inkotanyi Tutsi regime for far too long. We want freedom. Tutsis have discriminated against Hutus in the colonial educational system, in government, in social welfare programs.

"Listen to me; solutions are not provided by foreigners. White people have abandoned us, as expected. If you rely on them, you end up eating garbage. Counting on white people for help, on their lies about this or that is a waste of time. They only care about their interests. Rwandans have learned their history and are saying no to a repetition of history. The removal of the Tutsis is the only way to break out of an historical cycle of discrimination and oppression."

Finn entered Marta Davide's office. On the muted television screen, a church burned against a cerulean sky. She stood, sifting among the pile of dispatches dated April 14, 1994, which had arrived in the morning mail from various towns and cities in the country. A gold cross swayed against her ebony skin.

"It says that in Byumba the Interahamwe soldiers may have killed a Spanish priest, Joaquin Valmajo," Marta said, her tapered fingers on the desk. "The UN peacekeepers will be driving to

Byumba. We should go. We can't show weakness in front of the Hutu regime."

"Ten Belgian soldiers were killed yesterday by the Interahamwe," Finn said. "This revolution has nothing to do with weakness. From a political standpoint, it's about saving one's ass."

"You mean one's white ass," Marta said.

"That seems about right," Finn replied.

Already countries were buttoning up shop in Rwanda, sporting blinders and speaking political babble, as thousands perished in cities, fields, homes, schools and savannas. At night, the moon appeared transposed, bereft at the blood-soaked Rwandan fields.

"We have to be proactive," Marta said.

"I'll go to Byumba," Finn said.

Marta slapped his cheek—so hard his ear rang. "We're a team, Eddie. And you'll need a Hutu woman to bail you out when trouble comes, which it will."

"We'll join the next expedition of UN peacekeepers. Wear their banners and be part of the convoy. Then we'll skip into Byumba."

"A decent plan. I have a friend at the UN. I'll give her a call and see if we can catch a ride with them. But I doubt they'll let us go to Byumba."

"Let me handle that," Finn said.

A naturalized American citizen, Marta had lived for years in Rwanda with her grandmother, and was fluent in Kinyarwanda, the national language. She was wide-shouldered and slim-hipped, wore her wiry hair in loose cornrows and sported burgundy beaded earrings that matched her lipstick. Her nails were unpainted, and when she spoke her eyes crinkled in the corners, as if transmitting an encrypted communique. Finn regularly labored to decipher the message, but he could only paraphrase its context, leaving him perplexed and enthralled with her beauty. Gunfire erupted from the street.

Finn peeked out the window. "I can't see a thing. It's probably near the checkpoint."

"Solomon," Marta said, positioned beside him, shaking her head.

She was almost equal to him in height. The air conditioners blasted cool air, but even Marta's cherry blossom perfume could not erase the stench of decaying human flesh that drifted from the Kigali streets into the American compound.

Lorraine, Marta's assistant, scurried into the office. She spoke in careful English. "I just got word. We stay the night. People are being slaughtered in the city. I'll make arrangements."

For two days, Finn dispatched his daily obligations without ambition. As a Security Investigator, his routine consisted of research into the use of counterfeit documents and undercover residences to unmask human trafficking. But the havoc, excluding the embassy grounds, based the Kigali districts in an antediluvian era that rattled any person of common sense.

He picked up his office phone and dialed his residence, expecting Jocelyn to answer. There had been no reply to his telephone messages on the answering machine. He could not envision her situation in Byumba. Frustrated, he took the stairs to the carpool pen. In an authoritative voice, he informed the caretaker, Jules, that he needed transportation.

"Not today," Jules said, seated on a bench, rotating his hamburger.

"I want a car," Finn said.

"You just told me, and I told you to take a flying leap. I'm not sending a car out in those streets to be hijacked and for your sorry ass to be carved up and used for dog food. How about a bicycle?"

A corrugated steel overhang insulated the cars, those in use and in need of restoration, from the sun. Standing fans circulated the muggy air. One mechanic drained a radiator.

"Do you have any horseradish?" Jules asked. "It's one of the culinary American sauces I fancy."

"What are you talking about?"

Jules bit into the hamburger. Finn recalled his Buddhist text, which taught that to foil ego, one should assist those with rudimentary needs. "Hold on," Finn said. "I have Beaver Deli Horseradish in my office. Let's bargain. Horseradish for a car."

"You're joking," said Jules.

"I'm being sincere. What do you want for a car?"

"It's too awful a day to get out of joint. So, bugger off."

"How about this one?" Finn indicated a vehicle with a UN insignia.

"That's a jeep. Say, Cedric, what's the status on those wheels?"

The mechanic, squat, with a bulbous nose and scarred cheeks, cleaned his hands on a dirty rag.

"Fit and ready," Cedric said. "But it's committed to a UN peacekeeper."

"What's his name?" Finn asked.

"Ivan somebody," Cedric said. "He's Swedish, I think, with the look of an albino. Wouldn't you say, Jules?"

"You can practically see the blood pumping in his veins," Jules said. "Do all Swedes have such sickly coloring?"

"He's the only Swede I've met."

"I once met a Finnish dude who never ate fish. He preferred fowl. He left Rwanda due to salmonella poisoning. You could practically see through the guy by the time he boarded the plane."

"Then why are Scandinavian women built like brick shit houses?" Cedric asked.

Jules raised his thumb and crooned melodically, "Under my thumb. They rule."

"No wonder those Nordic guys are ghostlike," Cedric said. "Wilting under all that feminine trauma."

"I bet they're all like that Swede, Ivan. Fairy men with a Mr. Magoo delivery. *'Gee, you Rwandans speak good English.'*"

Jules and Cedric laughed. Finn sized up the UN jeep. "I'll call this Ivan," he said, "and get in touch with you."

"Yes, do that," Jules said. "And don't forget the horseradish sauce."

Finn spoke with Invar Bjorklund, Swedish UN peacekeeper who agreed to take both Marta and him on tomorrow's outing north, which was scheduled to depart at six a.m. In the morning, when Finn met Invar at the car pen, he was precisely as Jules had portrayed him, a gaunt man with a creamy countenance and a round face that befitted a postulant nun rather than a groomed peacekeeper.

Sitting on the hood, Cedric pulled the jeep's ignition key from his shirt pocket. "Going my way?" he asked.

The convoy consisted of two trucks and a jeep. All three had UN insignia, as if this made the convoy invincible and gave them a pass to travel to any region in the country. Cedric wore aviator sunglasses, a 'Led Zeppelin 1968' black T-shirt, and an imitation Rolex wristwatch. Invar took the front seat, with Finn and Marta in the rear. As they journeyed north, eucalyptus trees shone against High Sierra peaks, and heat shimmers rose from the two-lane road.

Near Murambi, a checkpoint had been established, and three militiamen signaled the convoy to the side of the road. One militiaman strolled up to each truck and was given the same information: this is a UN convoy and should not be prevented from its objective. With each response, the militiaman saluted in medieval homage, told the operator to stick around, and within earshot, spat on the asphalt. At the jeep, he beheld Marta in her maroon blouse and the white-shell earrings that contrasted with her black features, and said, "Boss, I'm thirsty."

"I've got what ails you," Marta said with a dazzling smile. She fished into her knapsack and showed the neck of a whiskey bottle. "And if you let the trucks go, two packs of American cigarettes." She held the Marlboros before her chin.

The militiaman beamed and said, "Happy trails."

He took the whiskey and cigarettes and allowed the convoy past the checkpoint. Cedric gunned the engine, and the crew ignored the two dead men in the ravine. That evening, they holed up in a clapboard farmhouse, ate chicken sandwiches for dinner with tepid Urwagwa, a local liquor made of crushed bananas, and slept in bed rolls. During the night, lightning flashed, the expanse ragged in a misty rain as the breeze contained the blistered remnants of a recent wildfire that had despoiled nearby hills.

Near three a.m., Finn heard wailing. He stepped onto the porch and glided back in time to his Merchant Marine days. At sixteen, he had fled from his father's abusive control, a border patrol officer in Tecate, Baja California—his sole parent, who had spent his free time in bowling alleys and in striking Finn with his hands when he botched a chore. Using a fake ID, he was confirmed as an ordinary seaman in the Merchant Marine. He had zero knowledge of ships, and after a week of sickness, disorientation and fantasies of mermaids, he adjusted to the tempo of the sea and the contours of the ship, *Norwalk Victory.*

The austere Rwandan topography kept him at sea, a tether to those months on the *Norwalk Victory*, where he'd learned to handle perilous waters and personal threats that oftentimes ended in fistfights, which he usually lost. It was his ferocity that bonded him with the other seamen. Nowadays, the memory of the seascape kept him balanced, and to maintain this inner equilibrium, he would remember how the ship's engines initially had made sleep in his bunk intolerable, and later became a white noise of respite from the day's toil.

In the morning, on the road curving parallel to the forest, he wondered whether he would find Jocelyn in her home village of Byumba. Her predicament weighed on his mind. The convoy was a hundred yards in front. Hidden in savannah grass, an antelope cantered across the road, wavered, and dashed into the bush. Cedric tugged the steering wheel, and the jeep hit a pothole and fishtailed, marooning itself against an ikawa tree.

Shaken, the four disembarked. The air was overripe, due to the vegetation and the remnants of a hog, eaten to its skeletal carcass. As Cedric popped the jeep's trunk for the jack and the spare tire, Marta meandered onto a sunny trail. Finn called out a warning, but she defied him with a backward flip of her hand, as though she were strolling in paradise. Minutes later, Finn tracked her to a cluster of African redwood trees. She was on one knee taking photographs of a naked dead girl. The fractured bones of her chest, where she had been clubbed, pierced her skin.

Looking closely, Marta said, "She has no eyes."

But Marta could not have spoken those words, because Finn remembered the girl's eyes, open and blank. The dead, he discovered over time, are smooth operators. The body twitched, and a palm viper slithered out from the girl's waist, darted between Marta's legs and into the underbrush. Bewildered, Marta stumbled and toppled on top of the girl, dropping her camera. Finn picked her off the corpse. As she weaved haphazardly from side-to-side, Finn recorded her chagrin. A thimble-size bone jutted out from Marta's shoulder. Finn took her elbow, steadied it against his ribs, extracted the bone and tossed it away. He guided Marta to the jeep.

Glancing toward Cedric, who stood with Invar, peeing in overgrown vegetation, Finn shouted, "Where's the village?"

Cedric answered, "Two kilometers north."

In the front seat, Marta gasped, gazing at the wound and the line of blood dripping over her forearm. From the medical kit, Finn applied Betadine, butterfly stitches, and a gauze pad.

"Maybe you should stay with the convoy," Finn said.

"I'm going to Byumba. I'm responsible for the Spanish priest, Father Valmajo."

"This is just a village inspection."

"Try and stop me," Marta said, fiercely.

With the jeep's tire repaired, they drove north on an unlined asphalt road that protruded from decades of tropical weather. The sun had bleached the road the color of maize. In the countryside, crops had been sheared to the root's stem and farm plows discarded. On the outskirts of Byumba, house doors dangled from busted hinges. They parked in front of the post office on the northeast side of town. Marta went to the local schoolhouse to unearth the whereabouts of Father Valmajo.

Cedric and Finn strayed into an arid field where they witnessed the mutilated bodies of men, women, and children murdered with bayonets, knives, and machetes. The bodies lay where they had fallen. Some had been trucked over and cast into pits. As Finn circumvented an elderly man with a bullet hole in his face, he practically tripped over Jocelyn. It was the grey in her hair that had stirred a remembrance. A worm wriggled in the wound at her throat. Her upper lip was split, and dirt coated her ears. Her earrings and rings had been stolen. There were teeth marks on her cheek, and Pharaoh ants crept over her naked breasts.

Finn attempted to see the devolving milieu from Jocelyn's viewpoint: the exodus of thousands of Rwandans to foreign shores, the forgotten dead and the molested women and children. At an uprooted bush, a foot stuck out of the ground, and bloodied spears were propped against the wall of a hut. He swayed from one side to the other, as though he were on the prow of the *Norwalk Victory*, stunned at a rose-red sea after the slaughter of whales. He could not stop that butchery and now had been unable to prevent Jocelyn's death. He fondled her brow. An action he had never done in life. He fixed a handkerchief over her face that barely hid her throat. 'Safe unto heaven,' Finn thought bitterly.

Cedric sniffed vapor from a glue stick into each nostril. He offered it to Finn who accepted. "Now you're one of us," Cedric said, "like the homeless of Butare."

Cedric etched the sign of the cross against the sky and walked toward an acacia tree. Halfway up a hill, Finn glimpsed figures at the tree line. Whether they were scavengers, soldiers or poltergeists he could not determine. He had the inclination to holler, like one on a deserted island. Placing the glue to his nostril, Finn inhaled until he choked. He doubled over, sucking air into his lungs. Regaining his self-control, he looked uncomprehendingly at two sandaled black feet, close to his own. Three slaps on his shoulder blades further allayed his seizure. Finn straightened and took in the woman's tattered blood-stained meringue dress.

"Who are you?" he asked.

She pointed with her black arm at the countryside. "My village. I ran away with my daughter. She's hiding in the forest."

"Come with us," Finn said. "I know a retreat where no one will violate you."

"This is the way of my country," she said in a meek voice, the corners of her mouth pleated in thin lines. "Are you with the United Nations?"

"I am."

"I didn't know the United Nations would just let us die. We were always listening on the radio how they were here to help us. But when the killers said we were going to die what did the UN do? Their consulate became a fortress against Tutsis."

Finn wished to steer the conversation to another topic, but all that greeted him as he screened the meadow were mass graves. "Where will you go?" he asked.

"My sister's village. Life may be safer in her village. But I don't know."

"There must be another choice."

"Don't fool yourself, mister. We live the life we're given."

Finn led her and her daughter to the red brick church. On the steps, the mother and daughter halted, shivering, observing the jagged holes from grenades and, without a word, walked toward town. The priest who had handed over Tutsi parishioners to the Hutu militia had fled. Inside, below a statue of the Virgin Mary were shelves of personal effects from the missing and the dead. Finn attentively reviewed the items—ticking wristwatches, an amulet, a bloodied silk scarf, nylon purses, wallets with photographs of people smiling, close-knit groups with arms around waists of friends and family members. With a fingertip he nudged the corner of an envelope and saw his name written in elegant script, E. Finn. He took the envelope from the shelf, sat on a pew where sunshine flowed through a damaged window, and read the letter.

Dear Eddie,

I sit in the church at night with people crying. The Coleman lantern is the only light. I took a car ride with a neighbor to Byumba who dropped me in the middle of town. There were no birds. The dead were in the streets, the fields, in houses, hung upside down in trees.

I walked to the school to get my son, Turgen, but he wasn't there. All the children were elsewhere, and the school building had been demolished and maybe blown up with a grenade.

I found my sister Florence at a neighbors' house. She told me her husband and his parents were dead, killed in the family home. Before long the Interahamwe showed up and took us to a field. Florence and I started to pray. In the middle of the prayer, we escaped and the killers took after us. Somehow, we got separated, and I fell into a ditch that had been dug to throw the bodies of slain Tutsis, and this is where the Interahamwe found me. I was taken out of the ditch and raped by multiple men. I don't know why they would want an old woman like me but men like this do not care how young or old a woman is. They are not human. Two other men took my sister, Flo, and raped her, and I have not seen her since.

The ranking officer, Gakuru, a policeman from my village, socked me in the face. He told the other militiamen to reduce my height because I had always been arrogant. This is how he and my neighbors always viewed me. These men used bats and hurt my legs. My ankle is badly sprained. When they hunted for other Tutsis, I went to the church for protection.

Luck shined on me. Turgen and my niece were in the church. But I could hear the Interahamwe assembling in the yard. I thought if I picked one child, we had a chance to survive. I look at my son and niece and they are beautiful. I couldn't manage both because of my bad ankle. My heart told me to pick one, and I did.

I limped to the church door with Turgen, and many other people began running, too. We opened the doors and fled. The militiamen were on the steps, and I fell. I put my body over my son. All the while people were falling on top of me, many layers, and then the militiamen started killing those on top with their machetes. They killed the first layer, the second layer and finally the third. As they were swinging their machetes and bayonets people's blood fell on us. I confess I was so thirsty I drank the blood that dripped into my mouth.

When the men came to my layer, a militiaman said, "This one is already dead." He stripped off my shirt and wristwatch. I woke in the night and tottered into the church because I could hear the militiamen close by. My son is missing. But I know he is alive because otherwise his body would have been close to mine.

I wish I could remember a quotation from the Bible. This way I could tell you the degree of loss I feel. But I am not that smart. I expect death to come soon, and when I die who is going to take care of my son? Who will be his guardian angel? Maybe you, Eddie.

In the church there are dead bodies. They rot in the heat. I wish I could say that I am not scared, but I would not be human if I said that. Things are terrible here. Who will forgive these men? Without forgiveness, my country will dissolve in this blood mania. If I live, I will try to forgive these men, because there is nothing I can do to bring back my family.

A part of me prays you do not receive this letter. This way I know you have left Rwanda and are living.

Jocelyn

Finn inserted the letter into the envelope. He would search for Turgen, and if he located the boy, he'd find one of Jocelyn's relatives. He was incapable of fatherhood. After all, he'd had meager contact with his own daughter for the last three years. Beyond the window, the towering sky highlighted the scenic mountains, and if one preferred, they could fall into the trap that this inner church sanctum was a fabrication, and the native setting reflected the true contours of the country. He let his mind reside in this rustic fantasy. But the illusion was fleeting, for the church was a charnel house. He laid a hand on his thigh to quiet his legs' unbridled jitters. Invar, the UN peacekeeper, ambled up to Finn, his face ashen.

"How's it going?" Invar asked.

"Getting by," Finn said. "And you?"

"When I entered the church, the dead bodies were stacked one on top of the other. It takes a lot of strength to carry a body. I didn't know that." He mopped his brow with his hand. "We're too late. Too late, Eddie. We should have had the capability to stop this."

"If you say so," Finn said.

Invar stared straight ahead, as if scouting for an edict to bring a quota of professionalism to the bloodshed. Instead, he plodded toward the church doors with the attitude that the sunlight could revitalize him. On the brick atrium, Invar looked east and then west, deciding which way to proceed, and, indicating neither direction, remained stiff as a mannequin. Finn placed the letter in his shirt pocket.

He exited the church, passed Invar, and took the gravel trail cushioned with jimson weed and newborn daisies. Browning foliage layered the hillsides, and Finn overlooked the corpses in the poorly dug trenches. He sat in the shade of the acacia tree with Cedric, who offered Finn his water bottle. Locals walked respectfully around the pair, due to the belief that the UN process existed. He watched Hutu government militiamen patrol the same track with machetes, automatic weapons dangling at their hips, and a pout that bespoke of a petulance that went unpacified.

A militiaman and a villager with a befuddled brow faced off in the grass. The militiaman flattened his hand against the man's chest.

"What's your name?" he asked the villager in a friendly manner.

The man trembled.

"Your name," the militiaman requested.

"Paul Disi."

"Are you from Byumba?"

"Yes."

"Is your family home near us?"

Wrinkles mapped his wizened face. The militiaman was shorter, thinner, and younger than him, and his army fatigues had been laundered. Disi shoved the militiaman's hand away and canvassed the area for assistance.

"Let me help you find your family, Paul," the militiaman said.

"No, thank you."

"I can help. This was once my village, too."

"I don't remember you."

"I'm sure you or a friend took a job that was once mine," the militiaman said in a tolerant voice. "But that's ancient history."

Two seasoned militiamen assembled behind Disi. They were joking, reveling in the story they told one another. Finn overheard their exchange. "Like a paralyzed monkey. You should have seen her. Her eyes were bigger than the moon. She fell lickety-split. Like slicing a green banana. Her body bent one way and her head fell the other way."

As if they had rehearsed this act, each militiaman selected one of Disi's elbows and carried him toward a weather-beaten barn. Disi wiggled his shoulders, begging for an explanation. Finn jogged onto the path after Disi. The well-groomed militiaman presented his palm like a guard at a school intersection, preventing

Finn from advancing. There wasn't another UN peacekeeper within two hundred yards. All matters of cooperation left the militiaman's face. The dead would be nameless for days to come, and Finn understood that once the UN peacekeepers hopscotched to another sector, the Tutsis would be susceptible, and the militia's Hutu machetes would re-start their bloody whirlwind.

Finn gestured at Paul Disi. "I want to speak to him."

"Speak to me."

"He has the answers I need."

"We have to interview him about his activities in the village. When we're done, he's all yours."

Paul Disi receded over a ridge. "I guess that's that," Finn said.

"You UN folks are refined people. You catch on fast."

"Yes, we recognize degenerate motherfuckers when we see them."

With the militiaman's pistol unholstered, Finn retreated until he came to a ditch. He intended to take in each facet of the militiaman, his uniform, the sun-dried creases on his face, the scar that arced from the corner of his mouth to the middle of his chin, the chili, coriander and peanut butter on his shirt collar. But the pistol garnered the majority of his attention. It was a six-shot revolver, and Finn's concern amplified. He kept his arms by his sides and resisted smiling. Smiling prey always find a grisly end.

"He's UN," Cedric said, standing alongside Finn. "An American."

"American. Dutch, English, French, German. I don't care about nationality. Did you hear what he called me?"

"No," Cedric said. "But you have important things to do with your time rather than create an incident for you and your family."

The militiaman froze. It was as though retribution had a name, and a nationality, and could desecrate anyone's household. No one in Rwanda wanted the familial curse of genocide, Tutsi or Hutu. "Did you hear what he called me?" the militiaman repeated.

"He's on drugs," Cedric said.

"We all should be smoking hashish. It brings civility." The militiaman spat on Finn's trousers. "He insulted me."

"He's an idiot," Cedric said.

"The asshole is an idiot, certainly," the militiaman replied.

"I'm a what?" Finn asked.

Cedric threw Finn into the ditch, pinning him on the wet grass. A deceased woman lay a foot away. Her body had begun putrefaction, the internal organs decaying, inflating her body. To impede the militiaman, Cedric raised a fist and holding off the blow to the last possible second, he peeked over his shoulder and spied the militiaman stalking a hill, the revolver holstered.

Cedric rose to his feet. "Let's go."

Finn sat up. Aware of the decomposing woman and his fortunate escape, Finn admitted his fault—the use of caustic humor to fight off episodes of alienation, adulation and depression. But these scraps of personality portrayed snippets of the man. He took the woman's hands and set them below her breasts. "May the road rise up to meet you," Finn said quietly. The words brought him tranquility. But that promptly waned as the woman's bodily fluids seeped into his shirt and her odious gases impelled him from the ditch. On their way to the church, Finn's feet were cold and flies nose-dived around him, landing on his neck and cheeks. He fell into a full-out sprint, barreling up the path, his endorphins ravaged, his mind a chasm except for the last image of Jocelyn and her slit throat, indicting the memory of his inability to defend her.

Days later, Finn's narrative to his superiors told of the UN's and the United States failure to safeguard the Tutsi people. The evacuation of UN troops and United States personnel was an act of cowardice, Finn wrote. The UN peacekeepers were ineffective and paralyzed and demonstrated no authority to exact change in Rwanda.

One example, Finn chronicled, unfolded at a technical school in the capital Kigali where UN troops were guarding two thousand Tutsis. The soldiers were authorized to abandon the school to help evacuate white outlanders. As the soldiers withdrew from the school grounds, groups of Tutsis rushed their vehicles, clinging to the doors in a futile effort to stop the troops from leaving. Some Tutsis begged for the soldiers to kill them because a bullet would be bearable compared to death by machete. The soldiers fired into the sky to drive the refugees away. Seeking asylum, the Tutsis raced across the city toward UN headquarters and the United States compound, whose gateway was barred and manned by armed soldiers. Both groups were intercepted by the Hutu militia and diverted to a gravel pit. There, the two thousand Tutsis were murdered.

Subsequently, Finn was ousted from Rwanda and posted, for the second time, to the American Embassy in the Philippines, where he knew the South China Sea cushioned the islands in a saintly haze.

CHAPTER 2

"I was chosen," Marta Davide said, "to make changes in the southern provinces."

"The Philippines isn't like your three-year posting in Bangkok," Lorraine said. "The risks in the south are legitimate, as they were in Rwanda, and the Muslim terrorists aren't pushovers."

"After two months at the American Embassy in Manila, my progress has been nominal," Marta granted, "but things will be different tonight."

They sat at a table at the Marriott Hotel in Manila beside the screened veranda, where twilight obscured the faces of people on the street. Lorraine, her former assistant in Kigali, was now the American Embassy Minister-Council's associate. A wind descended, marginally muting the jeepneys, buses and cars on Newport Boulevard and the vendors roasting meat, grilling *isaw*— chicken intestines—and cooking pork adobo in aluminum pots.

"I'm elated to be working with you again," Lorraine said. "Your communication skills are the reason the Minister-Council requested you." She picked up a burning cigarette in the ashtray, inhaled, and blew a wreath of smoke at the ceiling. "And your motley qualifications were a plus." She let out a short, bemused cough. "Motley. I read that word in a Toni Morrison novel. It means..."

"I know what it means. I'm a cosmopolitan bitch from divergent cultures. I was educated in the States and lived for years in the Philippines and Rwanda. My grandmother was Rwandan and her husband Filipino. My mother was born in the Philippines, in Pasay. Her husband, my father, was American, a black man from North Carolina, who dumped her once she got pregnant." Marta laughed. "So goes the veracity of men."

They drank mojitos, and the mint sprig gave Marta a measure of anticipation.

"Why did you decide to meet Captain Fuentes here?" Lorraine asked.

"The hotel has private security. Two armed men with shotguns guard the entrance."

"There are no safe precincts in Manila," Lorraine cautioned. "A few blocks east, people are living in shacks and mothers are raising their children in mouse-infested alleyways. Holdups are common. And don't wear jewelry. You'll be an easy pigeon."

"Quiet yourself, Lorraine. *Guceceka*."

Upon leaving Rwanda during the genocide, Marta began to lose her Kinyarwanda vocabulary. In Bangkok, as an embassy office worker, she strove to master the Thai language, but the five tones proved arduous, where a single word can have five contrary meanings. She longed to speak Kinyarwanda to Lorraine, but Lorraine had become accustomed to English, with a sprinkling of Tagalog. She dreaded the day when Kinyarwanda, the graceful language of her grandmother, bypassed all recollection. Then she would be left with English, its hard consonants and abrasive sentence structure culling her dreams into a singular, geometric landscape. When she was a child in the Philippines, she had memorized her mother's tongue, Tagalog, and her relatives' dialects —Illocano and Waray. Recently, her dreams had a fluttering of

Tagalog and Philippine vistas. In sleep, she attained comfort in this newfound commonwealth.

"The dope dealers often wander over from Tondo, like that guy," Lorraine said, gesturing at a sockless man in worn shoes, jeans and a threadbare Midnight Rambler t-shirt, who loitered near the hotel. "The cops are killing the dealers without a warrant. No arrest. The victim doesn't have to be a drug dealer. He can be a guy the cops don't like or someone who hasn't paid his dues. The graft is over the top."

"Honey, after three years away from Rwanda you shouldn't be so stressed."

"Captain Fuentes wants contraband from the Americans. That's why he contacted us. The Minister-Counselor sent you to determine how we can coordinate with the police and military and address the issues in the southern provinces. But corruption is everywhere, so nothing is guaranteed."

"It never is."

"You're even darker than before, and more beautiful," Lorraine said with a scintilla of venom. She looked at her plump belly. "Stay away from Philippine food. You'll only get fat like me."

Marta recognized Fuentes in the veranda's glass. On their third telephone conversation, they had discussed physical descriptions in preparation for this evening's meeting. He was a solid half hour late, a reasonable lapse since he adhered to Filipino time.

Lorraine raised her arm. "Here he comes."

At the table, Lorraine introduced Fuentes, departed, and took a stool at the bar. The waiter approached.

"Porterhouse medium-rare, home fries and salad," Fuentes said, without taking a menu. "And a double Chivas with a single ice cube."

"I'll have the same minus the Chivas, and I'd like my steak well done," Marta said.

The waiter smiled in a feminine way at Fuentes.

"I'm delighted to meet you in person," Marta said.

"You underestimated yourself over the phone," Fuentes said. "You're quite attractive. Statuesque. I like my women with a bit of height."

'My women,' Marta thought, 'and a steel pike in your eye.'

Fuentes's Chivas appeared in a snifter glass.

"I know our discussions are preliminary," Marta said, "but I do want to say that my government is interested in an amicable resolution to the dissension in the southern provinces."

Fuentes consumed his whiskey in two swallows. "*Masarap*," he said, running his tongue over his upper lip.

"Captain Fuentes, I want order rebuilt in the southern provinces and for the Abu Sayyaf to give up their weapons."

"As do I."

"Answer me. Can you stop the killings and kidnappings in the south? Is your power that influential?"

"I have leverage with these insurgents in the southern provinces. I'm their brother-in-arms. But zealots are difficult to predict."

"Unless you're a zealot yourself. Then you'd fit into the clan."

"Trying to get rise out of me, Miss Marta?"

"You are a member of the militia," she said. "Zealotry is in your groundwater."

"You're an endearing girl to have a meal with." He smiled. "I see a rewarding partnership ahead."

Fuentes wore a silk shirt known as a *barong*, closed at the collar and falling past the beltline, gabardine pants, loafers and a garnet gemstone ring complemented by an Omega watch. His teeth were well cared for, and his facial contours gave him the portrayal of an aged magazine model, glassy-eyed and jowl heavy. Sweat had formed at his armpits, and his cologne emitted a fruity odor.

"Are you Muslim?" Marta asked.

"I'm whatever the job requires. But I was born Catholic."

A bar boy brought Fuentes another double-whiskey.

"Have you ever been married?" Fuentes asked.

"Once. It was a disaster."

"I have a lovely wife and three children. Speak about your marriage. I want to get to know you. This way our negotiations can have a fruitful outcome."

Marta sipped her mojito and allowed herself this access into Fuentes's cordial graces.

"My father was in the American military, and I lived for years with my mother in the Philippines."

"Do you speak our language?"

"I do. After university in the States, I returned to the Philippines and lived with my mom. I was twenty-three, and she thought I should get married. She arranged a meeting with a son from the Tantacan family."

"I know that family. They pay their help slave wages and drive expensive cars. Rumors are rampant they traffic in dope. But they are only rumors."

Dinner arrived, and Marta carved her steak in half. She winced at the medium rare beef and piled the home fries into a tidy pyramid.

"On our third date, we had dinner at an expensive restaurant and in the car, he said he'd take me to my house—but he didn't. Even when we entered the hotel's parking slot with curtains on either side of us, I never doubted him."

"Oh," Fuentes said. "A love hotel."

"It was only when he closed the door that I became suspicious. In the room, he told me to take off my clothes. I said no, and he punched me. I didn't know what to do. He pulled apart my clothes and tied me to the bed."

"He's an awful man," Fuentes said, popping an artichoke into his mouth.

"I didn't resist," Marta said.

"Pardon me?"

"He was to be my husband, so I didn't fight or yell or do all those things the movies and magazines say a girl should do."

"That is a common reaction, Miss Marta."

"If that happened today, I'd slice him up. Leave him with no nose or manhood."

The porterhouse blood on her plate darkened. Since Rwanda, she was of two principalities, the one where she stipulated that all meat and fowl be cooked well done, kissing the teeth of burnt. However, violence didn't repulse her. She had stored it in a personal cosmos, where she could nuke the emotion to smithereens, if needed.

With his knife, Fuentes sawed off chunks from the porterhouse. Marta ate her salad and fries.

"Is the food not delicious?" Fuentes asked.

"The steak is too rich for me," Marta said. "Where does your family live, Captain?"

"In Valenzuela, northern Manila. We have a house and a yard with papaya trees."

"Why not in the southern provinces?"

"I need to look after my family. Life is cheap in the south. There are warlords, literally, like those in the feudal ages, where in certain locales a man has ultimate say over life and death. If you print a negative word in the newspaper, you'll end up compost in the jungle."

"How did you become the contact for the southern provinces, Captain Fuentes?"

"I'm engaged by the Philippine militia, and I'm sent to Mindanao and other southern islands for a variety of reasons. Most importantly, I deliver on my word to the Muslim terrorists. I also have relatives in Mindanao with major league friends."

"The other day, I stopped by a Muslim facility in Manila where they have education classes. The people were busy. They were even organizing a blood drive."

"There are over one hundred thousand Muslims in Manila. They are Filipino, plain and simple."

"And why is the south so hostile?"

Fuentes wiped his mouth with the napkin. "In the south, the Muslims are the majority. Historically, religious separatists expect to procure their own township. The Jews fight for the state of Israel. No anomaly there, really. Every few years the Philippine government complies, in theory, to allow Muslims in the south to draft their own constitution, impose their own tax system and other laws. Then the provisions blow up. There's a beheading, which I believe a Rwandan girl like yourself is well versed in, or the kidnapping of tourists, or an assault on a village occupied by the Philippine military. Or some such tragedy. And poof. Negotiations up in smoke."

"Thanks for the history lesson, but I know all that." Marta paid by credit card, leaving peso notes as a tip. "Is there any specific information you can give me how cohesion can be achieved in these southern provinces?" She wolfed down her food while he spoke.

"Simply, the Moro Islamic Liberation Front group doesn't get on well with the Abu Sayyaf. The Sayyaf is the most radical of the Islamic terrorists in the southern Philippines. Last year the Moros were helping the Philippine military pursue the Abu Sayyaf gunmen responsible for the beheading of a Canadian prisoner in Sulu. As you can see, either group squeezing for independence of a Muslim majority in the south is a precarious business."

"Then how can we reduce the violence in the south?"

Fuentes stuffed two toothpicks into his pocket. "If you still have an appetite, Miss Marta, I know a vendor with the best halo-halo in the city. Follow me. I see there is more to discuss."

On Roxas Boulevard, amid the clamor of street vendors and traffic, neither spoke. At a crosswalk, Marta thought Fuentes was inclined to take her arm. To dissuade him, she kept her hands in her skirt pockets to eliminate any sexual advance. His military posture, stern vertebral column, mirrored the photographs her mother kept of her father in his American Air Force uniform.

At Intramuros, they stopped at a concrete wall, dwarfed by the branches of a lamio tree.

"Philippine history has outlasted turbulent times," Fuentes said.

He jerked a thumb at the sizeable acreage behind the wall that preserves churches, universities, houses and government buildings. Intramuros, a 17th century enclosure of fifty streets, had been devastated during WWII and reconstructed, but still retained the Spanish architecture with its stone slabs and bastions.

"I know the history of Intramuros," Marta said. "My uncles and aunts were killed inside the grounds when the Japanese sieged the country in 1942."

"Your family were loyalists." Fuentes wrinkled his nose at the diesel and the polluted waters of Manila Bay across the boulevard. "If you omit Jollibee's, and the other fast-food joints with their ugly neon and let your mind wander, you can practically see the way the shore was four hundred years ago. Majestic, with traders selling all brands of merchandise and the sea water pristine."

"I can do that. My grandmother told me I had special abilities. In the evenings, in Kigali, sunbirds would talk to me."

"You are a talented woman," Fuentes said, as Marta sidled to the curb.

Traffic whirred by her, and orioles traversed the face of the moon. Within her imagination, she teleported to a distant time where Spanish galleon ships weighed anchor in Manila Bay and the sailors traded silver for Indonesian spices and Philippine textiles. On the wharf, in clay pots, exotic plants of tamarind, avocado, guava, papaya and pineapple were sold to local farmers. Soldiers in hanging sleeves, knee-length baggy trousers and rapiers bargained at the seaside markets, and vendors hawked indigenous wares. Marta gravitated to this era where allegiance and faith were inseparable, and the enemy was as distinct as the bowsprit sail on the galleons. Behind her, against the evening sky, cathedral spires shone in spotlight. College students exited Intramuros from one of the universities, gossiping in Tagalog. On the other side of the street, half-naked boys, lounging on the parapet, jumped into Manila Bay. Marta could hear them laughing.

Fuentes jockeyed to her side, and said, "We have to do all we can to preserve our country from the Americans, the Chinese, the Muslim terrorists. We can imprison the sex vacationist, but what do you do with terrorists who kidnap and kill the innocent? What did they do in Rwanda?"

"Nothing. We never saw it coming."

"But we have time here," Fuentes said. "But only if we act decisively. We need to cloak ourselves in disguise like the vampire *tiyanak*. We'll take the form of a child in the jungle. When the terrorists come, we'll revert to our former selves and let our claws and fangs devour them."

"Vampires?" Marta asked. "Really?"

"I'm talking symbolically."

His fetid breath reminded her of Kigali, and how the dead lay unburied for days in the city heat until carted off to a cemetery or incinerated in crematoriums. The crematorium soot stained each day's activities, so that it was easy to imagine the dead being sprinkled onto one's Corn Flakes.

"Do you know about revolution?" Fuentes asked.

"Too well."

"For us to succeed we must use treachery, a key element in any revolution. In order for a militia to destroy its enemy they need to adopt new warfare strategies. Delude the opposing forces. Create a phony story and support it with bits of legitimacy. Propaganda is your brother-in-arms. It sways public opinion. That is how we destabilize the terrorists by developing a seductive scenario. And once timetables are finalized, tyrannize the troops with an iron fist. This is how you subjugate the oppressor."

"You make it seem simple."

"The plot has its loopholes. Yet, it's worthwhile. I have already discussed this strategy with Lito Gregorio. He's a devoted Abu Sayyaf commander in Cotabato. I've told him only the benefits for him and his militant cronies, and a gambit to alleviate warfare. You'll meet him soon. But have no fear. He prefers young boys."

"I need specifics about the process in order to conduct an agreement for the southern provinces," Marta insisted.

"I'll tell you in a week." He kissed her neck and Marta cringed. "You remind me of a jade vine. They are rare and expensive flowers."

Fuentes went south on Roxas Boulevard, and she presumed that he aspired to make them cohorts. Fraternal twins, it occurred to her. She had read that, from thousands of miles apart, twins can intuitively know when the other is in jeopardy.

Marta crossed the road, dodging cars that honked at her—a crazed woman daring to be impaled on a bumper. On a dead-end lane, a beggar lounged, half-asleep on cardboard, in front of a railing, and Marta dropped peso coins into his plastic cup. In response, he adjusted his dirt-stained trousers. He could have been any age. Street living had obliterated the calculation of years. She sat on the parapet, as the rail-thin boys in Manila Bay splashed each other, their faces glistening in the moonlight. On his feet, the beggar nodded his head as if listening to a heavenly seraph, and Marta queried which domain, the beggar's or the boys', possessed the more relevant forecast.

She could not take her eyes off the beggar, as the boys frolicked, shouting in the background. In her mind's eye, she had seen this beggar before, perhaps panhandling at the love hotel where her ex-husband had cinched her to the bed like chattel. It was possible the beggar had been transplanted from a far-flung era to this juncture for an errand not yet known. As her thoughts circled, she captured a last-minute snapshot of the beggar staggering toward the road, his cardboard mattress hanging over the railing.

*****

Richard Rudolph pulled aside the second-floor window curtain and stared at Ifugao Street. It was late afternoon in the Barrio Barretto, as girls walked to the bars, employed as bartenders, waitresses, hostesses and dancers. The sky, a grey dome, confined the high humidity. Rudolph had been standing for an hour. The pimp was sure to come by. His niece had been AWOL for days from the bar, Shenanigans, and word from the street grapevine was the pimp had a bounty for the girl's recovery. His niece told him she had slept with the pimp. "She's a lonely lady. And she buys me chocolate."

'Love for sale,' Rudolph thought. 'Now, time to spit-roast her.'

From the bed, his niece used the television push-button control, searching for a program. She wore shorts and a blouse with the word Esmerelda on the front.

"Why don't you leave well enough alone?" she asked.

"If I did, Meryl, your aunt would murder me. Then where would I be?"

"In the same situation, Uncle. A fat man who can't go home 'cause his marriage is on the rocks. Aunt Carmelita is angry at you. She saw you at the massage on Mendoza Street."

"You know nothing of it. Hush your mouth."

"Don't worry," the girl said in a pleasant voice. "No one loves you."

Meryl was sixteen and petite for her age. Her face had been sullied by a bootleg whitening cream. He had raised her with the ideology to be a polite young woman who could upgrade herself with the education he had paid for and the groceries and housing he supplied to her and her mother, a housemaid. He professed that his deficiencies had somehow been engendered in the girl.

Before he could bark a response, he saw the pimp on the street, hauling a bag of snacks. She was a solid two-hundred pounds, medium height, with leathery arms and bovine calves that suited a rugby player. With the window ajar, Rudolph listened to her volatile wheezing. Dressed in a beltless magenta dress, she carried an umbrella to shield her from the sun. Sweat dripped from her hairline. The seed of frenzy expanded in his belly, identical to the internal intoxication he had experienced in the Vietnam War as a sniper.

After a failed mission, he had been warned about his dereliction of duty. Hours earlier, he had lain prone in the sawgrass on a hillside in Vinh Loc. He'd clicked off the rifle's safety and tempered his inhalations. As he sighted the Viet Cong troll through the rifle scope, one on a drawn-out roster on the U.S. government hit list, he tactfully finessed his index finger around the trigger, since he preferred a hair-trigger that called for only three pounds of pressure.

He fired and the bullet bore into a lorry tire. He had not purposely missed. For a past reckoning, Rudolph suspected, a *devas,* a Buddhist spirit guide, had blinded him. Ruled by muscle memory, he discharged the spent shell and slipped the second round into the chamber even though he could not see. The sawgrass tickled his chin, and the tropical sun scorched his buttocks, as it arced westerly over the mangrove swamps, swaths of jungle, villages, invisible anti-personnel mines—toe poppers and Bouncing Bettys—and napalmed plantations transfigured into moonscapes. Rudolph prayed. A Catholic scripture and then a Buddhist benediction. But it was only when he ejected the round from the chamber that he regained his vision.

Once Rudolph disembarked from the helicopter at Da Nang Airfield, he quaffed four Tiger beers within ten minutes and, anxious the beers might dull his wits in front of the captain, he swallowed two Benzedrine tabs. Twenty minutes later, as his heart began to pulse to The Rolling Stones's *Jumping Jack Flash,* he smoked a Thai stick joint with Sergeant Wolfe, who had forty-eight hours before rotating to the States. Wolfe had been on a binge for a week, with the apprehension blues gnawing at his paranoid machinations. Wolfe wanted out of Vietnam, the wet that stuck in his fatigues and nostrils, the bugs that inhabited nearly every device and human crevice, the killing and the army hierarchy, who still formulated a winning solution to the war. In the head, Wolfe had peed blood for ten days. Antibiotics were inconsequential. The medical personnel called it a poor-ass justification for a medical discharge. Nonetheless, Rudolph saw Vietnam digging her depraved claws into Wolfe's bladder. And, Rudolph conceded, the only thing in store for Wolfe in the States was guzzling Altes beers on the stoops of Detroit's crumbling shanty towns and factories, unemployment and a boxed-up rage that might erupt at any time inside a Zipperheads bodega.

"I have toe crud," Wolfe said, sitting up on the cot and showing Rudolph his naked feet. "Man, raw meat couldn't look worse."

"I'll give you two to three odds those toes fall off before you're out of here," Rudolph said, exhaling the sweet Thai stick smoke.

"You're a warm, fuzzy, snow bunny, Rudolph. Go fuck yourself and pass that doobie over here." Wolfe inhaled. "Quality shit."

"Didn't you used to feed the big cats at Binder Park Zoo in Battle Creek, Michigan?"

"That was another epoch, man. I was just trying to make some bucks and go to technical college, only to end up in this primeval forest."

"Hey," Rudolph said, pulverizing a mosquito against his knee, "hide those monsters before I wig out." The Benzedrine incited Rudolph's manic swings at the mosquitoes inside the wood-wall hut. "Say, what shoe size do you take, Wolfie? Twelve, thirteen? Nah, I bet those puppies are a perfect fourteen. Back home you can wear Italian leather or Keds and never have to lace up another pair of combat boots for the rest of your life. Just don't get a job on a factory floor 'cause then you're neck deep in the grunt life and you'll lose your shit fast as hell."

Wolfe passed the joint. "Thanks for the pep talk. You're a pal," he said. "Now go blow yourself."

At 1600 hours, Rudolph expounded to his superior officer on the assassination debacle. He recited the military lip jargon for the fugazi, and the instant he transitioned into his personal vernacular, he knew he was fucked.

"It wasn't cool, Captain Pemberwell," Rudolph said, standing at attention. "I had the gook in my crosshairs, and I swear I was gonna pop him one in the skull, so his comrade pals would know you don't screw with the U.S. military, 'cause tomorrow it could be your head being shredded by an SR-25. I see you know where I'm coming from, Sir. We're on the same wavelength. Zeroed in. And everything was going as programed. Scarcely a flurry of discord. My nuts resting comfortably in my new boxers—a present from an old flame—without a worry of the yellow sac spider getting to my revered sack. I was buttoned up. No openings, Sir."

"Captain," Rudolph said, his posture leisurely dissolving. "I had him six feet under. Then I felt a reptile on my leg. But I didn't terminate. I had my training. I was stone-man. Boom-down, cool. However, I couldn't get the idea out of my brain that it might be a coral snake or a king cobra or a red river krait. Well, you get the idea. When I fired, the snake bit me. The bullet flew, and I blasted a soldier's kneecap. Then I skedaddled out of there and made it to base on a Bell Sioux Huey that should be in mothballs. The contraption practically disintegrated mid-air. No fucking lie, Sir."

"So," Captain Pemberwell said, eyeing his coffee mug emblazoned with the seal of the 25th Infantry Division, "how long before you kick the bucket?"

"Pardon me?"

"The snake, Corporal. They're poisonous. How many hours before you dee-dee out of this crapshoot?"

Rudolph grinned. "I lucked out. Not poisonous."

"But I am, Corporal," the captain said in a scholarly voice. "I'm submitting the paperwork for a dishonorable."

"You can try," Rudolph said, belligerently, "but I have a stellar record."

"That sleazeball had to go, and you fouled up, Rudolph. I'm done with your insolence. Get out of here."

"I didn't foul up. I eliminated all the distractions, the screaming birds, a girl being raped on an oil drum. Locked on, man. Locked on I was, Captain, Sir."

"Get your dogface out of my tent, Corporal."

"Who are you calling a dog?"

Rudolph's knuckles rotated so they would connect hard and fast, crunching the captain's aquiline, waspish nose, spraying blood in a Jackson Pollock design on the tent walls. Then one of the bennies flatlined into a Lone Ranger Sahara where all Rudolph tasted was sand on his teeth and a tropical vapor that restricted his vocal cords.

"Right, Captain. Right-O," Rudolph said, with a half-ass salute. "Do your worst."

Rudolph had matriculated over time to dispose of hateful emotions. 'Yes, moving on toward enlightenment,' he told himself, watching the fat woman waddle on Ifugao Street. Just warn the pimp in a genial way. *You're finished with my niece, Mama.* No need to feud with the broad. She wouldn't dare send a Filipino motorcycle gunman after him, which would cost five thousand pesos, a hundred bucks, maybe less, to kill someone in this hick town.

He said to his niece, "Bolt the door when I leave. I'll be here in time."

"In time for what?" Meryl asked.

"To slide you over my knee, pumpkin, and spank some horse sense into you."

"Enjoy the high life," Meryl said, aiming the television control at the screen. "But bring me a steak sandwich. I'm starved."

*****

In the rear room of Shenanigans, Rudolph dithered in the doorway, where the girls donned western attire with fringed tops and skirts and plastic six-shooters. The walls and the ceiling were painted a mottled grey, but the parquet floor was decorated with pink stars—a bogus harbinger, insinuating that a hatful of gold awaited each girl at the bar. Rows of lightbulbs were strung across the ceiling's beams. Two girls in panties applied makeup before a full-length mirror, and Rudolph delivered a goofy smile. He was a recurrent pest at the bar.

40

"Shave that beard, Mr. Rudolph," the tall girl called out. "Then you'll be *guapo*."

"He's too old to be handsome," her friend said, tying her halter top.

"I think he has potential, Nicole," the tall girl said, giving Rudolph a view of her naked breasts.

"He's the bear about to eat a honeycomb," Nicole said, "but he doesn't know the nest is full of bees."

"Eat whose honeycomb?" the tall girl asked with a wry grin.

Withholding a response, he entered the mama-san's office. Angel chilled in front of the air-conditioner, her hands raised so the frosty air streamed into her armpits.

"You're a sexy woman, Angel," Rudolph said, tapping a cigarette from the L&M soft pack and lighting it with a Zippo.

Angel grunted before the soothing waves. Rudolph closed the door with his boot heel. He moseyed over to the glass aquarium tank containing Angel's coral snake, nicknamed Speedy Gonzalez. Rudolph tapped on the tank, and Speedy glared at him.

"There's feces stuck to Mr. G," Angel said. "Would you mind picking it out?"

Rudolph mashed his cigarette out in a tortoise shell ashtray and rapped on the glass with emphasis. He had the definite vibe that Speedy was sizing him up, evaluating his opponent. If provoked, Speedy would launch upward, dislodging the wire mesh at the top of the tank and sink his fangs into Rudolph's face. Rudolph's knuckle hit the tank: no response. Resting on a bed of grass and weeds, the snake's amber-and-black bands were ringed with gold stripes. They dueled eye to eye, and only when Rudolph stuck his tongue out and wagged it did Speedy rise from a coiled posture and shake his tail.

"What the hell are you doing?" Angel asked, smacking the top of Rudolph's bald head.

She raised the wire mesh, lifted Speedy's lithe body from the tank, and cuddled him in her arms, as one would a somnolent cat. She petted the slick scales, dug out the morsel of feces, and jettisoned it to the floor.

"I want Meryl in the bar," Angel said. "Unless you want to pay her permanent bar fine."

"Pay?" Rudolph said. "You're looney. Yeah, a real looney tune. Don't you agree, Speedy? Now what would Elmer Fudd do in this comic animation? I think he'd yank a shotgun the size of a pitchfork from his trousers and pop one in his nemesis's ear. Ain't that so, Speedy?"

The flare of revulsion resurrected inside Rudolph. A flush spread upward to his neck and bile coated his throat.

"I like the way she puts her mouth between my thighs," Angel said, tickling Speedy Gonzalez's head. "She's expert at that act. Many customers have told me so."

"Let's be respectful," Rudolph said, striving to extinguish the internal fury.

'Just talk, man,' Rudolph said to himself. 'That's all this is. She has no wizardry over you or Meryl.' He recalled Nietzsche saying —"*Without music, life would be a mistake"* —and foresaw restraint. But in his hand, he clutched a Balisong knife against his outer thigh. He flicked his wrist, exposing the blade. 'This too will pass,' he thought. The snake nuzzled Angel's bosom, and his lungs smarted from the aquarium's rotting banana fronds and regurgitated grasshoppers. The tank was warping his mental health, raising the barometer of hostility he maintained from meditation and non-incendiary acts of beer drinking.

"My niece is a kid," Rudolph said, standing in front of Angel. "She's going to school."

"An awesome idea. I'm sure she could blow those schoolboys for some decent pocket change. When was the last time you were in the classroom, Teacher?"

"I work…I work…say—"

"Chill your jets, Richie," Angel said, swinging Speedy's head at Rudolph.

The snake hissed and two fangs drooled a mucous liquid. Instinctively, Rudolph guided the Balisong blade to his hip, the steel pointed at Angel's midsection, and burrowed the blade tip just above her bellybutton.

"Now be cool, Richie."

"There's nothing cool here," Rudolph said.

He tried to rid himself of the tank's filth, which resurrected a bleak history. His ire rekindled. 'Install yourself in the vault of well-being,' he told himself. But the terrain was a swamp, and every notion of goodness sank into a wasteland. He clamped Speedy's throat with his free hand, immobilizing the head. Angel's eyes widened. Her lips puffed out and, as she sought to hold onto the body, Rudolph whipped the Balisong blade onto the snake's neck, severing the head in one neat swipe. Speedy wiggled in Angel's embrace. Crestfallen, the mama-san's arms went rubbery, and the snake's body plunged to the floor. Rudolph tossed the head to the ground, and with his boot toe crushed the snake's skull. There was the noise of a critter being squashed—a lizard, a gecko, or a gerbil.

Rudolph pressed the blade tip in Angel's ear. She stank, as though she had soiled herself.

"Anything you want, Richie," Angel panted. "Anything."

It occurred to him that he had taken what he needed, but he extended the moment, and said, "Find another girl to charge your battery. Meryl's not working this dive."

He twisted the blade tip into Angel's inner ear, as if scraping away a layer of wax.

"Enough, Richie," Angel pleaded.

"I'll say when its quitting time."

"I have money."

"I'm not Judas Iscariot."

"Who?"

"An apostle who betrayed his loved one for thirty pieces of silver."

"I have gold," Meryl blubbered.

"I won't be banished to the ninth circle of hell for gold or kisses or an infatuation. One ear drum is sufficient for the likes of you."

He folded the blade and left Angel sweating, her fatty arms shaking like sand-filled softballs. He bid farewell as he strolled by the girls, smoking cigarettes at their cubbyholes. Before reaching the bar, he retraced his steps to their room.

"I won't be falling by any time soon," Rudolph said.

"Okay," the girls said in unison.

"But I'd like to take both of you out for a meal. A peace offering for any bad karma I may have sent your way. How's that?"

"We'll see you, Mr. Rudolph," Nicole replied.

"I mean it."

"I know," Nicole said. "I'm your friend."

'It's paramount to have friends,' Rudolph thought. At the hotel, Meryl had departed. The television was on, and she had not written a note. He chucked the steak sandwich he had bought at the outdoor food grill onto the bed.

The pale-shingled bars, restaurants, and shops on Ifugao Street glowed a tangerine hue, as the sun melted above the horizon. The coloring reminded Rudolph of the first time he had seen the Pacific Ocean at dusk. He was fifteen years old, sleeping in the Malibu sand dunes with Janice Mulligan, a seventeen-year-old black girl who read Gwendolyn Brooks poems to him in a blanket made up of summer moonlight. He would often ponder why God had blessed him with the easy ability to recall, without reservation, her body next to his, when the years that ensued revealed only the Almighty's mercilessness.

One block east, wind rippled the waters of Subic Bay, and Rudolph relished the sea air on his cheeks. At the jeepney stop, Rudolph helped a grandmother onto the jeepney's stair, and once seated on the bench, he set her groceries on his lap. Six passengers sat on one side of the jeepney and seven on the other. No one spoke an impolite word. Rudolph crossed his beefy arms to give the Filipinas on either side of him as much space as possible. When the jeepney stopped at Jasmin Street and the grandmother stepped off the last stair, he handed her the grocery bag, and she said, with a smile, exposing a missing cuspid tooth, "*Salamat.*"

On J. P. Rizal Street, he hopped off the jeepney and headed westerly, passing a shuttered pharmacy where the paved road compressed into an earthen artery. Within minutes, palm trees, gladioli and chrysanthemums surrounded Rudolph and an exquisite blue early-evening sky spread contentment over the field. As the artery shrunk to a well-worn trail, he stepped on the two-foot square slate tiles he had installed on a layer of gravel years ago. He reveled in the mango orchard he owned and the trees he had nursed from saplings, and his pulse rate lessened. A bee flew under his bearded chin. He was nearly home.

In the coconut tree that shaded his house, an osprey fluttered her wings in a low-hanging bough. Through the screen door, Diana Krall sang in her stylish contralto voice from the cassette player. Inside, Carmelita painted with watercolors on her canvas. A cat, asleep on a copy of Robert Graves's *I, Claudius*, purred loudly. Chicken adobo simmered on the kitchen stove.

"I've used up the lemongrass Eddie Finn gave us last month," Carmelita said, placing her brush on the easel.

"He's a cheap bastard," Rudolph said, pulling off his boots and socks in the doorway.

"I thought you owed him money?"

"Exactly. He won't let me off the hook."

He kissed her cheek and inhaled her lavender soap, and though her hands were hardened from years of manual labor, her fingertips prune shriveled and lines etched the corners of her mouth, he remembered her as a limber, young woman with a hard, telling stare that awed some men and aroused others.

"You ass," Carmelita scolded.

"It was all a case of mistaken identity, dear heart. I wasn't in Lila's Massage."

"I know that, *Bobo*. You idiot, how could you leave Meryl alone in that hotel room? She came home in tears."

"Tears?"

"She's a child."

Rudolph mulled over how to inform Carmelita of Meryl's sexual escapades at *Shenanigans*, but he figured she was mindful of such happenings and that Meryl's blunders were due to his negligence. 'There's no winning here,' he mused. He admired the sensual Cezanne-like style in Carmelita's painting of apples, oranges, and a half full bottle of wine.

"I'll take care of her," he said.

In his study, the books were organized in alphabetical order on teakwood shelves. On the desk, the typed manuscript had pen-written corrections. Standing, he reviewed a single sentence for five minutes, immersed in the complex structure and a phrase that needed restoration or excision; a police siren neared.

Carmelita placed a spoon near his mouth with a pinch of adobo broth. "Here," she said. "I bought the chicken at the market and not the store. It's usually tastier from the market."

Rudolph swallowed. "Delightful."

The siren grew louder, and he anticipated seeing a police uniform. He tapped his trouser pocket, wishing he had ditched the knife.

"I think I'll add chilies," Carmelita said. "Who do you think they're after this time?"

"Probably some champion of the people," Rudolph said.

At the front door, the sky was lit with stars and the night scented with the hint of hyacinths. The cat trooped over Rudolph's feet and scampered into the garden. A litany of cicadas buzzed from the trees.

"What did you do this time?" Carmelita asked, staring at the side of his face.

"Just being me, I guess."

"They gonna haul you away again. I have some money stashed. The police have taken a bribe before."

She dipped her hand into his pocket and clasped the Balisong knife.

"I know someone who can help," Carmelita said.

Rudolph draped his arm around her shoulders. "He's got to have some mighty *cohones*."

"I don't know about that. Look. It's Sergeant Reyes."

The khaki police uniform came toward them. Reyes's hand was clipped onto his holster, and he wore a forlorn expression on his face. Carmelita exposed the blade, and Rudolph took the knife from her and threw it on the kitchen table, jarring a vase of sampaguita flowers, which teetered but stayed upright.

"Be a good girl now. Smile and feed Sergeant Reyes some adobo."

"He don't deserve my adobo," Carmelita protested.

"We don't want it to go to waste," Rudolph said, as Reyes halted in the doorway's light. "Sharing is a sign of providence."

*****

The girl slept with her knees drawn up near her belly, the blanket below her chin. Finn sat against the cushioned headboard. Shortly, Criselda pulled off the duvet, and Finn listened to the sound only Filipina feet can make on a polished pine floor. From a chair, she knotted a towel around her buttocks and thighs. At the bassinet, she sniffed the zinnia flowers in a plastic bowl and entered the bathroom.

The shower, the terse smile when she re-entered the bedroom, her arms caramel-colored from province farm labor—which embarrassed her—was familiar to Finn but did not ease his desire. She combed her wet black hair from her forehead to her shoulders, the shampoo scent intoxicating. He craved to ferry her back to the bed and feel her skin on his own. Each garment—underwear, blouse, denim vest, and plaid shorts—had been carefully arranged the previous night on a chair. She dressed, facing the window, and he questioned if her remoteness had to do with her eagerness to leave and her awareness that he was no longer a young man. She stood at the foot of the bed.

"I'll see you tonight," Finn said.

"Is that so?"

"Yes."

"Okay," she said with plangent compliance, affirming that his words, like most men who visit bars, comprised atoms of truth.

Finn wore dungarees, a t-shirt, and flip-flops on the walkway. Criselda's gait was quick and self-assured. A boy in black trousers and a purple short-sleeved shirt with a stenciled porpoise gathered flower petals with a pole from the pool.

The sun was absent in the chalky sky. Finn stretched his hand out into the morning half-light. Lahar, the volcanic ash that intermittently sprinkled earthward from Mount Pinatubo, freckled his palm. The ash wafted from the decapitated mountain, less than twelve miles away. Though the volcanic eruption transpired years earlier, minor seismic tremors still ensued.

They followed the Oasis Hotel circular driveway flanked with coconut trees, plastic pink flamingoes and tidily built houses. A Caucasian man and a Filipina tended to their front lawn and the mimosa flowers that faced the roundabout. There was the early morning fragrance of frangipani. For several yards, a rooster pranced near Criselda. As they neared the compound's gate and the jeepney stop on Fields Avenue, Criselda stepped away from Finn. There were no surveillance cameras, which echoed Finn's requisite for privacy, the main criteria for his renting a room at this aging one-story hotel. He could retain his anonymity, a fleeing commodity in western nations.

"You can go," Criselda said.

"I'll stay."

"Good-bye," she said, her eyes trained on the southern side of Fields Avenue.

Her cleft chin tightened and her eyes glassed over, and when the jeepney approached, he re-entered the circular drive.

In his room, the bell chimed and Finn unlocked the door and peered outside. "Burt, what do you want?" he asked irritably.

"Sorry to interrupt, Mr. Eddie. It's time we go to the jail."

"Take a seat and switch on the television. I need a shower."

Burt kept his shoes on, poured himself a glass of water, and dialed to a Filipino channel. "Where have you been the last three weeks?" Burt asked.

"On holiday," Finn answered, entering the lavatory.

The two weeks in Palawan held no stationary marker in his mind. It was as though, in that southern Philippine archipelago, he had been blown overboard without compass or clock. Nearly every day, Finn scuba dove one of the World War II Japanese wrecks: The *Akitsushima, Olympia Maru* or The *Irako*, which lay three nautical miles from Coron Island, and ten to forty meters on the sea floor, depending on the ship. Most days, he was accompanied by sightseers. He explored gangways, engine rooms, a wheelhouse and battered decks, and visualized the ships undamaged, floating on Coron Bay.

On a Wednesday morning, due to steel-grey storm clouds and portending squall-force wind traversing Coron Bay, he dove alone on The *Irako*, the deepest of the three ships. As he descended, Finn marveled at the breadth of the ship once it came into view. The *Irako* appeared nearly whole, resting on its port side, its bow inclination at a one-hundred-and-ten-degree angle. He entered the ship through a rupture in the hull. After swimming past a bicycle propped up against a cabin wall teeming with razorfish, and The *Irako's* sentry perch, he tarried, holding his position by gripping a black coral-crusted anti-aircraft mount. He had expected to savor this submersion most of all, since he was the sole diver, and he had the sea and the wreck to himself, but the ship's desolate passageways caused an aberrant feeling in Finn. A foreign entity reigned in this crippled ship, beyond its steel and The *Irako's* osmosis into an undersea habitat. He could feel the continuation of the fallen dead who had been killed from the U.S. Air Force bombing of The *Irako*, in 1944. Cold wracked his body, and he shivered. His breathing accelerated. A turtle swam past his face mask. He checked his regulator. He was feeling the effects of oxygen toxicity; he had rented a bad Nitrox gas cylinder from the boat's operator. A school of barracuda crossed within arm's length.

The sea darkened. Overhead, the storm was upon him. The cold chop forced him to tighten his grip on the mount. The isolation was crushing. Inspiration, regret, revelation had vanished. As a Merchant Marine seaman, he had never encountered this burden of solitude. 'You're always learning from the sea,' Finn thought, pawing a lionfish.

As if in an opium withdrawal, his abdomen cramped and he felt a detachment from the sea he never imagined possible. She had been the glue of his youth, the dominoes that had aligned and molded his character and provided him with a lens to examine himself. And now, he comprehended the sea's indifference, and the loss of her guidance was as colossal as his impotence in Rwanda.

After the shower, he shaved, and snuffed out the candle Criselda had lit on the toilet seat. In his boxer shorts, Finn joined Burt on the bed, watching a Filipino movie. It was a black and white, 1960s Tagalog film with the draconian theme of jealousy and vengeance. In the movie, the maid, a sixteen-year-old girl from a southern province, slaves for an affluent woman and her son in Manila. The son falls in love with the maid, but at a friend's apartment, a hoodlum rapes her. When the mother discerns the rape, she boots the girl into the street.

Carrying a rucksack, the girl passes a musical cabaret. Her eyes are swollen, and tears stain her cheeks. Finn recalled the bruise on Criselda's upper arm, and when he had inquired about it, she had spun about in the bed, and refused to speak. Who had given her the bruise, and could he have accidentally been responsible?

"You dummy," Finn bawled at the television. "Run away with her, forget everyone else and tell your mother to book a ticket to Hades."

In the movie's last reel, the boy shuns his home and eventually finds his beloved, singing in a Makati karaoke bar. Her hair is sculpted in lacquered waves, Titian red, Finn imagined, and her dress has a low, sickle neckline. With the song over, she departs the karaoke bar with a man in a striped sports coat.

After the credits, Finn said, "The mother was a real bitch."

"The Philippines are poor," Burt replied politely.

"What does that mean?"

"Someone always has to be sacrificed. The mother has to live with her guilt, and maybe the son will start over, but..."

"But what?"

"I don't think so. The Filipino family stays together." Finn endorsed the Asian truism in family, the responsibility to the clan. Perhaps it was this absence of values that made his own country so dysfunctional: the bankruptcy of fidelity except to oneself.

Finn dressed in cargo pants, sneakers, and a loose cotton shirt.

"I worked for twelve years on Clark Air Force Base," Burt said, rising to his feet. "I did errands for the enlisted soldiers after school. Soon, I rose in the ranks and accomplished tasks for officers." He set the water glass on the side table. "I know girls who would give a lot of gold to be like that girl in the movie, because their life is very bad. Things are worse these days without the base. I miss the American military."

In his voice lurked the timbre of disapproval, the loss of the American occupation and hundreds of highly paid jobs.

"You can stop your wishful thinking. The American military won't be returning."

"We should hurry. The police are not always friendly. A man can die in our jails, even an American. And for what your friend did, it could be suicide."

"By gunshot?" Finn asked.

"Anything is possible. Even the well-to-do are afraid of the jails."

*****

Burt drove his reconditioned 1972 Chevrolet Monte Carlo on MacArthur Highway. A six-inch plastic Madonna hung on a beaded cord from the rearview mirror. Finn sat in front, and Burt's aunt and niece rode in the rear seat with a duck in the middle. The city's buildings symbolized the aged district: tea-stained, depicting a lethargic morning. Departing the city's hub, the paved road undulated, taking on the natural contours of the region's hills. At a flashing stoplight in front of the Holy Rosary Church, the duck squawked, and the girl pressed the bird to her hip.

Clamping the duck's bill, the aunt spoke in Pampanga, the local dialect, "This bird is sick," she said.

"Are you a duck doctor, auntie?"

"Don't talk gibberish."

"What's going on?" Finn asked. He stared at the old woman, the duck and the young girl with celestial eyes.

"We have to get out," the aunt said. "The bird is cursed."

"Did she say cursed?" Finn asked the girl in English.

"The duck's laughing at us," the aunt said.

"We'll sell it in the market, Aunt Phyllis, and then be rid of it," her niece told her. "We need the pesos."

"No. See, it's a devil bird. It has one blue and brown eye. Stop the car! I said, stop the car!"

Burt pulled over to the side of St. Francis Bridge. His aunt hobbled onto the roadway, the wind whipping her dyed black hair. She reached for her niece and the girl heeded, as did the two men. The sky was the color of ivory, and the unmoving bridge water stunk of sewage. On the roadway, jeepney passengers ogled at the eccentric scene.

"Let's go, Auntie," the niece said. "You keep the duck, Uncle Burt."

"This is cuckoo," Burt said. "Aunt Phyllis, get in the car. The weather's murderous today."

"Nephew, people, animals, and objects can be possessed. There are totems that bullets and bombs cannot reach." The girl took her aunt's hand. "If no one tells them it's the devil, darling May, then how will they know?"

May's eyes lit on Finn as if to say, she may be old but listen to her.

"Let them have the duck," Aunt Phyllis said.

May wore bell bottom pants and a canary yellow short-sleeve blouse, and her arms were wafer thin. She carried a book bag on her shoulder, and her wire-framed glasses reminded Finn of his daughter, whom he had seen only twice in three years. She lived with his ex-wife in a New Mexico suburb of pruned cacti and manicured lawns amid the unforgiving Chihuahuan Desert.

May led her aunt toward the city center. Before they had traveled less than ten yards, May glanced behind, and the wire-framed glasses clouded over in the day's glare. Finn wanted to yell that it was risky for her to be in this city with only her book bag and this shrew for security. His daughter should know better. She should have learned from their talks together, such as where to cross the street at rush hour and how to throw a fastball with your fingers across the stitched seams, and that the poetry of Andrew Marvel was for adults, men like himself, who had failed to satisfactorily master life's lessons.

He watched May and her aunt shrink to the size of rabbits.

In the car, Burt said, "Off with the duck's head!"

"Shut up," Finn said.

"Only joking, sir."

They pushed north toward the plains of Central Luzon. In the foothills, the mountains rose against the horizon in volcanic contours. A minority had excavated peaks, while others were wreathed with forests that housed cloistered sightseers in a nature retreat. Finn was tempted to drag out his daughter's picture from his wallet. There were still seeds of memory within him that had not dried up. The duck squawked, and he feared it, as the old woman had, emboldened by the thesis that not all is as it seems.

As the sun brightened, the morning fog dissolved. Caribous rigged with leather harnesses plowed the rice paddies. When the car contacted a newly tarred portion of road, the heat descended. Dust powdered the windscreen, forcing Burt to use the washer fluid and wipers. The road had warped from inferior asphalt. Farmers wore straw hats, and women selling bargain-counter commodities at outdoor markets, shielded from the sun by beach umbrellas, fanned themselves with yesterday's *Philippine Star*. Finn and Burt unbuttoned their shirts and kicked off their shoes. The earth appeared to have rotated off her axis.

Around one o'clock, the route petered into a circuitous lane, which led them to a gravel lot. The jail was small and mean. In the yard, two burly greyhounds slept. Flies swarmed their eyes and ears, and when the insects stung the dogs' scrotums, they ground their bellies in the dirt. Inside the building, a police officer in a teal-colored shirt worked at a paper-cluttered desk, the piles weighted with cartridge boxes. A fan squeaked. At the window's sawed-off metal bars, Burt discussed the circumstance of the jailed American, and Finn sat on a chair with the duck on his lap. A crucifix was attached to the wall above him.

"Any last appeal?" Finn asked the duck.

From a doorway, a girl of three or four, topless, in plastic shoes, came toward him. A bandage, with a splotch of blood, or iodine, on thin gauze, was taped to her knee. Her belly pressed against Finn's thigh, and she stretched out a hand and petted the duck. The police officer hustled over and spoke in Ilocano, a northern Luzon dialect, and the girl shambled away.

"Mr. Finn, I remember you from the American Embassy New Year's party," he said, his English crisp. "You were drinking champagne from the bottle and dancing with a tall strawberry-haired woman. In the middle of the song, I saw you trip and fall. You were riveting to watch. If you were that drunk in my borough, I'd have arrested you."

"Today, I'm sober as a judge," Finn said.

Cradling the duck beneath one arm, Finn rose and passed Reyes his American Embassy calling card, embossed in gold lettering. Reyes skimmed the name and logo and pocketed the card.

"Major...."

"Sergeant Reyes," Reyes corrected him.

Burt grinned from the window.

"Sergeant Reyes, I have some papers for you," Finn said, and presented the legal-size envelope. "Simply stated, this gives you the authority to leave the American, Richard Rudolph, in my care."

Reyes lifted the flap and counted the U.S. dollar bills.

"What happened to the girl?" Finn asked.

"A bomb exploded in a local restaurant. It caused pandemonium in the community."

"Who did it?"

The girl's absence made the mundane room confined and sordid.

"An Islamic group. My guess is the Abu Sayyaf. They're heathens."

"I didn't think they came this far north."

"They stray from their southern provinces. Anything to spread anarchy and the word of whoever they worship. Last month a bomb exploded close to our sports stadium. Eight people were killed. Luckily, my niece and sister were spared."

"Positive news, given the flighty nature of a terrorist."

"A week later another bomb exploded in the local market, killing my sister and three of her friends," Reyes said.

"Sorry to hear that."

"Are you a church-going man, Mr. Finn?"

"Not these days."

"There's no saving you, then, eh?"

"It's a constant battle between me and my spiritual advisor. But I think the playing field is changing."

"Playing field?"

"I've begun embracing the idea of miracles," Finn confessed, "and the realization that there are things out of my control, be it love, rebellion, genocide. I know that any one of those acts can ignite global violence. It doesn't matter how you prepare a defense to these upheavals, desire one or the other. Frequently, God is simply demented. Then the avenging angel arises. Don't deny her existence, Sergeant. I've seen her. The carnage isn't pretty. Fields and cities running with blood. Brother betraying brother. Religious tabernacles gutted. But she has mysticism. So, I've pried apart the portal for the arrival of miracles, you might say."

"I didn't picture you as a church going man. Now you talk of miracles and genocide together as though they are siblings, Cain and Abel. That didn't end well in the Bible."

"No one would deny that. But you must hold onto the miraculous, or the idea of the miraculous, in order to delay your journey to the graveyard and the sentiment that tomorrow you're next in line to fall under her axe. I've met military men, screwball civilians and kid soldiers who see life as a one-way highway to God's little acre. No penance. Just the old dirt nap. So, they hack away at life without regret." An ache blossomed behind Finn's eyes. Even his physical body was morphing. "All roads lead to the cemetery. Why cause such a fuss, Sergeant? One neighborly action here or there, what does it get you anyway? Yet, I think miracles can evade a calamity, to some degree. But maybe it's all hullabaloo. Better to drown oneself in single malt Macallan whisky and baseball games. Wouldn't you say?"

"You should know that God and love reside in the Philippines."

"Yes, the Philippines is a country of faith. But it's my job to find those who commit crimes, prove my case, and throw them in prison."

"I didn't know you were a policeman," Reyes said.

"I'm a certified American government investigator with some authority in the Philippines." The duck shivered, as if it had come to terms with its imminent fate. "By the way, did the police catch the bombers?"

"Not yet. But we will. Behead every terrorist, is what I think." Reyes shoved the envelope into his hip pocket. "Burt mentioned the story of the duck. Have you ever seen the devil?"

"Twice," Finn said.

"Ah, you may be worthwhile after all." Reyes pointed at the duck. "Take the bird and come with me."

Finn followed Reyes into the lot and to a four-by-four-foot square wire cage, where Reyes told Finn to deposit the duck, which he did. In the sunlight, Reyes's features were haggard, and his cheeks had brown moles that matched the constellation Perseus.

"I'm glad to get rid of your Rudolph," Reyes told him. "All he does is talk, all day, all night, to anyone who will listen, and when no one is there to listen to him, he still talks. He's batty."

"But is he unhurt?" Finn asked.

The duck was eating a turd eggroll, and Reyes jarred the cage. "As best as can be, given the circumstances. Is he a friend?"

"Most of the time."

"We don't like his type. He gives the Philippines a bad name. Do you carry a gun?" Reyes asked.

"No, I never have."

Reyes pulled his pistol and aimed the barrel at Finn's nose.

"I once shot a man in the face," Reyes said. "It was the only time I killed someone. What's the bounty on your head?"

"Not a *centavo*." Finn's voice fluttered at a low octave. Reyes held the trigger. "Sad to say, my government doesn't value her employees."

"But you could get me more money for the reindeer?"

"Reindeer?"

"Yeah, the reindeer man."

"Oh," Finn said, "you mean Rudolph."

Skittish that Reyes would lose his decorum, Finn checked for an escape route. A greyhound, which had relieved herself, scratched at the roots of a palm tree. She was imposing, with shark-like teeth.

"The money I gave you, Sergeant Reyes, is mine," Finn said. "It's all I have. I'm sure you've guessed that by now. The Americans wouldn't give a penny to get Richard Rudolph out of jail."

"But I have my family to support."

Finn patted his pockets and stopped as the greyhound snarled. "I wish I could help. But I'm out of cash."

Finn considered those from whom he could elicit a loan, but the list was short and neither person favored him at this point in his life.

"You are a brave man to come here with only Burt and your envelope. I could say I want to keep your American. What would you say to that?"

"I'm doing my job."

"To hell with your job," Reyes said.

"Absolutely," Finn said. "To hell with it."

Reyes swabbed the sweat from his upper lip with his shirt sleeve. Four diamond scars marred the fleshy part of his forearm.

"On Sunday mornings, I go into the market and search for my sister," Reyes said. "I know I won't find her, but I hope that her spirit will forgive me. I should have protected her."

Reyes languished in the dominion of what-has-been, and Finn appreciated the outlook. Spurred by a remembrance, such as the graves in Rwanda, he would transition from a plane of uncertainty and dispatch himself to one of fortitude, where he could give an order to underlings to breach a house that detained child prostitutes. If he misread the situation, the sex traffickers would relocate the children or kill them if they were a nuisance. Success remained a gamble. Where most men sought reassurance from a higher power for flubbed assignments, Finn had shelved such piety. To liberate one child sex worker could not be imperiled by pious vacillation.

"I can relate to wanting to help someone you love," Finn said. "We are both in exile."

"Have you ever buried a sister?" Reyes asked.

"No."

"Or someone dear?"

"That type of loss never fades."

Reyes lowered the pistol. "Go, get your fugitive," he said in a dismissive manner. "I'll barbecue your duck. And I'll think of you and your friend when I give its bones to my dogs."

*****

Captain Fuentes monitored the knife from the opposite side of the table, with the blade poised above the anterior muscle of the woman's forearm. She had two semi-healed lesions from a previous ceremony, and now she was prepared to make a fresh incision. Her eyes were partly closed, and he had misgivings regarding her intended objective. He sat far enough away to swat the knife from her hand if she lunged at him. She lowered the blade until it touched flesh. The incision, two inches in length, was done with deliberation. The knife was sharp; the steel glistened and implied its own volition. There was a look of contentment on her face as the blood oozed onto the edge of each separated skin fold. She had nerve, and though Fuentes anticipated she would cease now, she angled the blade for a second round. A minute ticked by. The knife's pommel rested on the table. She made the second incision a half inch above the most recent one. This one was deeper than the original, and the blood dripped past her forearm, onto her wrist, into her palm, composing a henna-like diagram, that of a flowering lotus.

Gratified at her performance, his stomach grumbled. 'A person with her capabilities has the makings of a patriot,' he thought. But Fuentes debated whether she had the perseverance to wield the knife on others. That takes repulsion, he said to himself. And few women can summon such an emotion.

It was mid-afternoon, and they sat on the bar's patio beneath an awning in Quezon City.

"We could use a gutsy woman like you in Mindanao," Fuentes said. "A woman of courage, who isn't afraid to shed some blood. Someone else's, though."

"Are you serious?" she said with contempt.

"Put the knife on the table, Tala," Fuentes ordered.

She laid the knife in the ashtray, and Fuentes folded a napkin on her forearm.

"Where's your medical kit?" he asked.

"Inside, under the bar."

Fuentes tramped into the dreary restaurant, retrieved the kit, and settled in his chair. Tala's blood lines were beautiful to him, as if she were physically offering herself. Meticulously, he took gauze pads, Betadine and medical tape from the kit and laid them on the table. He cauterized the two lacerations with Betadine and stemmed the blood to a trickle with two gauze pads and finally the medical tape.

"I'm broke," Tala said, "and three months overdue with the mortgage. My boyfriend said he'd help out with money, but I haven't received any from him. He lived with me for a month. I took care of him. We had marathon sex sessions. When I call, he doesn't answer. I continue to write to him. He swore he'd give me money for the restaurant."

"What's his nationality?"

"Denmark."

"You trusted him, and he lied to you." Fuentes watched the pads darken with blood. "What are you going to do?"

"I don't want to return to the bar. I need other options. Maybe I could be a dental assistant. Those girls are paid well and have regular hours."

"I'll need to change these pads again."

"You're my uncle. Can you help me?"

"I'm not really your uncle, you know that. You're Lito's niece. He's a colleague of mine in Mindanao."

"He terrifies me," Tala said. "Word is, he's murdered people."

"I wouldn't know. I'm a pacifist."

A Caucasian man with shoulder-length blonde hair, a Fu-Manchu mustache and pasty complexion entered the restaurant. He shouted for assistance and thumped the countertop. Within a minute, he approached the table, and seeing the blood on Tala's bandages, he vacillated, prepped to inquire about a selfish issue, either a request for a beverage or an explanation for the budding scene.

Fuentes glared at him and said, "We're closed."

"No problemo," the man said. "But can I have a brewski for the road?"

"We're out of beer," Fuentes said.

"I'll get him one," Tala said eagerly, rising.

"That's kind of you," the man replied.

Fuentes figured the *dayuhan* had been bar hopping all night and was coming off a methamphetamine rush. Most likely, he still had a bundle of cash. 'Take him to Suzy Q's for tequila shots,' Fuentes thought, 'and mug him in the toilet.' The idea had its appeal. Too bad Lito isn't here. He'd like this faggot. In his pocket, Fuentes carried rope that could be used as a double-looped garrote. In tough scrapes, he had used the garrote on a rival. Done skillfully, the garrote can choke a man into submission.

"I'm Sal," the man said.

He rolled his shirt sleeves and wiped perspiration from his nose. The posture of intimidation was artificial, which galled Fuentes. He recognized inferiors, and the boy coarsely exuded this character.

"Yes, have a seat," Fuentes said playfully.

Sal joined them and a minute later, Tala gave him a Budweiser. "Would you like a menu?" she asked. "Food isn't a problem. If you have friends invite them over. We never close. God wants me to run this tavern. Her name is *Summer*." The sign above the entrance was carved from wood, written in script and varnished a cadmium yellow. "I go to church, and I own *Summer*. You're always welcome."

The gauze pads had darkened, and Tala crooked her arm inward, away from Sal.

"That's a bad cut," Sal said.

"It sure is," said Fuentes, pushing the medical kit toward Sal. "Help out the pretty woman, Sal."

The sun shone directly behind Tala's short frame, and the light illuminated her ears, giving her an elfin quality.

"Sit," Fuentes told Tala. "Let Sal redress the bandages." He intended to kick Sal's chair, misfired, and connected with Sal's shin. "Sorry. You don't have to be a doctor, boy. Do the right thing and help Tala. She's a beauty, isn't she?"

Sal took the medical kit, and Tala seated herself gracefully and extended her arm.

I've never done anything like this," Sal said, unfastening the medical kit. His hands trembled, and he licked his lips. "I'm not sure what to do."

Fuentes picked up Tala's knife, the ridge crusted with blood, and tapped the tip on the table. "It's like music, Sal, the old one, two, three. Do you tango? You'd look pretty in a dress."

"What the fu—"

"One, two, three," Fuentes repeated. "One, rip off the bandages. Two, clean the wound with Betadine, and three position the bandages on the wounds. Does the flow of blood scare you? This is just a minor abrasion." Sal took one of the bandages. "Carry on."

Sal peeled both bandages from Tala's arm. She did not wince and fixated on Sal's eyes. He squirted drops of Betadine on the two wounds and the blood reconstituted to a silty brown. Holding the gauze pads, he dawdled, perplexed by how to rig them onto Tala's forearm. Deftly, Fuentes took the pads from Sal, an action he had performed on the battlefield for soldiers, planted them firmly on the two wounds, and secured the pads with medical tape. He took two additional gauze pads from the medical kit, knowing the blood would seep into the first layer, and after taping the second layer of pads, he packed up the medical kit and lit a cigarette.

Tala folded her hands in her lap, the bandaged forearm masked from view by the table. "I was chopping veggies for burritos, and I cut myself with the knife," Tala told Sal.

"Is that how it happened?" Sal said in amazement. "That's terrible."

"It's a crime," Fuentes said.

Tala's brown eyes sparkled, and her cheeks inflamed. This boy was her savoir, a foreigner with money to bail her out from her desperate financial hardship. To the leeward side of Tala, Fuentes observed the two-story, red and blue opulent tile-roofed co-ops and the North Luzon Expressway—a washed-out asphalt strip scintillating in the tropical sun. Further east, the cluster of tin-roofed dwellings that the impoverished occupied in this Quezon community were crowded together like ant farms. As Sal polished off the dregs of his beer, the pitiful boy-man infuriated Fuentes; Tala deserved someone with grit. He would be an easy mark at Suzy Q's. He bet he could pawn him off to a local gangster as a drug mule.

The stagnant, bucolic day sapped his energy. Fuentes flung his cigarette to the dirt; the desire for such a dismal episode at Suzy Q's dissipated. There would be payback for the shakedown, and he had scant influence with the authorities in this municipality. He ached, though, to choke Sal with the garrote in front of Tala. Just for a modest period of time. She would learn, then, that those who watch, while another person inflicts injury on themselves, also suffer. But he cared too much for the girl for such a demonstration, and he had an appointment he needed to keep.

"You have things under control, Tala," Fuentes said. "I'll speak to your Uncle Lito about saving this shit-hole. He'll be willing to help you out."

"I like it here," Sal said in a caring manner.

"You're a darling," Tala said.

"Comrades to the end." Fuentes rose to his feet. "Tala, use Betadine and bandage the arm three times a day to keep away infection. I don't want anything to happen to you."

The Subaru's leather seat was hot and sticky, even though Fuentes had lowered the windows and parked in the shade of a bani tree. He picked a worm off the clutch and hurled it onto the gravel. After he started the engine, he drove out of the lot at high speed, kicking granite pebbles into the oil pan and exhaust, so that they rang like shards of glass on a marble floor. The craving to use his garrote persisted.

After thirty minutes, Fuentes stopped on hard-packed clay. Music blared from speakers. The Ferris wheel in the carnival, twenty yards away, simulated a whirl-a-gig against the darkening sky. Drawn to the gigantic wheel's allure, the colorful lights, and its dizzying arc, he heard peoples' screams. Nearby, the roller coaster dipped and swerved, screeching on steel rails. At the end of the ride, the boys and girls staggered away, giddy. He headed toward the clamor, and a tumescence took hold. Lovers strolled on sandy lanes inside the carnival, and girls with faultless brown skin, clad in their school uniforms—yellow blouses and maroon skirts— roamed in packs of three and four. Children ate caramelized banana on a stick, frozen yogurt and grilled sausage. Fuentes went toward a canvas tent apron decorated with the figure of a midget wearing a bowler hat. The billboard in front of the tent advertised a sword swallower and a woman in a leopard leotard who could invert her body until she peeked at the audience from between her parted legs.

Fuentes bought a ticket. The tent was nearly full, with twenty-five to thirty people. A ruckus festered, with eager souls ready to shed their mundane reality. A father propped his son on his shoulders to get an unobstructed view of the stage. In the corner, two teenage boys swallowed from a pint whiskey bottle. There were no windows or ventilation. The tent, sodden with sweat and mold, was lit by oil lanterns. Fuentes maneuvered near stage front and stood in the company of a man in his thirties, high on marijuana. Fuentes recognized the aromatic scent.

At seven p.m., the emcee mounted the stage in front of a moth-eaten backdrop. He was dressed in a charcoal overcoat, a creased pimento shirt buttoned to the collar, and shiny rayon pants. His cheeks had a high gloss to them, and his eyes spoke of a career in these carnival productions. To silence the crowd, his arms spread wide, as if anointing each rube in the tent.

"You are about to see," he declared, "a tour-de-force that has bewitched kings and queens and presidents. Monarchies have idolized these performers. These feats will amaze and shock. If you need to use the comfort room, do so now. Bladders have been known to weaken upon observing these entertainers. Let's begin."

He loosened a knotted rope, and a banner displayed William Shakespeare's *King Henry VI, Part II*

"...I'll make thee eat iron like an ostrich,
and swallow my sword like a great pin, ere thou and I part."

The sword swallower stepped on stage. Fuentes had expected a man with an athletic physique, but a woman appeared. Chubby, with pumpkin-colored hair and an anemic coloration, her green-black lipstick transmitted the look of a ghoul rather than an attraction. She was stoned. Her pupils were black feral saucers, and she avoided eye contact with the audience. The tent's temperature increased, and the confinement was testing his patience. He had other interests to attend.

"Meet the one and only Lady Marguerite," the emcee said, gesturing grandly at the sword swallower.

Lady Marguerite wore a black corset, a leather miniskirt and mesh stockings. Cardinal red, aquamarine and lime-green tattoos in the caricature of eyes, skulls, monoliths, and a dragon's head coated her arms. A flower lily was tattooed to each breast with a naked woman twined with a serpent in the center of her chest. On the knuckles of each hand were printed letters, and Fuentes squinted to comprehend the meaning. He read the word *sword* on the knuckles of her left hand and *sport* on the knuckles of the other one.

"Do it, man," the weed smoker beside Fuentes yelled. "Swallow the load."

Someone jostled Fuentes from behind. Voices jeered for a demonstration of Lady Marguerite's skills. An object whacked Fuentes in his neck. He stuck his hand in his pocket and squeezed the garrote. Oh, you devil, I sense your predatory appetite. Soon, he said to himself, you will have liberty. The boy, seated on his father's shoulders, was swinging his leg, repeatedly nailing Fuentes, who bulled his way to the side and encouraged the man and child to his spot.

The emcee exited and Lady Marguerite unlatched a brown case, the lid facing the audience. The first sword, the length of a baby Python, eighteen inches long, epitomized a crucifix with its bauble handle and black steel. She presented the sword to the audience, as if cradling a priceless artifact. Then she tilted her head upward and, with a brief hitch in her arm, held the sword tip over her mouth. After a mighty inhale, she broke her elbow joint and the sword descended. Her throat swelled, and her thighs became rigid, centering her body. She wore high-top purple Converse sneakers. With the hilt above her mouth, Lady Marguerite stretched her arms out, the way a ballerina concludes her performance. The applause was restrained. Someone threw popcorn onto the stage.

"A lousy starter pistol," the weed smoker cried. "Get real, man."

Lady Marguerite removed the sword with the same effortless motion. She placed it in the case and withdrew another sword, this one over two feet in length. Her biceps flexed as she steadied the heavy steel. With flair, she swiveled the sword like a spigot in quickening revolutions. Fuentes welcomed the upsurge of exhilaration among the spectators, and he imagined fighting the

Philippine military with a cutlass in the Mindanao jungle: severing ears and noses, puncturing larynxes, livers, and spleens, blinding the wounded. His body sprayed with gore, and surrounded by howls and wailing men, his optics constricted where there was no other aspiration but the destruction of the enemy.

Lady Marguerite raised her chin, and with the tip angled due south, she lowered the sword in one seamless movement. With the sword halfway down her gullet, there was a negligible wince, almost imperceptible. On her mouth, a laceration, nearly a paper nick, the width of single hair, broke the symmetry of her green-black lipstick. The sword, now three-quarters inside, had passed her trachea and epiglottis, skirted the bronchi, and entered the upper and lower esophagus. Her face blushed. Fuentes noted her self-discipline to quell the gag reflex. A quasi-silence blended with glee stewed in the tent.

"What's that on her leg?" the weed smoker asked Fuentes. "Do you see it?"

"Don't talk," he said.

"I think she's pissing herself."

"You should leave."

"Are you kidding me?"

"Out the door," Fuentes said.

A bubble rose from her mouth. Staring at the tent's pinnacle, Lady Marguerite dislodged the sword, raising the steel from her esophagus until the tip surfaced. The applause was considerate, and Lady Marguerite abruptly vacated the stage.

"What a joke," the weed smoker said.

"Shut your trap." Fuentes said. "She did her best."

"I'll say what I want."

"Get out of here."

"Are you a Jew? You look like a Jew. I know there are Philippine Jews."

Facing the man, Fuentes poked him in the chest with his thumb. "I mean it. And, if you stay, who knows what could happen to you? A knife might pop up out of nowhere and find its way into your gut. I bet you've never been slashed by a knife. It happens fast. The knife shows up in a man's hand, a hand like mine, a stranger. Then the stranger stabs you two-three times, quick as lightning, and next you're bleeding and the blood soaks your shirt and pants. Yeah, listen up. Scared shitless, you clamp your hands on your belly and run shouting for help like a madman or fall to your knees to hold your insides from spilling out, and it'll be the first time in your life you realize you're made of silly putty. Do you get me? You deaf?"

"Okay, okay," the man said in compliance.

Slack-jawed, the weed smoker slunk away, mumbling to himself, sweat beading his forehead. Fuentes loosened his shirt collar. The tainted tent air held fast in his lungs. He coughed, and he recalled the whore he'd discovered in a Manila hotel room four months ago, murdered for an obscure motive. He had befriended the girl. When she hadn't shown up to clean his condominium, which she did on a weekly basis for extra cash, he'd scoured the city for her. It took less than two hours. She had signed the ledger in a low-class hotel, The Carlton, along with a Robert Arlington. Guided by an intuitive source, his God, or an internal divination, perhaps even his love for this girl who worked tirelessly at menial jobs to feed and clothe her parents, brothers and sisters, the only financial benefactor for her family in Davao, whose land had become fallow, and who had lost two uncles and three aunts to Typhoon Unsang—two hundred and eighty lives drowned on a capsized ferry boat, at night, in monstrous waves—Fuentes entered the room. He detected the odor of a corpse, which no bleach could mask. The maid had overlooked the bouquet. He yanked the blanket and linen off the bed. She had been stuffed between the box spring and mattress. He gently laid her on the floor. The signs were obvious. She had been strangled to death. Management telephoned the police, and he prayed for her that Sunday in church.

Fuentes checked his watch, bullied his way out of the tent, and hastened to the pre-determined location. At the shooting gallery, Marta was squeezing the trigger of a pistol, pumping water into a smirking clown's face.

"You're late," Marta said.

"A road accident."

The pistol's water subsided. "I almost won. Just another second."

"Let's talk over there," Fuentes said, gesturing at a buttoned-up stall.

The ground was soggy. Two ten-gallon water barrels had been tipped over. At the stall, the Ferris wheel's lights cast a rainbow on the thinning puddles.

"It sure is a gorgeous night," Fuentes said. "An evening for lovers, wouldn't you say?"

"I know nothing of love," Marta replied.

"That's dishonest of you. But we'll let it pass for now."

"Are you alone?" she asked.

"Too often."

"So, no one's shadowing you?"

"I live a lonely life."

"You're a shameful man."

"I have carried out your every request to this date," Fuentes said. "That should prove my credibility."

Fuentes smiled, nodding his head, using these suggestive devices to ease her hostile posture. He recalled the *hantu demon* with his unkempt hair, coming to his home when he was a teen, using the same technique, incessantly nodding and smiling, to extort money for groceries from him and his mother. At the kitchen table, as Fuentes began to pass pesos toward the demon, he stopped, as terror lanced an inner nerve. He abruptly reneged on the concession. In an effeminate rotation of his wrist, the demon departed, and the following morning, Fuentes's bicycle had been stolen, the chain sheared from its Proteus lock. He had learned, then, that monsters and djinns roam neighborhoods and cities and occupy the same dimensional plain as his own.

"I know someone's after me, Captain," Marta said.

"Precisely who?"

"I never see them. But they leave the same brand of cigarette butts at my apartment house, on the pavement in front of my favorite restaurant, in taxis I ride in, at the local newsstand, outside the American Embassy on the bench where I eat my lunch. There's a man's cologne at all these locations, musky, like he hasn't showered for days."

"I'm a man of hygiene, Miss Marta."

"Take me seriously."

"I can protect you."

"No, you can't. You're a scoundrel."

"Now, you have my number. But I am a man who adheres to a private canon, too."

"And what's that?"

"Wreck those who do me injustice."

Fuentes's smile withered. Whatever response he made would not satisfy her.

She took an envelope from her purse, as if acknowledging a prescient commitment. "This is for you," Marta said. "The data in the envelope has the location, dates and troop strength of the Philippine military in Mindanao. This is a show of fealty. A guarantee that the United States wants a truce in the southern provinces, which can be viewed as a collaboration with the Philippine government and the Abu Sayyaf."

"You're a courageous woman," Fuentes said. "This dispatch will convince the Abu Sayyaf commanders the government desires a solution to this interminable conflict. I'll be honored to deliver this letter to the people in charge."

"The presumption is this will spark a chain of events where other extremist groups will negotiate with the United States."

"Yes, a leap into a less hostile global order. Your idealism is noteworthy. Yet, there's a flaw in your scenario. Nothing progresses the way it's planned. All one has to do is read history. It's full of transgressions, charlatans, and cutthroats."

"One has to try," Marta said sincerely.

"That is often a calamitous fact."

Fireworks scaled the night sky and exploded in a shower of Roman candles, receding in cones of light.

"When do you leave for Mindanao?" Marta asked.

"In a day or so. Arrangements need to be made. This could change the tide of the war in the southern provinces."

"This is a mediation, Captain Fuentes. I trust the content won't be used to retaliate against the military. I've seen what can happen when information is corrupted."

"You're all alone," Fuentes said, "aren't you?" She was challenging to read, and the pheromone of cowardice and evasion was not present. 'Those are commendable traits,' Fuentes thought.

"This doesn't come from your superior. Is there someone else that knows you've given me this package?"

"An associate."

"Are you sleeping with him?"

"Get your mind out of the gutter, Captain."

"You're a loyalist. I see that now."

"Get real," Marta said. "Don't spew that rubbish. Here, this is yours."

Fuentes took the envelope, weighing the virtue of passing its contents over to the Abu Sayyaf. The luxury of having military logistics swiftly paled. These men, the rebel commanders, functioned on revenge, and Fuentes mediated whether each commander would kowtow to the letter's details and view it as a means of negotiation with the government. The enticement was overwhelming, addictive in nature, to ruthlessly kill as many Philippine soldiers as possible. Wouldn't such a victory also send the Philippine government to the bargaining table? The math was basic, and satisfaction flowed from the calculus and possible outcomes.

"I'm obliged to you for this," Fuentes said, depositing the envelope in his pants pocket. "Marta, one day you may find yourself in a life-and-death struggle. I'd like to show you a way to defend yourself."

Fuentes removed a knotted rope from his pocket. "This is a garrote. It's a weapon. Someday, it may save your life."

"What are you up to?"

"Let me show you how to use it."

He stood behind Marta and ran his fingers lightly over her thick braids. He had never touched the hair of a black woman or been inside of one and he relished the sexual fervor.

"In all likelihood, your enemy will be standing when you come from behind," Fuentes said.

Marta swiveled her head so that she could see him from the corner of her eye. "What are you going to do?"

"This is only meant to demonstrate a way to pacify your enemy. The Philippines can be a hostile country, especially in the lower provinces."

Fuentes stationed the garrote below her chin.

"This is a simple device, really. All you need to do is slip it around a man's throat. Piano wire, a telephone cord, even your belt can be used. I have tied a single knot in the rope. Once the rope is around the villain's throat, position the knot against his windpipe." With a finger, he grazed the soft space above her collarbone. "The knot goes here. Then jerk tightly while you bring your knee into his spine. He'll quickly succumb."

Directly above the Ferris wheel, sparks scrolled downward, landing on top of the fabric above each car. Fuentes had tightened the garrote on Marta's throat, so that she could feel the tension and grasp that even this mild constriction could raise anxiety in an adversary. He heard the shrieks from the Ferris wheel before Marta raised her arm and pointed at the skyline, as the cars, one after another, ignited in flame and smoke. He released the garrote and watched the Ferris wheel take on an incendiary glitter. As the fireworks ascended, exploding in a charismatic display, the Ferris wheel kept circling, and with each cycle, cars were set alight, the exhausted rockets torching the fabric and foam seat cushions. The flaming fabric fell onto the people in the cars, igniting their clothes, burning their hair and skin. A girl jumped from a Ferris wheel's car at its apogee, her arms and shirt on fire. She landed on the ground, her ankles snapping from the impact. She writhed, pounding a fist into the weeds. The Ferris wheel gyrated; its revolutions piloted by a timing apparatus. A tall boy charged out of a car, the side of his body on fire, his hands overhead, as if holding onto the imaginary front risers of a parachute.

Marta was in full gallop toward the Ferris wheel, and Fuentes matched her stride for stride. They threaded in between the seams of the dumbstruck crowd. The thick curtain on the side of the wheel caught fire, spewing patches of scalded cloth. At the ticket booth, the boy in charge reeled from side to side, paralyzed as the combustion spread with a calculated intelligence.

Fuentes spoke in Tagalog. "*Itigil ito*!" he yelled. "Stop it!"

HILLS OF COTABATO

Terror-stricken, the boy scooted away from the glowing curtain that spewed balls of smoldering fabric in all directions. Elevated by the evening's gusts, the fabric sent people scurrying. Screams cleaved the night. Another person dove from a car, clawing to ease his descent. Fuentes entered the booth and saw nothing that could curtail the wheel. He hastily scoured the area and located a metal box opposite the ticket booth, sprinted over, opened it, and gleaned an off button. Excitedly, he pressed the red button, craving the wheel's speed to diminish, and when nothing happened, he rapped the heel of his palm on the button. Within moments, steel ground on steel, and he saw the gearbox smoking, the wheel looming before him, still spinning, and the rabble shouting from the burning cars as they sailed onward. He inhaled the roasting rubber flanges, melting iron wires, gleaming foam and plastic as the noise, firelight, and carnival food reviled him. The Ferris wheel light bulbs burst, and its engine ruptured in an orange ball, followed by billowing smoke. Fuentes feared the Ferris wheel would breach its foundation, but then the wheel, with a self-anointed resolve, decelerated.

Fuentes hurried to the platform and yanked people from each car's doorway, gripping their arms, snatching their burning shirts, hauling them out, feeling the heat on his face. Some ran headlong into a chain-link fence while stragglers squirmed on hands and knees, coughing, vomiting—an irregular sway to their carriage that proved a pernicious force had entered their bodies. He spurned their mewling and theatrical cries. He fisted a boy in the nose who sat immobile in a car and plucked him from the flames in the nick of time. Others bailed from their cars as they neared the Ferris wheel's nadir.

Fuentes thrust passengers into Marta's arms, who shepherded the ones too afflicted to walk. Hot cinders seared his shirt. His body wove in outrage at the irrationality of tragedy. Marta and two other Filipinos wrapped towels around those ablaze.

Tossing aside one charred towel, Marta retrieved a discarded jacket and smacked at the flames that crept up a child's arms and trousers. The fire ate into the boy's brown skin, fat, and muscle. Dropping the jacket, Marta tackled him to the ground. She clawed at the tough dry soil, shoveling dirt onto his torso, suffocating the flames. His sobs were silent. Marta pulled off his burnt socks and sneakers, and a Filipino volunteer carried him to a makeshift medical tent.

The Ferris wheel rotated and a man, just past the wheel's apex, leaped from his car, flames searing his beard. Fuentes looked away from the falling man. As cars spun by, he wearied of the incessant moans. This was not his job. Strife could only come from this service. The fireworks had ceased, leaving a smoky, diaphanous cloud above the Ferris wheel. Still attentive, Fuentes beheld a girl three cars away, frozen in her seat. When the car entered the platform, he took her arm and tugged her against him. Her school uniform was sediment-stained, her eyebrows and hair blackened, her mouth gasping for air.

"You're okay," he said. "*Liyag. Liyag.* Darling, you're fine now."

"Where's my boyfriend?" she asked.

"Here you go," Fuentes said, handing her off to a volunteer.

Smoking embers boosted by the wheel's momentum performed a Tinkerbell-like dance in the cars. Passively, Fuentes dismissed the shouts from onlookers and the confusion in the park. In the sparse crowd, he observed the weed smoker from the sword swallower tent on his knees, praying, toking on a spliff. Sprawled in the muck, one of the jumpers, his head deformed and apparently dead, raised an eyelid. He whistled through broken teeth. Fuentes presumed someone would go to his rescue. Neglected or unseen, not a single sole bustled toward him. He watched as the jumper issued a final exhalation, the visible eye that of a vulture staring into space.

At the medical tent, people bleeding and broken berated the personnel. A derangement had taken hold of them. They reminded Fuentes of men wounded in battle, in need of absolution amid a barbarous jungle. Police sirens converged on the carnival.

On her knees, the boy's dingy sneakers smoldered in the notch between Marta's legs. Hunched behind her, Fuentes smothered her singed, braided hair. In exhaustion, she leaned against him.

"Is it over, Captain?"

"That would be my guess."

"What about those people?" Marta asked, eyeing the medical tent.

"The cavalry is here."

Ambulances and police cars surrounded the Ferris wheel.

"Let's go before the police start their interrogation," Fuentes said.

"Because?"

"In the end, explanations can only harm us."

"I see. We don't want to leak our mission."

"Now you're talking, Miss Marta."

Fuentes helped Marta to her feet. She regained her bearings and walked across the near-empty carnival grounds. The air was chilly, the crescent moon a comb in the tangle of stars. As they approached the entryway, a man bumped against Fuentes, his slender frame bending against Fuentes's brawn. For some reason, his comportment terrorized Fuentes, and when he glimpsed over his shoulder at the man, he was moving his hand the way a cheerleader might twirl a baton at a high school football game. A chill jolted his heart, rejuvenating the buried knowledge he had laid to rest as a teen, when the *hantu demon* had visited his home in Bohol. He grasped that this creature's behavior, whether agreeable or heinous, was determined by how people treated him.

At the roller coaster, the demon's hips shifted in a comely manner and a sparrow-like carol from his throat carried toward him. The longer Fuentes observed the creature, the greater the *hantu demon* invaded his mind and perverted his sanity, manipulating the image of his adored mother, the demon's greed taking advantage of their poverty. The carol excavated each detail of that childhood morning memory. Fuentes ground his thumbnail into his palm, hoping the sting would replace the portrait of the undernourished boy at the kitchen table with the creature. It took all his willpower to regain his sovereignty.

"How are you feeling?" Marta asked.

"We're moving on to greener pastures," Fuentes said in a rough voice.

"Are you sure?"

"I got what I came for, so we're golden."

"That's a relief," Marta said. "I thought you wouldn't help me."

Fuentes laughed. "My dear, you will be hugely respected in Cotabato."

CHAPTER 3

Finn and Rudolph drank beers in a bar on the outskirts of Burnham Park. Burt was holed up in a gambling den, throwing dice on a heat-warped plank. A squad of black ants crept up the nickel-plated strut onto the tabletop. Using his index finger as a catapult, Finn sent an ant sailing into a ray of daylight. The Temptations's "Just My Imagination" played on a musical Motown loop. Finn dusted another ant off the table.

"That's very Zen of you," Rudolph said. "Feeling better?"

"Miles," said Finn.

Finn recalled the duck, which had deserved a jubilant fate rather than the one Sergeant Reyes had in mind, such as a ward at a children's petting zoo.

Rudolph pulled photographs from his wallet. "These are my wife's cousins. All cherries." The Filipinas were dressed in scanty dancing outfits.

"Adorable," Finn said.

"So, I think my cousins are pretty. What's it to you? It never bothered you before. If you're lucky, I could introduce you to one of them. You're not a bad-looking guy."

"I bribed Reyes to get your ass out of jail. And for what?"

"These girls are my family." Rudolph replaced the photographs. "What's eating you?"

Finn drew a smiley face on the frosted beer mug. "I get it. This was a pissant rap. Catching you in a massage parlor with your pants off and your pecker wagging at some fifteen-year-old girl was a police snafu. The cops wanted to bust someone, an American, and they targeted you. Is that your story?"

"It was all smoke and mirrors, bro. Smoke and mirrors. The cops needed some cash for a gambling debt, a dope deal gone south, a new motorbike, whichever. Revenge, if the truth be told. Someone wanted to get even with me. Vengeance is a compelling factor in this country. You should know that. Yeah, the cops stuck me in that louse infested jail cell and took the bribe."

"You're innocent as a barfly."

"Now you see. The fog's clearing."

Finn ordered another round of beers beneath the slow-revolving ceiling fans. Sitting on stools at the counter, Finn noted two Philippine police officers evaluating Rudolph and himself from the bar mirror. They spoke in muted voices, but the look of contempt was unassailable. They were underpaid, taking graft from bar and club owners to complement their salary. For any petty infraction, a tourist could pay off the cops or be jailed for days. But Finn was a diplomat, of sorts. In another time, he would have bought the police officers drinks, a way to stay on congenial terms. Instead, he pushed the plastic ashtray to the edge of the table and ate a stale pretzel.

"I need some money," Rudolph said.

"I'm broke. Sergeant Reyes took my savings."

"You always have some bucks squirreled away. That's one of your loveable faults, Eddie. You see the potential for failure, where I recognize that failure is a concept that can be slung on its butt and called a triumph."

Rudolph had a way of reading him. 'Carmelita's aptitude for prognostication must be rubbing off,' Finn thought. The idea that Rudolph could get near his inner ruminations irked him.

"You always have a go-to stash," Rudolph said, signaling the bartender for fresh drafts. "You did in Rwanda, I bet? That's what makes you an effective bureaucrat. You're groomed for the fallout."

"The fallout?" Finn deplored being wrested back to the Rwandan genocide, the blood rivers, and the acrimony. The memories had yet to expire into the surreal landscape of remembrance. "You want to know about fallout. I wrote a letter exposing the real version of the ethnic cleansing in Rwanda to the American Embassy echelon, and they didn't want to hear it. Or they didn't want to confront the turmoil. So, they exiled me here, where the corruption is so ingrained that multiple arrests won't scratch the surface of criminal activity. If anything, it would hurt a number of innocent lives."

"Take your head out of your ass," Rudolph said. "This isn't the last train to Clarksville. You have political juice and that's a useful elixir these days."

"I was an effective investigator in Rwanda, such as stopping children from being sold into the sex trade. We imprisoned some head honchos. Now, I'm here to make inquiries about international water pollution crime in Southeast Asia. Did you ever hear of such a crock?"

"So, you screwed up in Rwanda by telling what really happened. Whoever could have prophesied that madness? Time in that hell hole messed you up, Eddie. Your humor is perverse."

"I see that as a godsend," Finn said.

"Not from my side of the table, bro, and I'm the guy who's watching over you."

The bartender dropped off the beers; the incident with Sergeant Reyes should have unnerved him, but it had left no impact. 'You're evolving in an affirmative light,' Finn thought. Yet, an imaginary ligature around his rib cage was choking off his airways, and he concentrated on his respiration. After twice silently reciting the *Namo Amituofo* Buddhist incantation, he reclaimed a modicum of normalcy.

"Amigo, return to the Land of Oz. If I don't repay the loan, you can always find me. You've known me for years. You know where I live, and my haunts. Have I ever bailed on you?"

"Let me think about that."

"I'm a respectable man, Eddie. And I swear on a stack of Bibles you'll get the money. How about it? This is primo karma, the likes of which boomerangs with benefits."

Finn sipped from the mug.

"How many years you been in the P.I.?" Rudolph asked.

"Four years on my first posting, and now three, this go-around."

"Head home to the embassy and stay in the city. You're out of your element in these sticks. The girls like your type in Manila, a real charitable American. But keep your guard up. The Philippines can be bad for one's health. You've got deeper lines in your face than you did two years ago. Now, tell the dudes in charge to re-assign you. A cushy stateside gig might cure your ailments."

"That ship is long gone." Finn's last trip to the States, after a two-year absence, had been disappointing. It wasn't the change to the environment that had troubled him—the vagrants on the pavement pushing grocery wagons laden with pots, plastic tarps, and bits of clothing, the dog-eared, ragged natives disgracing the National Parks, tossing trash on hiking trails, the muzak in elevators and malls, or the contaminated lakes where fecal waste washed onto shorelines, killing fish, and desecrating the fishing holes. Rather, he felt ostracized from his own countrymen, and vexed by the motherland, which was more alien than any republic he had lived in.

"The Brazilian Ambassador's wife was in the newspaper last week," Rudolph said. "Her husband, the Ambassador, still has the face of a weasel. Why she'd give up a fling with you to stay with that muskrat is unknowable."

"Are you blackmailing me? I don't give a damn who reads about my life."

"We've all got ugly details we want submerged, so don't say you couldn't care who flays the Eddie Finn life-book."

"I tell you again—"

"Chill out. You'll break into pieces if you keep this up, and we're inside a fucking saloon."

"I'm together."

"So how about the loan?"

The street was desolate except for a Filipina on the sidewalk toting a plastic bag of rice and pork, shouldering the blazing afternoon sun. 'This generation needs bona fide heroines,' Finn thought.

"Carmelita's a grand lady," Finn said.

"My wife has got soul. The Creator produces her kind once in a thousand years."

Finn piled ten thousand pesos onto the table. Rudolph snatched the bills, swayed to his feet, and cocked his short arms in a fighter's stance.

"Know I'm good for this bread. I'm off to the can."

"Enjoy yourself."

"I can see why you rub people the wrong way."

"It's a new art I've been cultivating."

"Be careful it doesn't gobble you up."

"Thanks for the tip."

"Just looking after a brother," Rudolph said, checking his fly and heading toward the comfort room.

*****

Finn, Rudolph, and Burt drank Red Horse beer in the car. It was twilight. The rutted mountain road descended at a precipitous angle, so one couldn't determine where the road's shoulder ended, and the jungle began.

"Are you married, Burt?" Rudolph asked.

Alone in the rear seat, Rudolph tossed an empty beer into a paper bag and grabbed one from the cooler.

"Yes, I have a wife," Burt said. "She's Pampangan."

"You can't count on Pampangans. But maybe you lucked out and got a gem. I'm sure you did. And you, bro, do you have a Filipina wife yet?"

"I'm not that lucky."

"You aren't lucky, I know. Now, let me expel the falsehood that's been pinballing in your head for decades that mentality supersedes carnality. The gospel is—nothing supersedes carnality. I'm thinking of the sixteen-year-old virgin who gave me a letter last week at my home in Zambales. I make sure she spends an hour a day pumping water from our spring, the upper body exercise making her tits grow by leaps and bounds, and at the same time keeps my mango trees merry."

Rudolph drained his bottle, retrieved another beer, and flicked the cap off with a Swiss army knife. "Why do humans lie about the fact that we spend most of our time thinking about sex? However, the luckiest ones spend a decent portion of time actually doing it, and they—including you, bro—are the shrewdest of the bunch. Forget the politicians, the politically correct faggots and dykes. I'm talking about human source and need. All right, enough venting of Baudelairean spleen on this point. But I see you get my meaning."

Burt cranked the volume on the radio, and the car moved lazily on a stretch of graveled road.

"Who's singing that song?" Finn asked.

"That's Kevyn Lattau," Rudolph said. "One of the best jazz singers. Her father was my Kafka teacher at UCSD in California, eons ago. To get even with that asshole, I sold Kevyn and her boyfriend some Mex scag. Her boyfriend died of an overdose. That's how seriously I take literature and bad teaching. Anyway, the scag must've helped. Gave her some soul, so she could sing the blues. Listen to her. Man, her father was one of those German ultra-conservatists who was in the Hitler Youth gangs, so she needed some motivation. I'm glad I could do my part to help her become a jazz musician. Amazing how many academics you can detest. Egotistical, hateful, fucked-up people. Almost as bad as preachers."

"He's a lunatic," Burt whispered to Finn.

"The hell I am. And I wasn't in jail for banging a pubescent like that prick cop Reyes charged. And you, Eddie, came to my rescue."

"With an envelope of cash," Finn said.

"Wouldn't your wife pay to get you out?" Burt asked.

"She probably thought it would reform my nature to spend time in the hoosegow. And she was pissed off 'cause she assumed I was getting a blowjob in a massage. Man isn't made to be monogamous. If I had money, I'd have a flock of lovely mistresses."

"Would you desert Carmelita for these mistresses?" Finn asked.

Leaning forward, Rudolph thrust his fingers into Finn's thigh muscle in a crocodile lock. "I'd be dead without her. She can ride a horse, tend a garden and out bargain any man."

"My mistake," Finn said.

Rudolph slid back into the seat. "She salvaged my life fourteen years ago, and I shared with her the blessings of Buddha, meditation, and tranquility."

The windows were lowered, and Finn gave himself over to the mountain. The burr of the car's engine mingled with the bird songs and the redolence of dove orchids, Philippine palms and staghorn soothed his nerves. As the car's speed slackened around a forty-five-degree bend in the road, Finn saw two figures in the headlights, beside the speed limit road sign. The headlights roved over their spindly forms, and Finn, striving to get a second view, peered through the rear window. He was tempted to tap Burt on the shoulder and insist on a U-turn. Jocelyn stood in the darkness, an apparition from Rwanda. She wanted Finn. He had not completed a task, or perhaps she was here to issue a warning, concerning his inept effort to protect Turgen, her son. 'There are no such things as ghosts,' Finn told himself, now staring out the front windscreen. But a nugget of doubt lingered, and Finn probed the possibility of a ghostly hinterland in his mind. It was best to keep such beliefs to oneself.

"How are you holding up?" Rudolph asked.

"Right as rain," Finn answered.

Burt drove with one hand on the steering wheel, and if he relinquished control of the wheel, they would sail off the mountainside. The image excited Finn, and then he felt ashamed. Death was not to be mocked. 'She's no diva,' Finn thought. 'Nothing of the sort. She's a broker of souls, a mainline junkie, who exhibits her face when nothing and no one can be saved. A real bitch.' Death had appeared the evening after his father's burial as he embarked to a local tavern. In an alley, she stood against a fire escape ladder, her lips puckered, bare-breasted, six toes conspicuous in each stiletto heel, enticing him to purgatory with the words, "Follow me, sonny".

The car straddled the road's center line, and Burt whistled to Eric Clapton's "Layla" on the radio.

"Epicures knew the truth," Rudolph said. "A blessing is a robust body and a serene mind. Or you can take the poor man's perspective, put your money in jars and bury them in the garden. That's what I should do with your bread, Eddie. But it will help Carmelita and myself in our daily lives."

Rudolph howled out the window, "Werewolves of London!" He opened another beer. "If God listened to the prayers of men, all men would swiftly perish, for they are ever praying for evil against one another. That's Epicurus. He also said we should have friends to help each other, and to know joy in life from sharing knowledge and experience. That's why I have eight women in my home in various stages of virginity."

As they cruised on the Cordillera Mountain Road, the air became leaden from the high humidity and the valley's lights came into view. Finn consumed the last measure of his beer. In town, traffic was bumper to bumper and the street lamps emitted a tangible vapor. Grilled food sizzled from charcoal rotisseries. Zigzagging drunkenly on the sidewalk, a man with a military crewcut glared at his wallet, which had fallen to the pavement. His stab to retrieve the wallet fizzled. He cursed, held onto a parked motorbike, and picked it up. His girlfriend stuck her arm out and he gave it to her. She jacked dollar bills from the wallet, tucked it beneath his belt buckle, and withdrew down the boulevard.

"That guy's in for a stormy night," Finn said.

"Shorter than you might think," Rudolph said. "He's got no wing man, so he's easy pickings."

"Where should we drop you?" Finn asked.

"I'll crash in one of the strip motels and go home tomorrow. You'll get every peso returned, plus interest."

Stalled on Fields Avenue, Rudolph pulled on the door handle near a two-hundred-peso-a-night flophouse where the whores, he informed Finn, cooked rice and stinky fish in the hallways and fed you for free if you were kindhearted. "And if they were unattached after a night's drudgery in the bar, they may sleep in your bed for no charge if they deemed you *guapo* and you bought them a late-night snack. Amen, brother."

Rudolph saluted from the sidewalk. Moving on, the neon signs implied a vast labyrinth of bars and restaurants. Without warning, Burt braked. A young girl, perhaps five years old, had ambled into the roadway, and Burt's headlights ensnared her in their glare. The woman who sold bagnets, a deep fried, crispy pork belly, at one of the food stalls, towed the girl away, shouting in a tirade of Tagalog profanity.

"I almost killed her," Burt said.

At a yellow stoplight, Finn said, "I'll bail here. Expert driving today, Burt."

On the strip, motorbike operators who sold dime bags of weed, played checkers on flimsy cardboard in an empty lot, and punters, half-drunk, meandered from bar to bar. Ignoring a hostess girl, who shouted out his name, Finn ducked into Stingers. He took a stool at the counter and asked for a Miller beer. The girls, shirtless, in skimpy vests and skirts, mingled with the customers and served drinks. Finn requested the mama-san to join him.

"Where's Criselda?" he asked her.

"She go to Manila," the mama-san said. "You want to meet a new girl?" She gestured at a chunky girl on stage who danced to the classic rock and roll tune "Bad Moon Rising" as though she wore leg braces. "How about her?"

"No. That one," Finn said, pointing at the girl with alabaster complexion picking glasses off a table. "What's her name?"

"She bar fined," the mama-san said.

"I don't care. I want to meet her."

"She's out of your league," the mama-san said, placing her fist on Finn's lap.

"What's her name?" Finn asked, removing her hand and drinking from the beer.

The mama-san put an ether-inhaler up her nostril. "No name," she answered, after releasing the spray. "Choose someone else."

"She must have a name. Give it to me."

"No name she has."

"Well, let's name her. How about Priscilla?"

"No name. She has no name. You *busog*. Drunk. Don't touch her, hansum man."

"Criselda, where is she?"

"She with her boyfriend," the mama-san wheezed into his ear.

Finn deposited a one-hundred peso note in the tab cup. On Fields Avenue, he sidestepped speeding jeepneys and throngs of paired couples for the evening. Two men in Hawaiian shirts exited an alley, laughing, giving each other high-fives. Beneath a dim alley light bulb, a woman in a short dress sat on the ground in the alley, one leg set at a forty-five-degree angle. Finn edged toward her. She was sobbing; a tissue plugged up a bloodied nostril.

"Where's my shoe?" she asked. "Where's my shoe?"

Finn scanned the alley. "I can't see it."

Her makeup was smeared, and her square chin and broad shoulders typified a well-conditioned swimmer.

"Shit," she said, her voice reduced to a normal range. "I just bought these heels. Can you check? I'd feel like a dummy with only one."

Finn prowled the length of the alley and pinpointed the shoe behind a wooden pallet. The heel was broken, hanging on by fabric. Within spitting distance, two rats clashed over an apple core. The duel had drawn blood, and the shorter rat had been blinded in the left eye. To mediate the dispute, Finn's foot quashed the apple. Instead of an amiable truce, each rat raised onto its hind legs. Retreating, Finn strolled up the alley until he reached the woman. She took the shoe from Finn, and he watched her battle to slip it on. With an outstretched arm, he endeavored to assist her, but she swung a fist, which connected against his ribs, the blow surprisingly violent.

Standing on her own, and taller than Finn, she said, "My purse. Where's my purse?"

There was malice in her voice. She had shaken off the assault from the two Hawaiian shirts, and he'd learned from experience that she could be volatile. Such types, known as Billy-Boys, swallowed estrogen hormone pills, a process to aid the transition from male to female, which routinely caused drastic mood swings. Finn always made it a policy to give such women ample passage on the street or in a bar.

She hobbled over to the spangly bag resting on a door mat and looked inside. "I've been robbed. Find everything," she demanded, as if urchins would pile forth from the two buildings' clandestine passages. She fetched a comb and wallet near her feet. "Please help, mister."

Finn found her compact mirror and lipstick case in a puddle of water. The cheap compact was totaled, and he was unsure of the color of the lipstick. Near the brick wall, he discovered her keys and, as he reached over a rusted, chainless bicycle, he heard another Billy-Boy scream from the mouth of the alley and come charging toward him. She was a towering figure and even in high heels, she ran at an alarming pace. Completely vulnerable, the body blow sent Finn reeling sidelong, crumpling to the knees. The compact and lipstick flew from his grasp. His head bounced off the brick wall. Flustered, Finn attempted to rise before the second onslaught.

"Stop! Stop!" the woman said. "He's helping me."

"Oh my! Oh my!" her friend cried. "So-so sorry."

The friend lugged Finn to his feet. Even in the hazy light, her heavily made-up face and putrid perfume disgusted Finn, but he smiled, nonetheless. He retrieved the compact, lipstick, and keys. Reaching the woman, he handed over the paraphernalia. She fondled his shoulder, the gesture apologetic in its grace.

"Well, that's it," Finn said.

"Thank you. Don't forget me."

Finn dawdled, uncertain how to respond. He blew her a kiss, made his way to the street, and hailed a trike. The breezy ride to the hotel further sobered him. Passing the American military cemetery with its rows of white crosses, he smelled mowed grass, which was groomed habitually by a Filipino groundskeeper. The crosses had no end. There were sporadic lamp posts on the gravestone lanes. The only semblance of life in the midst of the flowerless graves were the leafy trees. He tried to resurrect the vanquished, but it proved fruitless. A weariness stole over him. He shut his eyes and thought of all he had been and had possessed and what he had lost. The trike hit a speed bump, and his head struck the canvas roof. 'Serves you for drifting,' Finn thought with a grim smile.

At the Oasis front desk, the pretty receptionist gave him his room key, a handwritten message, and asked, "Mr. Ed-dee, are you sick?"

Finn grinned, feeling his upper lip stick to his gum line. In his room, he showered and brushed his teeth. As he assessed his features in the mirror, a bluish knot had begun to form on his forehead. Someone knocked, and he opened the room door. Criselda stared warmly at him, smelling as if she had come straight from a bath. She wore a round-collar white blouse and ironed trousers, with a gold Catholic crucifix at her throat. Silently, he took in her beauty. It was as if he straddled two colonies, and this one before him, illiterate and youthful, was his way forward.

"Can I come in?" When he stalled, she asked, "Do you have a girl inside?"

"No," he answered.

"I wanted to surprise you."

"I'll call by the club tomorrow."

"Never you mind. It's your life."

"It's not what you think," he said. "I'm just bone tired."

"I don't work the bar anymore," Criselda said, and strode away.

He wanted to call out to her. All he required was fifteen minutes without interruption and a pastoral setting, where she would listen to the oldest story of a man in need. He closed the door. He would see her later in the bungalow on Senega Street, which she shared with her twin cousins, sixteen-year-old bar girls, Tempest and Teresa.

From the closet, he retrieved a leather bag and unhitched the latch. He took out the pipe, a marble-size ball in tin foil, and his Zippo lighter. He positioned them on the bed sheet, peeled the foil, chipped off a sizeable opium flake, and nestled it in the pipe. With the Zippo lighter, he lit the opium, moist and brown and perfect. 'Precision leads to pleasure,' Finn told himself.

His lungs inflated, and there was a tickle on his tongue, as if he were inhaling nitrous oxide. Smoke eased out of the pipe's stem and spiraled up from the bowl. Each time, Finn exhaled the smoke in identical puffs. Satisfied, he set the pipe aside. The room had the dimension of promise and clarity. He thought of taking a swim and drinking a glass of Fundador whiskey.

He drew again on the pipe and the bitter flavor and saccharine aroma pacified the day's misadventures. Since morning, he had sought this excursion, the descent into a familiar subterranean tributary. He lowered the air conditioner and fell asleep to its placid hum and entered into a mystical state that was as close as practical to the death he wished to reach.

CHAPTER 4

Marta had spent the early morning at a local spa. After the massage and a shower, a plump Filipina had begun her manicure, clipping the nails and then filing them with an emery board. She spoke incessantly about her German boyfriend who sent her money from abroad, which was always a mere pittance to meet her requirements. Her skill was deft and painless, and Marta approved the pastel nail polish she had chosen. After applying the topcoat to seal in the color and prevent chipping, the manicurist guided Marta's hand under a light source to dry the nails.

"This should take a few minutes," the manicurist said. As she packed up her tools, she asked, "What should I do with my stingy boyfriend?"

"You're pretty and charming," Marta said. "There are other men who will give you money. Don't make yourself sick over him."

"That's sound advice."

"Is he an expert lover?"

"What? I don't know."

The manicurist checked Marta's nails and slid her other hand below the light source.

"It's none of my business," Marta said. "I apologize."

"He's old and not all that strong in that department."

"But the equipment still functions?"

"Mostly. But I make do." The manicurist further trimmed Marta's nails with the emery board. "Almost done."

She removed Marta's hand from the light source, appraised the nails and blew on each finger. 'A gesture of sexual interest,' Marta thought, 'hesitant yet brazen.' This appealed to her. In a world of liars and fictitious love, she preferred the idea of unfettered expectation. 'The here and now,' she told herself. 'This has value.' Intuitively, she knew that governments would be highly served by a conclave of women.

"Double the money you want from him," Marta said, giving the girl a hefty tip. "He'll come begging and think you're highly desirable. And if he doesn't call or write or visit, there are other men worthy of your affection. I'm half Filipino. I know his type."

"Oh, I didn't know you were Filipino."

"I am," Marta said, touching the glass door. "Don't lose your soul to this man. He's not worth it."

"I'll take your advice, miss."

Another customer sat on a bench, reading an old *Vogue* magazine.

The manicurist said, "You have a tender heart."

"Only a handful of folks might say that of me nowadays."

"Then they're kooks."

They both laughed in supple peals, as if they were two schoolgirls sharing a secret that would unravel for years to come. A trike took Marta to the Oasis Hotel and, as she entered the lobby, the pleasure she had acquired from the spa evaporated, the extreme humidity staining her shirt with sweat. She entered the room with a key and sat Indian style on the bed. The curtains were drawn, and a garland fragrance, similar to Thailand's *phuang malai* string of flowers that canal boat, taxi and bus operators arranged on figurines of the Smiling Buddha, scented the air. Finn released a congested snore from his nasal cavity.

"Eddie, stop playing games," Marta said, pinching his cheek. "What do you think you're doing?"

The tremolo scolding awakened Finn.

"Atta boy," Marta said. "You were choking in your sleep. These torrid climates never did agree with you."

Finn pulled on the duvet until it covered his chest.

"How did you get in?" he asked irritably.

"I said I was your wife."

Marta switched on a table lamp. Finn's face was bloated, and his lips belonged to those of a child, pink and fleshy.

Marta asked, "Was it a loving dream, Eddie?"

"I was dreaming of you," he answered, blinking, recalibrating his surroundings.

"Did I survive?"

Marta's hands were in her lap, and she saw him take note of the silver ring on her middle finger, the ring he had bought her in a bazaar in Kigali, Rwanda.

"I thought you were in Spain," Finn said, "getting laid under spruce trees with your German fiancée."

"He's Austrian."

"Marry me. What do you think of a Buddhist ceremony? It's my new religion."

"You're a capricious man."

"But loveable," Finn said, tossing off the duvet and standing ill-at-ease on the pine floorboards.

Nice belly, Eddie. You've really let yourself go to pot."

"I don't care about my weight," he said, grabbing his pants from the floor and yanking them on with a grunt. "I helped build a church last month in Quezon City. I was a boy again, swinging a hammer. It has a gable roof and the maple is aged, and I think the church will last for decades, if no one blows it up. We installed stained glass, and the altar is oval, so people can light candles during communion."

"That's an interesting admission for a man without faith."

"I told you, I'm a Buddhist."

"Then God is dead for you."

"I always permit a margin for the improbable. I have various sacred relics and a shelf of theological texts. That's the romantic in me."

His religious view had become superficial, whereas Marta had yet to reach Finn's level of detachment.

"What did you do when the church was finished?" she asked.

"I came up here. I had an assignment."

"I thought you would be on your knees begging for forgiveness in the new church."

"I wanted the simple pleasure of building a structure, using a hammer and nails, and a level, so that the angles would be true."

"Did you find Jocelyn's son, Turgen, before leaving Rwanda?"

Finn sat in a chair. "I did. He was living in an orphanage, and I located a relative willing to take him. The boy blamed me for his mother's death."

"That should have been expected."

"What do you mean?"

"It's always prudent to assign the blame on another, an American for example, rather than one's own country. If he blamed Rwanda, he'd only grow up with hate, and that can pervert a child's mind to do terrible things."

"When he's older, he'll come for me."

"Don't be so melodramatic, Eddie. It'll only be a knife to the ribs."

"That's comforting," he said.

Finn reminded Marta of the drunks in Kigali who sipped counterfeit alcohol in alleyways. Chattering among themselves, or throwing curses at passing cars, they were cut off from welfare. Narcissism had incinerated their appetite for life. To them, one hour was like any other in the day.

"Ever since Rwanda, I pray," Marta said. "Almost every night I do. You must think that queer."

"Rwanda was a bad place," Finn said. "It's inconceivable for anyone to adjust to mass killings. And if you do become used to that carnage, well, you consign others to danger."

Marta hunted for Finn's cigarettes, pushing away his books, a magazine on deep sea diving, and a coral cameo brooch pendant, which reminded her of her grandmother, a piece of jewelry a woman of the early 20th century might wear.

"I have a new job," Marta said. "I'm now the Minister-Council's assistant at the American Embassy in Manila."

"Impressive."

"The embassy sent me to see you. There's been a kidnapping, and they want you to take charge."

The cigarette pack on the television was empty. Marta's belly felt the same way her mouth did—funky, and in need of a cigarette to mollify her rising anxiety.

"Do you mind if I use your shower?" Marta asked, taking off her polo shirt and unhooking her bra.

She removed her pants and panties. Her breasts seemed undersized, in contrast to the days and nights she and Finn had shared intimacies in Rwanda. She prized her thickening waist, her stout thighs. In the last year, she welcomed her physical metamorphosis. It was as though her body proclaimed an exterior confidence. These are magical hips, she told herself. They can mesmerize a man. Deftly, she unraveled her braids, snipped to shoulder length after the Ferris wheel fire. An arm covered her breasts, leaving her lower half exposed. Finn's silence revealed he had acceded to her independence. Whatever affiliation they had once fostered together was history. She entered the bathroom, and her body unwound beneath the cascading shower water. After soaping her loins, the bathroom door handle shook.

"Go away," Marta said. "I don't need you in here."

"I know that."

"I sure hope so."

"I understand your anger."

"You understand shit."

Finn rapped on the bathroom door.

"Don't come in," Marta said.

Finn jiggled the doorknob.

"I'm okay. I'm in the shower. I'm peeing in the shower. Couldn't be better."

The wood creaked from Finn's bulk. "Anything I can do?" he asked.

The answer came quickly. "Don't go dopey on me, Eddie."

"I want you."

"Forget it," Marta told him.

"It's the big bad wolf," Finn said. "I'm coming in."

"Fat chance."

Marta dried herself with a towel, draped it around her body, and entered the room's alcove. Finn now wore a shirt, and Marta brushed her unbraided hair.

"Do you remember reading about the Chinese priest who was taken for ransom four months ago in the southern province of Mindanao?" Marta asked.

"I don't."

"The Abu Sayyaf were behind it. Last week, three American Peace Corps volunteers were kidnapped by these same militants. They were teaching locals English in Cotabato City, Mindanao. The American ambassador says he wants the Peace Corps volunteers and the Chinese priest rescued. This is your commission. Pay what you need to and take any action necessary but bring the three Americans and the Chinese priest home."

"What does this have to do with me?"

"You've been around this interplay before. The Minister Council, my boss, figures you'll know how to supervise this so-called diplomacy." She browsed the items on top of the bureau: Finn's wallet, keys, handkerchief, a yellowed rabbit's foot, as though he had carried it since childhood. "Well, that's the game plan the embassy brains came up with. But the priest is part of the pact. He's important. I don't know why, and they wouldn't tell me. Perhaps Vatican authorities are worried. But we can't cut him out. Plum P.R. for the rank and file."

"Find another flunky."

"It's not a request. Can I use your toothbrush?" she asked from the alcove. "And find me a cigarette."

Finn foraged his pants pocket and tossed the message the receptionist had given him last night onto the bed. He inspected Marta's purse. Inside her wallet, he unearthed a photograph of Marta holding a rifle. Over her shoulder, a burnt-out village smoldered. He hid the photograph inside a book, Paul Cartledge's *Alexander the Great*. He sniffed her lipstick and licked the ruby stick. As if in pursuit of a keepsake, he nudged items aside and picked up a tin cylinder. He unscrewed the lid and upended the cylinder. Nothing. He banged it against his palm, pulled out a piece of paper, and gazed mystified at the words. All the while, Marta had remained in the alcove observing Finn. There were three names on the paper.

"Can I help you?" Marta asked.

"What do these names mean?"

"They're names of saints," she said.

"Saints." Finn's brow furrowed. "Genevieve isn't the name for a saint. Or is it?"

"Put everything back. I don't plunder your property, do I?"

"You can," he said. "Take what you want."

Marta grabbed the cylinder and the paper with names for children she imagined she might have one day and dropped them in her bag. Candidly, she had rejected the possibility of being a mother. She didn't know the date of this realization. It had simply nested in her subconscious until one evening, she ceded to its residence. There was no culprit. Blame was not part of the equation. Abstinence from conception was her decision and no one else's.

"I once thought highly of you, Eddie. But you're a derelict. So, get your act together."

"I will," Finn said. From the bi-fold closet, he retrieved the leather bag, placed it on the bed, and separated the latch. He took out the pipe and Zippo lighter and stripped the tinfoil from the opium ball. With his thumbnail, he chipped off a chunk, placed it in the bowl, and with the stem in his mouth ignited the Zippo and high-flamed the opium. He took a single toke.

Marta checked the message on the duvet. "How do you know Captain Fuentes?" she asked, waving the notepaper.

"He's a confidential informant of mine."

"Is he credible?"

"Fuentes is most cooperative when there's a first quarter moon. When it's a gibbous moon, he's mercurial. And he's a born swindler."

Fuentes's name aroused Marta. It was as if the menace she perceived from him had transported her into an impenetrable forest where tree roots split the earth in the distorted shape of human bones. Be prudent, Marta told herself. She scratched the shoulder scar she had received in Rwanda, on their trip to Byumba. Shaped into a hydra's tail, it was as though a sentient organism lived in the raised tissue and conversed with her.

"This Captain Fuentes," Marta said, "claims he has useful information about the Peace Corps workers' abduction. Maybe he can help you in Mindanao. He'll be in Manila tomorrow."

"I'll set up a meet," Finn said.

"And I know someone else, an ex-pat who's lived here in the Philippines for years and has contacts with the Abu Sayyaf."

"We should send in the military," Finn said.

"Or bomb them off the map, I suppose."

Finn gave her the thumbs up. "Maybe the U.S. Marines aren't busy. Those boys love a dandy barn burning."

"The American government can't do that," Marta said. "We have you instead, the embassy's Security Investigator. It'll be like your arrests of Triad sex traffickers in Africa and springing your friend Richard Rudolph from the northern Luzon jail. A payoff. That's what these groups want. The newspapers won't know about it. If successful, you'll be praised by the ambassador for the arbitration."

"And what are you here for?" Finn asked with a radiant smile.

"I'm your matchmaker with Jacky Ciros. He can broker the transaction."

"Jacky Ciros? I don't know him."

"Characterize him as a businessman emeritus these days."

"You mean Ciros is a former spook? Oh, that's just perfect."

"Don't get hysterical."

Marta emptied the contents of Finn's leather bag onto the sheet, exposing a fisherman's utility knife, a bottle of Hoppes Lubrication Oil, and a .22 caliber pistol. The Browning Buckmark pistol had been cleaned. As a teen, she had been taught to shoot a Marlin Model 60 rifle. She checked the .22 pistol's slide, ejected a bullet, freed the magazine, and laid both on the bed.

"What's that supposed to stop?" she said, tapping the two-inch barrel with the hairbrush. ?A hamster?"

"No," Finn said, "a man, or even a woman."

"Little boy toys."

Finn folded the tinfoil over the opium and set the pipe, Zippo lighter and opium in the bag.

"Why do you do that now?" Marta asked, a tenor of sympathy in her voice.

"It makes the day more pleasurable," Finn said.

She drew back the curtains, whipping up a cloud of sunlit particles. Finn sat against a pillow, and Marta acknowledged she was in a drama of her own genesis. She took the pistol, inserted the magazine, and pulled back the slide. Picking the .22 caliber bullet off the duvet, she pressed it into the chamber. She perceived consternation in Finn's face and a loss of color. Perhaps he'd noted the safety was on and Marta could not marshal the hate that the murderous act required. 'Smarter to clobber him in the face with the barrel than leave the weapon unused,' she thought. Though, the drama deserved an exercise of metaphysical theft. She laid the pistol at Finn's elbow.

"I'm going out for breakfast," Marta said.

"Those three kids are in a waking nightmare."

"We need to rely on one another."

"I'm your man," Finn said.

"Let's pray that's true."

CHAPTER 5

Jacky Ciros poured two teaspoons of sugar into his coffee and studied a crossword puzzle. The pencil tip rested at the five blank spaces requiring a name for the phrase *a biblical poem*. A smattering of early-morning regulars read the newspaper or shot pool at Margaritaville. Behind the circular oak bar, the staff spoke Pampangan and Wari. A wide-hipped waitress delivered a tray of creamers. Jeepneys and trikes shuttled in the dust of Fields Avenue. Marta entered and took the single available seat at Ciro's table.

"Let's pick up where our last conversation ended," Marta said, requesting a lemon iced tea from the waitress.

"If you have money," Ciros said, sniffing a creamer and shoving it to the far side of the table, "the Abu Sayyaf may negotiate. But who can predict what a guerrilla band will do when motivated by doctrine? The one saving grace is money, and that's what counts to these guerrillas."

Finn had shadowed Marta and pulled a chair over to the table. His fingernails needed shearing, and his hair had been flattened to his head with water.

Ciros said, "If you want a pow-wow with the Abu Sayyaf, I know who to contact in Cotabato. I know how to bargain with these guys, and I assure you everyone comes out alive." He aimed a finger at Finn. "And will he be going to Mindanao?"

"I'm in charge, Jacky," Finn said. "The American Embassy—"

"In charge?" Ciros erased a letter from the crossword puzzle. "Your designation doesn't mean squat to me or to anyone in the southern provinces. If you think so, and act that way, then the three Peace Corp workers are dead."

"I like that," Finn said. "You're the boss."

"I'm the only solution to their predicament."

Finn rolled his eyes. "You're a magician. What a relief."

"I'm a realist," Ciros said. "I find the best option and execute the proposal."

"How many times have one of your campaigns gone sideways?" Finn asked.

"Dumbass, mind your manners."

Criselda stood behind Ciros and nudged his shoulder. "I'm sorry, but I need pesos for the video game."

Ciros held out a one-hundred-peso note and told her to get change from the cashier.

"Hello," Finn said.

Criselda took the note from Ciros.

"Hello," Finn repeated. "Are you winning?"

"There's no winners in the game," Criselda told him.

"You've met Criselda before?" Ciros asked, as she went to the cashier's cage.

"She stopped me from hitting a drunk in a club. He was being disrespectful to one of the girls. I can't recall what happened. I know I hit him; I had blood on my knuckles. I searched for him. Someone told me the police discovered a guy in a barrel of rice. I let it go at that."

"I'm usually here to watch over Criselda," Ciros said. "But I was in Manila on business."

"So, you're a couple," Finn said.

"Yes, and I'm hopeful about our prospects."

"You are a lucky man," he said.

"It's not luck. I take care of her and her family." The two men observed Criselda as she controlled the video game's joystick. "She can play that game all day," Ciros said proudly. "Filipinos are affable people. But never cheat them, or else you'll end up fertilizer for a banana tree."

"When should we fly to Cotabato?" Finn asked.

"Tomorrow or Wednesday. I'll inform you of the exact date. And what price is the U.S. government willing to pay?"

"A suitcase full of dollars," Finn said.

"Eddie's an effective negotiator," Marta said, "and I'm sure the government will let him use his own discretion. They did in Africa."

"I like a man with a limitless bankroll," Ciros said. "All you have to do is be able to get the money. I can take care of everything else."

"The Americans are my responsibility," Finn said.

"It sounds like you want to go in with guns blazing."

"That was my original suggestion."

"Say, you might be useful after all," Ciros said with silken deliberation.

Finn came to his feet and noticed Marta's Kigali ring absent from her middle finger.

"I'll see you tonight," Finn told her.

"I have another engagement," Marta replied.

Before leaving, he paused at the mini-arcade and Criselda's video screen. "I'm sorry about last night. Is he your boyfriend?"

She aligned the stack of peso coins and answered, "He is."

"Why did you stay with me?"

"I didn't know if I'd see him again. No letter, no call. My family is poor, like I told you. They live in Samar. But now I'm with him."

A paddle blinked at the bottom of the screen and Criselda swiveled the joystick to repel the bouncing ball.

"Are you happy?"

"He takes care of me. But you have a girl anyway."

"Can I play?" he asked.

"No."

He whispered, "I miss you."

"Thanks. Me too."

Finn pocketed a peso coin from the stack.

"I'll see you soon," Finn said.

"Up to you."

"No, it's really up to you."

Finn stood on the wood-planked entrance to *Margaritaville*, close to the restaurant's window screen, attempting to decode Marta's and Ciros's conversation. A girl in a halter top, seated on a stool before the screen, smirked at him and Finn scudded to his port side. Marta had her hand raised, as in an oath, authenticating his veracity to Ciros.

Finn stepped into the street. In the outdoor market, vegetables, fruit and fish—croaker, moonfish and barramundi—were laid out on pallets and sprayed from a hose by a woman in a grungy smock. Farther eastward, above the mountain range, clouds were amassing, as a light rain began to fall in the waning sunshine.

*****

"Is he mentally stable?" Ciros asked.

Marta sipped her lemon iced tea. "No. I've known the guy for years, and he could blow everything sky high. He's no Cub Scout."

Ciros waited silently.

"The thing is, he gets carried away," Marta said, as if she needed the explanation to maintain her composure. "At times, he presumes he's acting as savior. But he's a harlot. And such a combination isn't dependable."

She lifted her blouse sleeve, exposing the ridged scar.

"I look at this and I know Eddie Finn. He's a man out for himself. In Rwanda, we were in a car accident. Later, my wound became infected, and instead of taking me to a hospital we spent half the day in a decimated village. It was our assignment. I developed sepsis, and now I've got a scar like Godzilla had drilled his teeth into me."

"He should have helped you," Ciros said. "But he assumed you'd live."

"In Rwanda a tsetse can kill you," Marta said. She wetted a fingertip and traced it over the scar. "Some people think scars are as glamorous as tattoos."

"Then we'll have to watch him," Ciros said. "He could mess everything up. Maybe he's out for himself, like you said, and maybe he's just ignorant and a klutz." Ciros picked his nose. "He may be useful. We could offer him as bait."

"That'll be a new role for him."

On the boardwalk, Finn had the jaded eyes and lined face of a man with too many questions, questions he should have answered years ago, questions that men usually answer stupidly or discard because of their difficult nature. But Finn held on to these questions, analyzed the enigmas and, eventually, remained baffled by them. He peeled away from *Margaritaville* and ambled toward the center of town, where one of the sleepy strip bars would be opening for the hardcore morning crew.

CHAPTER 6

Rudolph found the photograph of Carmelita in the trash barrel outside the flophouse on Fields Avenue. The Filipina he had bedded last night had discovered the photograph in his trouser pocket while she ransacked his clothing for money. She spelled out to him that she could excuse his adultery, because all men are unfaithful, but he had betrayed his wife, another Filipina, and that was a crime. Smitten by spite, she stole the photograph, hot-footed outdoors and hurled it into a trash barrel. Rudolph had chased after her. She fled, intimidated by his Filipino curses and the flabby girth on his hips. Curbside, Rudolph lifted the photograph off a ratty pizza box.

"Got you, my love," Rudolph said, sweating in the morning haze.

In the photograph, Rudolph and Carmelita stood on the veranda of their Zambalas home. Groves of mango trees were noticeable, and the rising sun laid a halcyon walkway in the pasture. Rudolph recalled the tropical fruit trees and the zest from the mango petals in the breeze. The blues, possibly John Lee Hooker, could be heard from the stereo inside the house. Carmelita's cousin, José, was behind the camera. He was a runty teen Rudolph had adopted, and who had died from a slipshod robbery, killed by the house owner, a woman, who carried a .38 Special in her handbag. In the photograph, Carmelita's thin arm curled around his waist, and a periwinkle kerchief was tied in her hair.

A trike's engine backfired, dismantling his rosy fantasy. Rudolph retired to his hovel, dressed, checked his wallet, and was grateful the girl hadn't stolen a peso. There was a loud bang on the door and Rudolph yelled, "Come ahead," and Finn entered.

"You look as if you just lost a testicle," Rudolph said.

"And you look like you just got laid."

"No man should sleep alone, and no woman either. Say, how did you find me?"

"There are only half a dozen denizens like this on Fields."

Finn sat in the room's solo chair. "Don't you like to sleep by yourself?" Finn asked.

"You must be mad, bro."

"Just slightly disturbed."

"My man." Rudolph reclined on the bed. "So, what's the problem? You wouldn't have come here if you didn't want my assistance."

"I'm going to Mindanao on holiday for some sun and surf. If you have some spare time, I could use the company."

Rudolph registered the glint of malevolence in Finn's eyes, the fickleness that unnerved people and made them privately curse him. 'The psychosis of bureaucrats,' Rudolph thought.

"Don't hand me that bull. Spill it," Rudolph said.

Finn shrugged. "I'm on an ill-fated government mission to Mindanao, and I could use a friend if things go haywire."

"Have some balls and tell your boss to off himself. The assignment isn't worth your life."

"Marta needs my help."

"That's bad news. You still have a thing for her, don't you?"

"No, not really. Maybe. It's closer to a bond."

"Does she give two shits about you?"

"I don't have that answer."

"Let's check the *I Ching*," Rudolph said. "Then we'll know what lies ahead."

"Is this necessary?"

"Positively."

Rudolph unpacked the velvet sack with the dice and the book that told of one's predestination. "Throw the bones," Rudolph told Finn.

"Where?"

"On the desk."

"That's it?"

"Then I'll research the numbers in the book. Give me your birth date."

Finn did. From Rudolph's embattled perspective, mankind eclipsed the black and white headlines. The warfare accounts that magazines and newspapers exploit and that regimes jerk off to with vindication had a purpose beyond television, video games and poisoned seas. There was the unknown and the knowable, and the pit where all misfortune lay. This, Rudolph perceived, with categorical certitude. Those who demonstrated these realities were the street waifs, the savants who sank farther into their own isolation, and the virtuous who had no clue that they had been deceived by preachers and politicians.

The dice hit the mirror, stopped, and Rudolph announced, "It says here this year is not your best, that love has been squandered, and you should spend all your money to know the bliss of a penurious life."

"Will I get married and win the lottery?"

"The *I Ching* is sacrosanct. Tomorrow, we'll go to the local temple. Maybe that will change your future, but it's doubtful. However, know this, I'll never mislead you."

Finn nodded and said, "There's another matter. I have to meet the cop, Fuentes."

"Why that creep?"

"Three Peace Corps volunteers and a Chinese priest are being held by guerrillas near Cotabato City. That's the reason for the trip to Mindanao. Fuentes wants in on the transaction. It's all about money. He's slime, and I need you with me."

"Give him the volunteers and the priest. The southern provinces are a nest of vipers."

"What are you saying?"

"You'll only screw things up. And when you do, those people will end up on a slab in the Manila morgue."

"I need someone I can trust. I'll pay."

"The bread is a plus, man, but—." He pulled a letter from a James Ellroy novel. "This is from Ollie, a pal of mine, my contact for weed," Rudolph said. "He got busted in Korea, and now he's in the Inchon Penitentiary for seven years. I sent him a box of books. I miss him."

Rudolph hauled out a typed manuscript from his military duffel. "I've been writing this book for fifteen years," Rudolph said. "It's about Vietnam. Yeah, another Vietnam War story. But this is the way I see it, but who's gonna publish it? The ideas in it —like me, I'm afraid—are so cynical that I must admit this is a truly monstrous, evil book. I know we've had Vietnam War stories up the yin-yang. There's no market for such a book, but I keep tinkering." His voice deviated to a softer decibel. "I've seen God a thousand times in this thing, plunged into the pit of rejection, and ravaged my brain until I got vertigo, and now that it's almost done, I'm still banging my head against the wall."

"What are your choices?" Finn asked.

"Choices?" Rudolph laughed. "My mother's dead. My aunts and uncle are pariahs. When my mom died six months ago, I was at her bedside. After the funeral, the relatives flocked around her Salvation Army furniture, her dilapidated home, her paltry possessions, and picked away at them. They're Kentucky hillbillies who can't read the newspaper, Southern Baptist bastards who use religion as a cloak to rob and rape. But I have the one jewel in my life: Carmelita, who still gives me a hard-on each morning. Were you ever married, Eddie?"

"For a brief period. My wife made me see my own cruelty. But I learned who she was, a user of people. I never saw the woman shed a tear, even when we divorced."

"You two made quite a duo. But you have a daughter."

"The one grace in my life. But she needs a stable father."

"You mean generous."

"Someone enlightened," Finn said.

"Don't sell yourself short."

"I write her letters, and she writes to me. If there are such things as blessings, she's mine."

Rudolph did not want to get into the machinations of Finn's former marriage. It would be a slog through a muddy minefield with emotional carnage.

"After the divorce, what next?" Rudolph asked.

"I applied for an offbeat diplomatic venue."

"To Asia?"

"Yes, and two years in Rwanda. In Kigali, when I couldn't sleep, I'd go to whorehouses. The girls would crouch on the floor behind a kerosene lantern hoping to be chosen. Some of them had lost a hand, an arm, a foot, to a land mine or possibly a machete. Tribal traditions at play. There is a curious beauty in the maimed. The first girl I slept with had lost her leg up to the knee. They'd do anything for 30,000 Rwandan francs or thirty bucks. But she was memorable in a way that's hard to describe. It was like bedding divinity. Still, you can't imagine the barbarism that took place and the peoples' resilience. On several excursions, I traveled to a massacred village."

"Why would you do that?" Rudolph asked. Finn was taking him to a landscape that deserved attention, acts propagated by villains, dictators, military regimes and callous men. It didn't matter if the territory was Sarajevo, Rwanda, Mindanao, or the hundreds of abducted children of Argentina. Such regions and events cure in one's recollection and demand to be divulged, even publicized, and heralded until they latch onto a global consciousness, if such an awakening is possible. 'Stay vigilant,' Rudolph concluded. But Finn was a buddy, and it was Rudolph's dedication to friendship that invariably quartered him in dubious alliances. One cannot scorn a kindred spirit, even if it means jumping into a cauldron of boiling piss.

"It was my job to investigate those villages," Finn said, "and I wanted to understand how people could be so inhumane."

"Hanging with the dead is no revelation," Rudolph said. "Was it redemption you sought, you sick cat?"

"Nothing of the sort."

"Then you were examining the human spectrum from decency to the indescribable."

"We all lose our way."

"Amen to that, brother."

"But I can't forget."

Rudolph touched his forehead. "You must be impaired in here to forget shit like that. All one can do is cram it in a drawer, seal it, chain it in, and live with the load."

"Do you ever think you should have helped out more when you were in Vietnam?"

"I was in a fuckin' war. All I wanted was to get out alive, and have my buddies come out in one piece." Rudolph believed a crazed, forgiving universe hovered over him. "I have enough problems caring for my soul and Carmelita's, her family… and you, to worry about populations. If you can help one or two people, and have killed no one, you've led an honorable life."

"That's why society is ass crazy," Finn said.

"It's the honest-to-God truth, bro. Now, what time do we meet this freakin' cop, Fuentes?"

*****

In his hotel room. Ciros drank a glass of Emperador whiskey. One bare foot scratched at the other, where a mosquito had bitten him. Criselda had neglected to remind him to wear his hat this afternoon, and now his skull was badly sunburned from the tropical sun. He breathed asthmatically.

Ciros said, "I'm here for you."

The meaning was unimportant. He tore off Criselda's towel, and before she could swing away from him, startled by her sudden nakedness, Ciros collared her wrist and dragged her onto his lap. He groped her thigh. Then she watched him disrobe. His jeans, the ones he had worn for days without a wash, fell around his ankles. The room's lamp was off, and the quasi-darkness comforted her.

On the bed, he pushed her head toward his groin, but she refused and told him, "No. I don't do that. Maybe only to my husband."

"Aren't I your husband?"

"No, I'm sorry. But you are not my husband."

"You little minx," Ciros said.

He rose to his knees and hit Criselda's inner thigh with a closed fist until her legs parted. He tweaked her nipples, and she bit her lip as Ciros's fingers clasped her neck. Then he struck her temple. The blow was impetuous. Her head caromed off the wooden bedpost, and she fell to the floor. With the room swimming in her vision, she took her panties from the foot of the bed and pulled them on. She scuttled backwards on the floor as the planks vibrated from his footfalls.

His penis drooped, half-erect, shrinking in his frenzy.

Ciros was humming a song with the dulcet rhythm of a lullaby. Gripping her thighs, he flipped her body over and drew her panties to her knees. His open hand spanked her buttocks in rapid succession, so that her body quivered, as if given electric jolts, and when he ceased the barrage, he kissed each cheek.

He belted her again. The depravity in his voice as he said, "I know you like this," made Criselda pray out loud to her Catholic God.

In short order, he was inside of her. The thrusts were hard, pushing her breasts and chin against the pine floorboards. He grabbed her hair, and Criselda took a fistful of Ciros's jeans to swing at him, but the undertaking was useless. The jeans slipped from her hand.

"No no no," she cried.

"I love you," Ciros said.

He let go of her hair, and the reckoning between them normalized, where Ciros fucked her and Criselda accepted the fucking until he came inside of her, withdrew his flaccid member, and relaxed against a wall, panting, his legs outstretched with Criselda curled on her side.

"We'll have dinner tonight at the Brown Derby," Ciros said.

Criselda went into the bathroom. She knelt on the bottom of the tub, the shower drenching her hair, her body, and then she squatted and scooped water inside of her, flushing Ciros out of her womb. She coughed twice, expelling more of him, ridding herself of his semen and stench. Naked, Ciros stood at the side of the tub. He was soft and slack-faced and sat on the toilet seat and watched Criselda without speaking. And when Criselda completed evacuating Ciros from inside of her, she shut off the faucet and took a towel from a shelf. She edged past him, left the bathroom, slid under the bed sheet, and when the bathroom door closed, she knew she would be alone for hours to come.

CHAPTER 7

Finn entered the casino on MacArthur Highway as town folks shoved peso coins into slot machines. The vermillion carpet and cobalt wallpaper imprinted with golden aquatic serpents heightened the casino's luxurious ambiance. As he descended into the casino, the serpents unfurled and expanded, their chartreuse tongues elongated, their slant eyes lethal, gazing at the room of gamblers. Someone had doctored the thermostat to a colder setting. Women wore sweaters, and their sapphire rings tapped the poker tables. The eau de cologne of old age battled the artificial lilac air purifiers, and people constantly migrated to the rear of casino, where high rollers tossed thousands of pesos onto blackjack, craps and roulette tables. Layered with a plush carpet, the windowless room created a carnal intimacy. Fuentes sat on a leather couch near the horseshoe bar, staring at a lava lamp, which glowed in the middle of the table. Finn took a seat on the couch and could distinguish Fuentes's brutish aftershave.

"Before we get to your business," Fuentes said, "I need an associate who can circumnavigate the rules. There's a Korean who likes private games. His preference is five-card stud. We'll arrange signs, you, me, and a friend of mine. We'll take all his cash, perhaps two-hundred-thousand pesos. All you have to do is contribute $1,000 U.S. I'll show you how to play."

Fuentes picked up the deck of cards from the table.

"You've got the wrong cowboy," Finn said.

"You should have some fun. There's no felony in ripping off a tourist."

"Another time."

"Oh well," Fuentes said. "Pay me 500,000 dollars and I'll negotiate with the Abu Sayyaf. Then you'll get the kidnapped American children."

"Respectfully, I don't want your help."

"That's impractical."

"I simply wanted to inform you in person that your assistance isn't needed."

"It would be a lapse in judgement not to employ my services," Fuentes said in a meticulous voice, tossing the cards on the table. "We've done business for years, and you have always received a fair remuneration."

"That's not a factor here," Finn said.

"You insult me."

"I'm sorry you feel that way." Finn regretted using the word, *sorry*. He had made a pledge to never speak the word again after he had seen his Rwandan driver, Cedric, fly three feet into the air, do a backflip, and hit the ground, after a land mine had disintegrated his legs. He remembered he had said he was sorry to the dying boy, and afterward had scampered out of the savannah grassland toward the Jeep. The word's inadequacy only made people sullen.

"How many dollars are we talking about for the Americans?" Fuentes asked, rubbing his raw bottlecap knuckles.

"Your participation isn't required," Finn said.

"You don't need Captain Fuentes?" Fuentes said with incredulity. "Everybody needs Captain Fuentes. Even you. I'm buddies with the Abu Sayyaf commanders. I have been to their camps. I'm one of them. Do you get it? I'm your inside man. I've infiltrated their lair." He motioned toward the Filipino clad in a tan barong shirt, who stood beneath a photograph of Ferdinand Marcos.

"It was a shame, Elwin, what happened to those two Filipinos who were arrested at the south entrance of Clark Air Force Base," Fuentes said to his bodyguard, now posted next to the couch. "The story goes three assassins inserted the two men into tires, stuffed them in like Tootsie Rolls. They spilled gasoline over them and torched each one. Both had been shot in the head. Thursday morning the police picked up the wife of one of the dead men. They'd found his driver's license. The wife identified her *awawa's* Levi belt buckle in the ashes. No one knows why they were killed. Some rumored it had to do with illegal gambling. This part is terrible, Eddie. A newspaperman wrote an article about the tragedy, and no one has heard a peep from him since."

"They say the Filipino military had a stake in it," Elwin added, shaking his head.

"Hush, Elwin. We don't want the American to think the Philippines are not civilized."

At the end of the horseshoe bar, Marta sipped a Bacardi Rum Coke. She held a look of apprehension, or at the very least one of concern.

"My American friend, is the lady with you?"

"I don't have a lady."

"I'm famished," Fuentes said. "When I was poor, we used to eat dog. Do you find that offensive?"

Finn came to his feet. "Not in the slightest."

"Did you know dog meat makes your dick strong?" Fuentes said.

"That's a new one."

"Once again, how much money will you pay for the American children?"

"That scheme is over. Give it a rest."

Finn took a seat at the bar. Clad in a short skirt, Marta stretched one silky black leg over the other, which glimmered in the bar light. Purple-tinted mascara highlighted her eyebrows, and she wore three gold hoop earrings in each lobe. Finn detected her Guerlain Idylle perfume, which he knew she applied to her breasts. It was as if he were staring at a reinvented woman, and he was unsure how to proceed, astonished that their relationship had been mysteriously expunged.

"Why are you here?' Finn asked her.

"I came here for a drink," Marta replied.

"Have you met Captain Fuentes?"

"Which oaf is he?"

"The guy in the yellow shirt."

"He's attractive."

"Listen to me, Marta. He's not going to interfere with us."

"You pulled rank, did you? I like when you do that."

He took the straw from her glass and curled both ends, leaving an air pocket in the middle.

"Pop it," Finn told her.

"I don't play your bar games," Marta said with rancor, getting off her stool.

At the archway to the casino, Elwin blocked her route. She said, "Watch where you're going, friend."

"Let her pass, Elwin," Fuentes ordered.

As Finn approached the couch, Fuentes called out, "American, you can't do this alone."

"It's copacetic," Finn said.

The lava lamp cast Fuentes in a volcanic tapestry. Finn could not take his gaze from the evolving patterns; it was as though Fuentes was comprised of only shadow and light, a bloodless man sheathed in sallow skin, and that his size was the result of excesses, extravagant eating, sex, killing and lies.

"Life never is this thing you call copacetic," Fuentes warned. "That's an invention spawned by amateurs and elitists."

"The government contract with the Abu Sayyaf will go off without a hitch."

"That's what those two thieves thought. That they were immune to anonymous forces."

"I admit, sometimes one encounters a negative fate," Finn said.

"Negative what?"

"One moment you're here," Finn said, "and then nothing. You're killed by lightning on a sunny day, mowed to the pavement by a drunk motorcycle punk, blindsided by a car on a motorway, stamped out by high cholesterol or felled by a massive coronary. Lights out, man. It doesn't get worse than that."

The lava lamp blazed intensely, further distorting Fuentes's visage.

"Death is permanent," Fuentes said, "but for some, it can take a while to die. And there are those, I hear, who like to watch the ultimate curtain call."

"That's eerie. The best to you."

Finn walked to the craps table where Marta shook the dice.

"Watch this," she said.

With a flick of her wrist, Marta threw the dice, and they came up seven.

"You won," Finn said. "Now, let's go."

The croupier stacked the chips in front of Marta. She told him this was her third pass, and she was staying. He watched her toss the dice from one hand to the other. She had the devil-may-care attitude of one lost in a summer field, friendless and unafraid. Nearby, Rudolph waited at a roulette table, eyeballing the scene. From behind, Elwin pushed Finn against a stone column.

"The captain wants to see you again."

"There's nothing more to be said."

"To be what?"

"We've had our talk," Finn said with finality. "That's it. *Maintindihan*?"

Elwin raised his barong shirt, exposing the revolver. His feline smile shrank, to emphasize Fuentes's instructions. From his periphery, Finn saw Rudolph charging at them in a full trot, arms outstretched, his irises huge. He grabbed Elwin's thighs, lifted his stocky frame, and heaved him to the floor. Elwin's pistol flew out of the waistband. On his knees, Rudolph unleashed an uppercut into Elwin's jaw, ramming the side of his face into the carpet. The second blow landed squarely on Elwin's collarbone, and a hoarse rasp broke from the man's voice box.

Rudolph rose and said, "We got to go."

Uniformed men with batons rushed toward them. With a hand on Marta's hip, Finn propelled her from the table toward the casino exit. She bumped into a waiter, and her chips scattered to the floor. The three maneuvered past slot machines, feckless patrons and a dragon, who scouted the retreating trio. A woman's chow-chow dog growled at Finn. They dashed out the casino doors and fled up MacArthur Highway, scissoring between pedestrians. Marta ran efficiently in her low-heeled shoes. At the end of the fourth block, they stopped before a smoking outdoor chicken barbecue stall. Rudolph, hands on knees, panted. The white hairs on his arms and chest shone with sweat, and the top of his head was scarlet.

Finn inquired, "How are you doing?"

"He's having a heart attack," Marta said.

"Is she with you?" Rudolph asked, amid rasping breaths.

"This is Marta. She's from the American Embassy."

Rudolph slowly straightened. "It's a privilege, Sunshine. Eddie has told me glorious stories about you." A jeepney roared past and Rudolph stared at a Filipina in the rear seat. "Did you see that? Not even a smile. Usually, an old fart like me gets a smile, but not today. Something's amiss. To blazes with them all. I need to sack out. See you in Shangri-la."

Rudolph gave them a cheery wave and sauntered off in the light rain. As he rounded the corner, he began shouting at someone and flapping his arms, as if in an apoplectic fit.

"Your friend's not right in the head," Marta said.

"What were you doing at the casino?" he asked.

"Partying."

Lightning creased the night sky. Marta was flawless, her face muscles taut, the lips indigo. But she wasn't the same woman he had known in Rwanda, and she would not be with him tonight, and that is where he desired her, partnered with him in bed and in the dreams that vaporize upon waking. She plucked an earring and tossed it to the pavement.

"Get out, Eddie," Marta said. "Go to Manila. Have the embassy boys send someone who can assist me. You're not up to this mission. Those hostages deserve a guy who'll give a thousand percent."

She headed to the crosswalk.

"Where are you going?" he asked.

"Not with you."

Finn watched her until she faded from view. At a newsstand, he bought *The Manila Bulletin*. The storm intensified, with raindrops the size of marbles, and Finn took shelter in the doorway of a clothing store. In the middle of the second page of the newspaper, an article, encapsulated in four paragraphs, explained the situation of the kidnapped American Peace Corps volunteers. The first paragraph stated there were two boys and one girl, all from a Chicago suburb of rectangular homes, pruned lawns, and low crime. A blurry visa-size photo of the girl was erroneously aligned to a story of a prostitution bust in Cebu City. Looking up from the newspaper and staring out into the rain, he spotted Criselda.

"Hey Criselda!" Finn shouted.

She came toward him holding an umbrella of polka dots.

"Where are you going?" he asked.

"I'm off to see my friend Annabelle. You want to come with me?"

She raised the umbrella, and Finn joined her. The rain gushed in widening sheets, and soon the rising water mounted the curb. She told him about the college she wanted to attend when she had the funds, and that she would study computers. They entered Sacred Heart Hospital and rode the elevator with a boy in a leg cast, slouched in a wheelchair.

In the shared unit, two geriatric patients were linked to IV drips, and they stopped at the foot of the third bed. A Catholic priest, in an easy chair, gauged Annabelle's cardiac monitor. His face was pockmarked, his cologne nearing the expiration date. He had removed his white collar and could have been mistaken for a street hobo, scrounging for coin.

Annabelle slept. She wore a nightgown the color of hay. Her facial shading was the beige of an onion with the same fragile covering. Near the priest, Criselda dropped to her knees, took Finn's wrist, and coaxed him downward. He yielded, so that she did not sense his resistance. With head bowed, he manufactured the face of his father in his mind, and in their discourse on baseball and San Diego's weather, he saw that father and son had the same chin, but that his father's eyes were brown and his were hazel, like his mother's, who lived in a mental institution, drawing charcoal Degas dancers with exaggerated limbs. 'Your future is secure,' he thought to himself. 'Incarcerated in a looney bin and diving farther into incurable neurosis.'

"Are you okay?" Criselda asked.

"What are you praying for?"

"I pray for my friend Annabelle, my mother and father, my sister Alma and my brother Caesar. I can pray for you, too. Do you want?"

"I'd be grateful."

After an inaudible recitation, Criselda sat on Annabelle's bed. "How do you feel, sister?"

"Hi," Annabelle said, roused awake.

"I have a letter for you. It's from that American soldier you dated." Criselda set the envelope inside the pillowcase. "Do you need anything?"

"Not now."

"Sure?"

"You're so helpful to me."

Criselda approached the Catholic priest.

"She tires easily," the priest said.

"We'll come tomorrow, Annabelle," Criselda told her friend.

They rode the elevator with a double-chinned nurse who chatted with Criselda about the latest news from Mount Pinatubo. On the street, she walked away from Finn time and again, to be doused by the rain. With each desertion, Finn readjusted the umbrella over Criselda, and when she paused at a lamppost, frowning, the hamlet caught off guard by the sudden deluge, he took her to his hotel. In the doorway, Finn unlaced and removed her wet sneakers. Criselda stripped to her panties and pulled on a terrycloth robe from the bed. On the television, a black and white movie featured people being led into a barbed-wire camp.

She asked Finn, "What's wrong?"

"Not a thing."

"Are you crying?"

"Do you know what's happening here?" he asked her.

"It's a movie."

"Yes, it's a movie about World War II and the extermination of the Jews by the Nazis."

"I don't know about that," she said, obstinately.

He muted the television. If he had been a younger man, he would have been dismayed with her ignorance of these facts, and that her education had not surpassed the tenth grade. But he did not care whether she knew or did not know that there had been such a thing as a World War. Her knowing or not knowing solved nothing, and he was damned if he was going to chronicle the Holocaust. She did not even know what a Jew was.

He stroked her flat nose. She brushed his wrist away, and he kissed her mouth. He removed the robe and shed his own clothing. On the bed, she guided him inside of her, and he felt her chest swell with air. Supported by his forearms, he watched her breasts shake with each movement of his hips and her eyes stare at him. They rolled onto their sides, and she wiped sweat from his brow and wrapped her arms around his neck and muttered phrases in a strange dialect. He came this way, his penis within her, her face beside his own. She would not let him leave her. Even when he found himself growing smaller, she wouldn't release him.

She slid beneath the blanket, and in a chair, he smoked a cigarette in the darkness. He could smell her in the room, a purity that made his own body feel weightless.

"Annabelle's going to die," Criselda said.

"Yes," Finn said.

"It is AIDS."

She began to sob. The lamentations were those of a child. He rubbed the cigarette out in the ashtray and sat on the bed. Her head was buried in the pillow. She did not stir, and he did not speak, and he waited for some time until she drifted off to sleep.

CHAPTER 8

"We are like the Philippine warrior Aguinaldo," Fuentes told Elwin. Rain peppered the roof of the parked vehicle. It was early evening. "We fight the Americans, and though we may retreat, we continue to fight them. I don't care how much our people take the American into our homes and how much our people love them, they are a bane for the Philippines, and we are rotting because of them. They do not offer our people or our women a better life. I see in Finn this same selfishness. Soon, we will ransom him, too, and then he'll know what it's like to be at the mercy of others with authority. He'll know the agony of defeat and see the coming of death. And I want him to watch those American children die, one by one, and learn that no one and no country is invulnerable."

"Why do you have it against this one, Captain?"

"Not just him. Yes, on second thought, chiefly him, Elwin. Because he thinks he can't be hurt. He thinks he has experienced all physical pain. And he's a fool to think that, and I want to teach him what the greatest hurt is."

"And what's that, Captain Fuentes?"

"Suffering."

"But everyone suffers," Elwin said.

Fuentes picked Elwin's wrist from his lap. He flipped it raw side up, removed a knife from his pocket, pressed a spring mechanism releasing the blade, and with a firm strike, scored

Elwin's wrist. Even as Elwin labored to free his hand, Fuentes refused to relent. He angled the knife's tip against Elwin's throat, and said, "I will kill your wife, your children, your cousins, your mother and… who else? And all else you hold sacred. The village will hold a grand Mass for you. But you will be dead, though the first to die will not be you. You will know the death of your wife and those you love before your time comes. Is that suffering?"

"Yes," Elwin said. "There's none worse. But does this Finn know of such a thing? Of love? And of such remorse?"

The rain and the arc lamps converted the thoroughfare into a surreal mural. Elwin's wrist bled, and he fumbled to knot a tissue around the cut.

"I have seen his eyes," Fuentes said. "They are women eyes."

"Are mine women eyes?"

"Yes, my friend."

"Now look at my eyes, Elwin. What do you see?"

Elwin held his gaze on the windscreen. Fuentes patted his cheek. "Look," he told him.

Elwin complied. "They remind me of an animal," he said apologetically.

"I have been told that before. A fisherman from my province once said I have the eyes of a whale. Eyes that show no light."

"I have never seen a whale," Elwin confessed. "But if you say you have whale eyes, I believe you."

Fuentes placed his hand into the rain and caught droplets in his palm. He stroked the wet against his forehead, and his lips parted. In the outskirts, a dog barked on Lankandula Street.

"This is what Eddie Finn will know when he looks into my eyes and realizes his suffering is only to start."

"You're scaring me," Elwin said.

Fuentes pointed toward the casino. "Here she comes," he said.

Elwin started the engine.

*****

The rain brought the suspicion that she was unsuitable for her American Embassy directive and her own internal mandate. Marta shouldered her way past two teenage boys sharing a joint, tripped over an exposed sewer pipe, and nimbly adjusted herself. There was one thing she told herself she wasn't going to do and that was to be with Finn. She wanted to inform Ciros how to utilize him. Water dripped from her nose and the street noise atrophied to a lull, due to the red stop light.

Once in Mindanao, Finn would be isolated, his docket amended by other actors, exaggerating his talent of persuasion. Seduced by these arrangements, he would be assured he was the sole agent to execute the negotiations for the Peace Corp youths. By enabling his executive status and inflating his ego, Marta would convince him to give her the ransom money. After all, she was Filipino, spoke the language, and had greater familiarity with the senior players than Finn. With her assistance, a higher success rate existed.

On her middle finger she wore Finn's Kigali ring, and on her index finger her lover's United States Naval Academy ring. Finn had never challenged the lie she'd told him years ago, that her mother had given her the ring for her birthday, which made her both despise and pity him. It also made it difficult to forget him. But now she had the solution of how to manipulate Finn. He was simply a pawn in her game of soldiers.

A car stopped parallel to her in the street.

"Come in, Miss Marta," Fuentes said, congenially. "I'll take you home."

Marta recalled Fuentes at the Ferris wheel, regal and self-reliant, and said, "I appreciate the lift."

In the front seat, the air conditioner functioned poorly, and a layer of dew filmed the windscreen, which Elwin cleaned with the cuff of his shirt sleeve.

"I'm staying at the Lewis Grand Hotel," Marta said.

"We'll take a slight detour first," Fuentes said.

Marta crossed her arms. "I don't want to."

"This will interest an embassy woman like yourself. If your friend Finn was here, he'd be intrigued, too. Once I show you, you'll recognize its importance."

"Take me to my hotel," she demanded.

"There's no hurry." Fuentes smiled, the automobile accelerating into the middle lane. "I find you very attractive. Don't you agree, Elwin?"

"Yes, beautiful like the moon," Elwin said.

"Have you ever seen the Sea of Tranquility from a telescope?" Fuentes asked Marta.

"No. Let me out."

"It's stunning," Fuentes said, ignoring her plea.

"That sea would be the ideal spot to make love," Elwin said.

"Legend has it," Fuentes said, "lovers have lost their souls to one another when gazing from a telescope upon the Sea of Tranquility."

"That's trash talk," Marta said.

"My apologies. But you should revel in the unimaginable. It's the way we'll save those Peace Corp workers."

"I'll change my thinking cap," Marta said, "but let's keep our feet on terra firma."

The rain decreased, and they motored toward Dau. In Dau, Elwin turned off the main road and took frequent side streets. Marta attempted to remember the route by memorizing landmarks, a tree splintered by lightning, a girl washing her hair in the rain, a tabby cat lurking in an empty truck tire. She went so far as to pinpoint the moon's bearing. But the moon defied logic, for it voyaged from one end of the sky to the other, whirled to her blind side behind a batch of clouds, and materialized directly ahead. Driving over a bridge and into a pasture, the car's high beams lit the bumpy road.

"I prefer your hair before you cut it," Fuentes said.

"So do I."

Elwin braked at the No Entry Road sign.

"We're here," Fuentes said.

When Marta didn't react, Fuentes reached across her lap and thrust open the door. Her shoes sank into the soil, and Marta saw only an endless field. The air was bittersweet, with the residue of three-day-old salted fish. In the near distance, the land rippled, the effect akin to stones thrown into a rural pond. Fuentes directed the torch, and Marta tailed him.

"A man telephoned and told me his fiancée was in this area," Fuentes said. "She had run away from him. Men do such terrible things to girls."

The road broadened, and Marta swung alongside Fuentes. The torch light projected a powerful beam. Soon, a leafless tree came into view. The trunk was the circumference of five men, and serpentine roots sprung from the soil. At the tree's base, manacled to the trunk by a chain, a girl sat on the soggy earth. Fuentes gave Marta the torch, knelt before the child, and spoke Tagalog. The girl replied in a string of blubbering non-sequiturs, and Fuentes told her to be quiet. Shielding the girl's head with his torso, he fired his pistol, dismembering the padlock. The report resounded in the night. Marta half expected a response, a farmer's shotgun perhaps, sparking in the dark. Fuentes disengaged the chain and hoisted the girl into his arms. With the torch on the girl's unblemished face, Marta estimated she was barely eighteen. Fuentes pushed the sobbing girl into his shoulder, and they doubled back to the car.

Fuentes rode in the rear, his coat wrapped around the girl's midsection, her body solemn against his corpulent physique. The noxious odor of the paddy field pervaded the car. Marta spun around. Fuentes's fingers cupped the girl's exposed breast. It was as though he was holding a dead mouse or a barbell. There was nothing sensual in the pose. The scene was purely for her entertainment. He titillated the nipple, and the girl yelped.

"Why would this man call you?" Marta asked.

"He knows if she was dead, he'd be dead, too," Fuentes said. "He's a thief, but he won't lie to me. I like that sort of man."

"He should be punished."

"Listen, Miss Marta," Fuentes said calmly. "In his head, he thinks he teaches this child and me a lesson. But the child will go home to her province with plenty of pesos for her and her family to live for a year, and the man will meet me in private to confess his sin. We both know there's no such thing as atonement." He kissed the girl's nose. "She's uneducated and poor, like so many, and eventually she'll start dancing in the bars. If you want, you can have her for a minor contribution to the lost lamb personal fund. She'd be a faithful servant. You would be doing her and her family a courtesy. What do you say?"

"I don't buy people," Marta said.

"You are as ignorant as Eddie Finn."

"I know how things operate. Remember, I'm Filipino."

Fuentes buttoned the girl's blouse. "Miss Marta, this child wants to be with you. She'll take care of your house, sleep on the floor with only a pillow at night. She'll tend to your needs, and she'll gratify you at any hour, and the mornings, too, if you want. And, if she refuses, I'll tell her to comply with your commands, and she will—for me. Have you no humanity? You are worse than the men who come here from overseas and screw our girls. You do nothing."

"I'm here to help our country. But I need a favor from you." Marta turned, cast off her shoes, and slid her hands up her thighs. She raised her hips, liberating her panties, and held them up before Fuentes. "I want you to give these to Eddie," Marta said. "We have to distract him from his assignment. You can say I'm your captive."

"What do you expect to gain with this silliness?"

"Money for you and freedom for Filipinos."

Fuentes told her to give the panties to Elwin, who pouted and pointed at the seat.

"How do you know this trick of yours will succeed?" Fuentes asked. "Who would care? A finger or an ear might have greater influence on Finn's behavior."

"He doesn't like you," Marta told him, and dropped the panties on the seat.

"I don't think he likes you, either."

"What are you talking about?"

"He's in love with a whore." Fuentes motioned Marta closer. "Again, I ask you, why are these undergarments essential to Finn?"

"He used to buy me this label. They're from France."

"So, you think he's a fool."

"He has that trait, yes."

"You two have much to learn about seduction."

At the Lewis Grand Hotel, Marta stepped barefoot onto the pavement. Fuentes lowered his window, and said, "I will meet you in Cotabato City, Miss Marta. I will preside over the transaction. Follow my instructions and we'll both be well compensated."

"Just make sure Finn doesn't alter our project."

"I'm your agent," Fuentes said, "and she," tipping his head to the girl, "will be watched over tonight. Just in case you were concerned about her health."

With the hotel room's table lamp on, Marta changed into a single-piece bathing suit. At the pool, she showered at the outdoor stall, removing the rankness of this evening's affair, and dove in. She coasted along the bottom, sensing the grouted tile floor, aware of the profound isolation. Using breaststrokes, she willed her way through the turquoise water, lit by aerial lanterns, convinced of her accuracy and strength. Ahead, the pool reflected the nighttime glow, as though fireflies skipped on the surface. With arms outstretched, she judged the neighboring wall. Her breath held as she made contact, and when she emerged from the shallow end, her knees stung, scraped by the pool's tiles. She abhorred the blood and was irritated at her swimming skill.

In her room, Marta bathed with a bar of soap and shampooed her hair. She wanted the gratification of impeccable cleanliness. She swathed a towel loosely around her hips. From the closet, she removed a miniature chess board. Releasing the latch, she laid the concealed syringe on the table. She wished to see the contrast between the inanimate table and the glass syringe that would soon have life, and methodically aligned the unused powdered heroin, a teaspoon, and a lighter.

Nearly a year ago, before her inauguration to heroin, she had foreseen a cataclysm, a fluid that when introduced into her veins would have the same melancholy as her abortion. But the heroin was passive and voiceless, and each time she brought out the heroin, the substance remained distasteful. In Phnom Penh, her Thai lover had coaxed her to try the drug, disclosing he would inject the junk below her big toe, so that no one would be the wiser. He was a former four-star food and beverage hotel concierge in Bangkok and had been hooked for years. Since their third meeting at a Sofitel bar lounge, he had dragged her into his tightening web of upscale clients and hotel staff, who furtively requested the white powder treat, whether in a hotel room or an off-road bathroom stall. And once in a Bangkok *soi*, he'd booted up, and inquired if Marta wished to join him. She always declined.

This evening, as she purified the syringe with isopropyl alcohol, she thought, 'I'm ready. I am primed for the trip.' Many a night, she had executed this Sacrament, removing the syringe, heroin, teaspoon and lighter. She knew the procedure; she had seen it done before. She had even cooked the mix for others, like her Thai lover. If she had not consummated the process for him and friends, then the ones who needed the fix would soon have lost their minds. So, she had strapped them up.

There were no other thoughts in her mind now——no person, no memory, no tether to propel her backward or forward in time. It was the ritual that governed her. With the instruments properly arranged, she opened the porch door, shed her towel, and contemplated the starless sky. She lusted for nothing, not a blessed thing.

As if in a trance, she glided her hand from her shoulder to her collarbone to her breasts. She teased her right nipple, and it quickened to her touch. Hearing the siren call from inside the room, she closed the porch door, surveyed the table with the instruments and the package of heroin, and whispered, "Tonight, you're mine." She laughed, and went to bed with the heroin intact, slept, and dreamed of a glass metropolis of liquid fire and immaculate bodies from a conquered nation.

CHAPTER 9

In the hallway to Annabelle's hospital room, Criselda warned Finn to be polite to the Catholic priest. His demeanor toward the priest the previous day bothered her, she told him. He had acted as if a brute consoled Annabelle and not a holy man.

It was an hour past dawn, and the priest was absent. Someone had taped Annabelle's nameplate bracelet to her wrist, to prevent it from falling off. The room was stuffy with an odor of stale milk. Criselda chose items from a steel cabinet. She arranged a T-shirt adorned with rockets, her underpants, jeans, a maroon jacket, green socks decorated with stars and sneakers with a Velcro seal on the bed near Annabelle's feet.

"We're going to church," Criselda said.

"Yes," said Annabelle, "but I'm very tired."

"My friend Eddie will help."

Finn smiled, and wished his cigarettes were not in his shirt pocket. Facing away toward a window, Criselda dressed Annabelle. He heard the ticking of the wall clock and Annabelle's rapid exhalations, as though she were in a marathon. Through the window, he watched boys in the playground throwing a baseball without gloves and girls rising and descending on dilapidated swings.

Criselda said, "It's time."

Partway down the corridor, Annabelle's legs buckled. Before her knees hit the linoleum, Finn entwined her in his arms, lifted her off the ground, her ribs, hard and smooth as fossils against his chest. Her hands on his stomach were surprisingly warm, and her scent was that of an orchid, as if she had been born from a flower. In the lobby, he questioned Criselda out loud whether they should return Annabelle to her hospital bed. Criselda disregarded his objection and pushed against the door. In front of Sacred Heart Hospital, she stepped to the curb to hail a jeepney.

"Am I heavy, sir?" Annabelle asked.

"Eddie. Just call me Eddie. And you're light as a feather."

Her lips pressed against his shirt collar, and Finn recalled his daughter, and it seemed to him that Annabelle weighed the same as his daughter when she was ten years old. Dressed in her Cinderella pajamas, he would carry his daughter off to bed after she had fallen asleep in front of the television. But there was a defect in this girl, as though a dipsomaniac had taken a corkscrew to her spine. Her body was cold against his now, and in the morning light, he saw purple marks on Annabelle's forearm, where the IV needle had been. Finn hugged her closer. He grinned, and Annabelle lodged a fingertip into one of the creases in his face. A jeepney idled at the curb.

"This way," Criselda called to them.

Cars and buses ballooned around them. Finn assisted Annabelle into the jeepney, ducking low, watchful of his footing in the aisle. Criselda and Finn sat on either side of Annabelle on the bench that faced the roadside. The jeepney driver stomped the gas pedal. They traversed several blocks. An old woman and a teen girl sat opposite them, and a boy of four or five wove against the teen girl's torso.

"*Kumustika*," Annabelle said to the boy.

The boy giggled, took a step, and balanced himself between the teen girl and Annabelle as the jeepney idled and two new passengers entered the vehicle. Once seated, the two newcomers passed their ten pesos forward. Annabelle clasped her hands in her lap. The brief color from outdoors had vanished.

"We're almost there," Criselda whispered.

"I'm thinking of my mother," Annabelle said. "She's coming from Leyte to see me."

"That should make you happy."

"I told her I'm pregnant."

"Was she surprised?" Criselda asked.

"I really am pregnant. At least, I daydreamed that last week. Isn't that crazy?"

"I think so."

"I'm just a whore," she said in English, in a lighthearted tone.

After another stop, the jeepney hurtled forward and the teen girl opposite Annabelle produced an orange from a brown paper bag.

"Are you hungry?" she asked Annabelle.

"*Hindi. Salamat,*" she said. "No. But thank you."

The teen girl peeled the orange for the boy and gave him two wedges. The boy set one wedge on Annabelle's knee. Annabelle took it and drew in the juice.

"*Masarap,*" she said to the boy.

"You look ill," said the old woman.

"Grandmother, please," said the teen girl.

The orange fumbled from Annabelle's fingers to the floorboard.

"You should be home in bed," the old woman scolded. "Go home and rest and eat."

"I'm taking care of her," Criselda said.

"You should do a better job."

"She does a good job," Annabelle said.

On the city outskirts, the three stepped to the curb. As the jeepney wove behind a bus, Annabelle waved at the old woman, and the old woman gestured skyward, as if the answers to her tribulations resided in an ephemeral empire.

Perpendicular to the street, Finn envisaged a sculpted facade leading to prodigious church doors. Instead, they crossed into shadow and entered the church. The gateway was open-air, the interior of the church breezy and almost soundless, barring the voices from street stalls. Just after the nave, Finn could see a sunlit atrium with flowers, terra cotta clay pots, clipped grass and a limestone lane that led to another area of the facility.

Criselda and Annabelle sat on a pew close together, with Finn four seats behind them. The stained-glass windows colored the ten-foot-tall statue of Jesus Christ in a saffron light. A consoling gust from the street passed the unseen wall. Immersed in the silence, Finn's mind strayed, and he hummed to the Rwandan *Chants et Danses Rwandais* and pictured Rwandan girls and women with arms linked, their colorful skirts expanding and flowing as they danced in a circle of life. He tapped a foot to the seductive music. He knew, though, that the devil migrates without restraint in all regions and in each season. But in such gatherings, he hides in the tall grass, trembling.

Annabelle's face revealed a benign acceptance. A checkered bandana covered her hair, and wiry veins lined her jaw. Finn sank onto the kneeler, and Fuentes slipped noiselessly into the adjoining seat.

"I see everything you do," Fuentes said.

Finn kept the shock of seeing Fuentes to himself and took the Bible from the recess.

"A book can't redeem you," Fuentes said.

"That's the truth."

"But you read the Bible?"

"I have."

"That's out of character."

"I like the stories."

"Why are they important?"

Finn turned to the Gospel of Luke. "When my father was drunk, he'd entertain his friends with his grandiose adventures. They liked that about him—the way he could fabricate a story from a monotonous day into an amusing event. He was a born con man."

"I read he died of an overdose."

"No," Finn said. "He was a border patrol officer and was killed in a shootout at the Rio Grande."

"You're proud of him."

"Not really."

Fuentes glanced at the King James Bible. "So many of these fables end badly. I was once attracted to the telling of Lot and his wife, who was changed into a pillar of salt for disobeying the Lord by gazing at Sod'om. Do you know that she doesn't have a name in the Bible? She's only known as Lot's wife. When I was young, I interpreted the story as a cautionary tale that shows a person's miserliness can sabotage all motives." He sat back in the pew. "But now I view the story differently. Lot's wife was bored and bound to look at Sod'om. Even though God had warned her not to look at the city, she was seduced by temptation. It was in her DNA to do so. I realize we are the same as Lot's wife, in that no warning can ever suffice to deter us from temptation. So, we are all in need of assistance from time to time. Even you, and those two girls at the pew. And, your lady, Miss Marta. Your pilgrimage to Mindanao will fail unless you agree to my help."

"Keep dreaming," Finn said a bit too loudly, attracting Criselda and Annabelle's disapproval.

"My, oh my, you have no idea of what's ahead," Fuentes said. "Tell Marta to get her priorities straight. The Abu Sayyaf are dictating the outcome of this trade. No one else. Can you see that?"

Finn closed the Bible, restraining his rage. "You're corrupt," he said, returning to the bench. "I don't believe anything you say. Maybe you pass pesos to the poor, but I know the final destination for you, and for me, is not strewn with garlands."

"True, no one will mourn your death."

"*Our* death," Finn corrected him.

"Next time, carry a revolver when you see me," Fuentes said.

"Why is that?"

"Cotabato is not nearly as hospitable as this church."

Fuentes skimmed his hand over Finn's crotch and marched toward the church's gateway.

*****

With Anabelle again comfortable in her hospital bed, Criselda went to her bungalow. Beneath an overcast sky at one o'clock in the afternoon, Finn took the Rabbit bus to Manila. Three hours later, he retrieved money from the American Embassy and transferred the sum to the Mindanao Consolidated Cooperative Bank. At his hotel, he packed a bag with the bare essentials. He disposed of all items that would classify him as an American government official, knowing that such recognition could result in his own abduction. He kept a photograph of his daughter in his wallet that did not, however, divulge her age; the image bolstered his adherence to the mission.

Darkness enveloped Manila: a brownout was in its third hour. As Finn rode in a taxi, the noise of the city emulated a sleeping bear, snug in its hibernation. Marta met him at the airline terminal with two tickets. Her face was drawn, as if she had been awake the previous night. She took his arm, escorted him past the police and toward the 727 Lockheed poised on the tarmac.

"I thought you forgot about me," Marta said, as she fastened her seatbelt.

"I made it, didn't I?"

"That's not what I mean. I imagined you were in trouble. Forget what I said the other night. I can't do this without you."

She was her old self again.

"We're not sleeping in the same hotel," Marta said. "And since that's the case, let's stay in close contact." The jet's engines fired up. "Ciros will meet us in Cotabato with his girlfriend. He said she may be useful since she speaks the dialect. He'll hook us up with the guerrillas. Then we'll pay the ransom and get out with the Peace Corp workers and priest in tow, all happy like little Indians."

"You're confident," he said, as they waited on the runway.

"I'm not going to let anything happen to you. But you have to do me a favor."

"Name it."

"You have to give me your word that you won't get involved any further than bringing the money together. I'll supervise the details. Stay in your hotel room. I'm telling you this for your security and the lives of those hostages. If you do what I say, I guarantee the Peace Corps kids won't be maltreated, and once home, they'll recite tales of your heroism."

Finn agreed. They soared into a brilliant sky. She squeezed his hand, the jet banked, and he valued her persistence. As the plane stabilized, the intensity on his hand escalated, as an object stabbed his knuckle. He saw she was wearing the Kigali ring, and the other ring, the one her mother had given her, was missing.

CHAPTER 10

The Abu Sayyaf soldier dragged the fat, freckle-faced boy out of the hut. His arms were tied behind him, his neck bore mosquito bites and his trousers rode low on his hips. He reviewed the jungle before him and the Philippine village of wild dogs. The soldier shoved him into a chair in the middle of the sunny yard. The fat boy breathed deeply from his mouth, his tongue resting on the bottom row of teeth. From the cover of a coconut tree, Fuentes appraised the American. He had seen the same fear on other pilgrims: Amnesty International infidels, Performing Arts social workers, Center for Investigative Journalism students, Jesuit priests and the conglomerate of missionary clergy, who grew obese as their flocks dwindled. Over months or years, these temporary good Samaritans all came to realize they were in enemy sectors, under threat, pillaged by poverty and disease, and their institutional and government machinery was as incompetent as their leaders to protect them from terrorism.

"Put a gun to his head," Fuentes said, in the Illocano dialect, to the soldier in a Boston Celtics shirt.

The soldier inserted the barrel of his AK-47 behind the fat boy's neck.

"Dance," Fuentes said. "Make him dance."

"He's shitting his pants, Captain," the soldier said.

145

"Take a picture of him dancing in his own shit. This will make the American government pay. They will not see the humor, only the tragic circumstance. But it will be entertaining."

The soldier wedged the AK-47 barrel into the boy's jaw. The boy's mouth shut. He rose, feebly, reluctant to surrender the chair. In remarkably clear English, the soldier said, "Dance."

The boy peeked at the soldier and finally at the two men sitting on a bench in the shade.

"These Americans have pig faces," Fuentes told Lito.

"You say they will pay millions of pesos if the Americans are panicked," Lito said.

"Yes, and the money will make even a short man like you tall."

Lito clutched Fuentes's forearm, snaring the spider tattoo. His thin fingers had the same puny vigor as the local grandmothers who toiled on the plantations, weeding cassava from the earth.

"This is my army, Captain. Remember Napoleon, and my hero, José Rizal? Both were shorter than me."

"My apologies, Commander Lito. I only meant to say that the Americans trade on fear. Give them fear, and they will deliver the money. And then your army will multiply, and all your demands will be met. And the most important one, an independent Muslim Mindanao." Fuentes bellowed, "He's not dancing!"

The soldier jabbed the barrel of the AK-47 into the boy's neck. "I have a college education. Dance or I shoot," the soldier said compassionately.

The boy lifted his legs and impersonated a jig, shuffling his feet, swinging his elbows, pantomiming a tune. Unable to attain a rhythm, he sagged to the ground. Wiggling from side to side, he resembled a three-legged cat on its flank, trying to right itself.

"Drop him in a hole!" Lito yelled, stomping his crocodile boots. "Take a picture, then shoot him, and take another picture.

We still have two others. This will really make the American stooges crap their pants."

"A genius idea," Fuentes replied. "The hole and the picture are attractive. But one less American will mean less money."

"We could take the Chinko priest from the other hut and shoot him."

"That would be a bad move. Even his death will reduce the ransom."

"Is that true? Priests can rot for all I care."

"Ooo-ooo, it is so," Fuentes said.

"What should we do with the fat boy?" Lito asked.

"Bring out the girl," Fuentes ordered.

The soldier kept the boy in the dirt with a backhand to his nose and retrieved the girl from the hut. She, too, had her wrists bound, though tied in front of her. The soldier led her into the middle of the yard. Fuentes came forward, wiping sweat from his brow with his shirt sleeve. The girl was in her mid-twenties, her black hair grooved with pink dye, and her eyes were the hue of balut eggs. She had the pointy ears of a monkey.

Within an arm's length of her, Fuentes said, "Take a picture of them."

Another soldier, with a Polaroid camera, hotfooted over and peered at the viewfinder. "I can't see him," he said, pointing to the American boy.

The soldier with the AK-47 booted the boy in the kidney, and said, "Please, stand up."

The boy struggled, and when he faltered, seesawing, unable to find his footing, he looked up, pleadingly, at the soldier, his head squirming, mimicking the anatomy of a trapped quarry. His wan face reddened. Then the soldier shot the boy in the ear. His body contracted like an accordion into the dirt. Blood squirted from the side of his head. The girl gasped and her eyes bugged out, as if she had never witnessed a death before. The soldier pivoted and ripped her blouse. She wore a bra, and he tore that from her breasts. She squirmed where the boy's blood pooled, losing her balance. On her knees, she shuffled one leg forward until she recovered her footing and, squaring her shoulders, she ran. Her hyper-gait reminded Fuentes of a television program of African giraffes eluding prey, loping across a wheat-shaded savannah, wary of cougars and hyenas, head bobbing in a telescopic pose. Scrambling toward the jungle's perimeter, she maintained her direction. The nearest village lay countless miles south. She was rushing eastward, where the dense jungle would surely swallow her. Fuentes watched her flopping breasts and her gallop that ended when Lito, who had raced after her, tripped her. The girl belly-flopped into rotting palm fronds, and Lito rammed his boot toe into her armpit, and rolled her over. The girl squinted, confused, her lungs pumping in short, intermittent breaths.

"I will have you tonight," Lito said to the girl. "I will fuck you in the ass."

Fuentes came over and spoke in an easygoing manner. "Miss, nothing will happen to you. The soldier who shot your friend will be reprimanded. This is all an accident. You'll be home soon with your family, eating steak and ice cream."

He helped the girl to her feet. Her bra hung from her neck like a bandolier, and he slashed it free with a knife. Prodding her shoulder, he led her to the yard, past the dead boy, who had not been moved, and whose jaw had fallen open again but lacked the petrified tenseness that had transformed his face when alive. Fuentes and the girl entered the hut. The other boy, thinner and taller, groveled in a corner.

"Is Tommy O'Connor dead?" the boy asked the girl.

The girl sank to the floor. "The bastard shot him," she said.

"Not this bastard," said Fuentes.

"Shit," muttered the boy.

"You two will be safe," Fuentes said, kneeling. "And no one will hurt you again, miss. You have the captain's sacred word."

He fastened the remaining buttons on her shirt, grasped her chin, dabbed the corners of her mouth with his handkerchief, and wiped mud from her cheek.

"You're just like our girls," he told her.

"I'm an American," she replied passionately.

"That won't win you any favors here," Fuentes said.

At the door, Fuentes extolled her courage to a lost cause, namely the education of the poor by way of English language lessons, when substantial change only happens in revolution—the killing of enemy soldiers, citizens renouncing their leaders, kidnappings, and the occupation of towns and cities. In the yard, the fat boy baked in the steamy daylight, drawing flies and beetles, and children enjoyed their football game in the area reserved for Islamic services. The soldier who shot him spoke with Lito in the shadows of a tree. 'It was a sin,' Fuentes thought, 'that your own people did not trust you.' That is always the beginning of the end of things, when skepticism of your confederates forces you to commit senseless crimes. Fuentes brooded on this fact. He did not care who would finally bury the boy. Soon the scavenger birds would arrive and mix with the red ants already feasting on the body.

Within minutes, a woman came into the yard. Stoop shouldered from years of drudgery, and wearing a straw bonnet, she spoke in a petulant voice to Lito and the soldier.

"Get this boy out of here," she said. "Be decent."

The two responded in silence. She confiscated the children's football and chaperoned them to the hospital that doubled as the school. Still, no one advanced toward the American. Presently, three women carried him on a stretcher to the western division of the camp, where the dead were processed for burial.

"Such craziness," one of the women said.

Fuentes re-entered the prisoner's hut and loosened the rope from the girl's wrists. She reeked of excrement and had developed a fever from poor hygiene, insufficient food rations and lack of sleep. Her teeth were white and straight, and he rejoiced in her seclusion. But the animus on her breath and in her eyes captivated him, and when she defiantly pushed her hand against his collarbone, she angled her fingertips at his throat. If given the opportunity, would she be able to drive a knife blade into her enemy's pulmonary cavity? He asked for her name, and she told him to go to hell. She loathed Fuentes, and this was the thing that thrilled him. He would tame this loathing, just as he had with the other American who lay listless on the floor. He put his hand on her breasts and pushed her against the wall.

"We won't forget our friend," the girl said, in a high falsetto.

"What friend?" Fuentes asked.

"Tommy," the girl said.

"I know of only two Americans to be ransomed. We never had a third American. And it would be quite easy for there to be only one. People get lost in the jungle, are eaten by lions, are drowned in the rivers, and fall victim to snakes and malaria. They are disposed of by leeches and die of forgetfulness and delusions. They are in the wrong place on a beautiful day when a bomb explodes. You're no exception. And if not for me, your pussy would be in every hut in this camp."

"When will we be free?" the girl asked.

"Everything depends on your American, Eddie Finn."

"Who's he?" they both asked in unison.

Fuentes strolled out the door, chuckling. It was like throwing a hex on them. In the compound, he observed a sudden flurry of activity. Men gathered up their weapons and spoke in fervent voices. Fuentes hollered at a boy with an M-16 rifle slung over his shoulder.

"What's going on, Carlos?" Fuentes asked.

The boy stalled. "There was a gun battle at the Matilac Mosque," he said, "and the government killed six of our people. The information from your woman was wrong. But the military evacuated. I think we're going to retaliate. So long, sir."

Fuentes was the sole Catholic among these Muslims, and he had a fleeting desire to make the sacramental action. As he did, Lito tramped up to him, his eyes dark-ringed and skeptical, as men congregated at the ammunition hut.

"Put the dead American in the car with the other fallen soldiers," Fuentes told him. "He will be a casualty."

"Your bitch lied to us," Lito said.

"Marta has admirable intentions," Fuentes said, but he could not discount the drubbing the erroneous location of the Philippine military troops had caused, which resulted in the demise of these Muslim soldiers.

"When do we get the money?" Lito asked.

"I'll set things up with the American representative tomorrow. By the way, you have powder on your cheek."

"Another one of your deceptions."

"No one should know you go to the hut where the boy sleeps," Fuentes said.

"You give too many orders. This is the south. You're paid only to consult."

"He's a child."

"The boy brings me comfort."

Fuentes did not care if all the terrorists perished. They were squalid, ruthless people, and he did not even regard them as Filipino. You do not shoot a man when he is worth money or is a commodity to be traded to enhance life for your village. The fat boy's death had been a waste. He had represented currency, and nothing had been gained. He would not miss him. He had not given him a second thought and never would. But there was a sweetness in his death, and the way the girl bolted for the jungle was sweet, too, and the image of eating her despair had the same flavor. Already the boy's blood has dried. This evening the moon will have an equal brilliance as tomorrow's moon. What changes? Tonight, he would strip away the American girl's garments. She must know that she has nothing to offer but her body, if her government foregoes payment. He would peel every stitch off her till her soul wailed.

Inside the hut, someone sobbed. Fuentes walked toward the gathering and stood beside Carlos at the ammunitions hut, the M-16 clutched in his hands, and he nodded at the boy's smiling determination.

CHAPTER 11

"Eddie, you have shit for brains for telling the embassy stumblebums I'm here with you," Rudolph said. "Because if I get hurt, you take the fall, and if I screw up you take the fall. Is this what they teach you at embassy school? In case you didn't think this out, when you add an unknown element to the mix, some kind of weird shit is gonna happen. Even me, bro, a guy who cares for you, would sell your ass for a bunch of mango trees. You don't know what you're dealing with in this southern archipelago."

Rudolph relaxed on the queen-size bed that had been fitted with a starched sheet, the blanket doubled over at his feet. "You think you've got it all wired. But you have no idea of the depravity these jokers are capable of inflicting. They have no boundaries, no integrity. But I'm your man. Under different circumstances, I wouldn't have made the trip. What's my mission? How can I help?"

"Do nothing," Finn said.

"Then why am I here?"

"I don't know who to trust."

"You're one piece of work."

"I told you I'd pay."

"Eddie, we'll swim this river together."

The Hotel Romeo was on Don Rufino Alonzo Street in Cotabato City. The room had an atypical configuration with two curved walls, a walk-in closet two feet deep, and a bathroom that could only be reached by inching past a wardrobe, which hinted of an undisclosed cubicle. A pint-size dormer, in the groove above a portico, had a view of the main street. Finn unlatched the shutter that showcased the diminutive town. A scant number of weary pedestrians made their way in the blistering heat.

"Listen to me, bro. I'm out on the street today minding my own business, checking out the clubs when this crazy shrew starts hassling me. She was too mean and too ugly to be one of those common whores, whom I dearly love."

Rudolph stared at the ceiling, as if replaying a sixteen-millimeter movie clip. "Years ago, I met this whore from Barrio Barretto. One day her sponsor showed up, a guy from Switzerland. She screwed me in the afternoon after she sent this jerk-off to the naval base at Subic to buy her a refrigerator. If she'd really loved him, she'd have let him buy the fridge off base, for a cheaper price. But she needed the time to tell me to stay away. She was cold, calculating, but her pussy was warm as cinnamon, and she really messed with my head. But you know that the language of whores is money."

"Not for all of them," Finn said.

"They've destroyed my life," Rudolph said, dismissing Finn's appeal. "But that's not so bad because all lives are destroyed in the end, and most long before the final dinGodong."

"She did a number on you," Finn said.

Rudolph pushed himself higher against the pillow. "She should have treated me decently. The Lord Buddha beseeched her. But she was a whore and grasping put her way low on the Karma wheel. In the next life she'll be born as a sea slug. Sad, isn't it?"

"If that's the Lord's plan, yes."

"So, this morning I told this dragon shrew to get lost, but she doesn't budge. I tell her again, and she puts her hand on my arm. I shake her off, and if her husband had been nearby, I would've thrashed him. I cut out. Then she starts running after me like a witch, straight out of *Macbeth*. But I shake her because she's old and carrying this sack of stuff. I'm on the brink of following someone into an alley and bludgeoning him. Give me the Thai Buddhist and Filipino Catholic any day of the week. Two days in this miserable rathole and my personality is changing in wicked ways."

Rudolph drained a beer and opened another.

"I have to figure a way to contact the head honcho of the Abu Sayyaf guerrillas," Finn said. "Ciros, the guy the embassy connected me with, says he can. But I don't know. He's had three days with no luck. He's been trying to fax the bastards. Maybe you know someone or some way to do it. If you can, find out without causing any sort of disturbance. I don't want anything to happen to you."

"You're a pal."

"See what you can dig up."

"How much cash do we have?"

Finn hesitated. "Twenty-five thousand for expenses."

"Dollars?"

"That's right."

"And to pay the ransom for the Peace Corp kids?" Rudolph asked.

"There's half a million dollars," Finn said.

Rudolph beamed. "You've sure got these bureaucratic dickheads bamboozled. We could boogie out of here with the loot. Those kids are goners, anyway."

"I can't do that."

"You're still glued to a morality flag," Rudolph said. He took a swig from his beer. "You think I'm a badass, don't you? I haven't been on a killing spree, so I'm law-abiding, but I do have an in with the local mob from a family marriage. Money is master in these islands. The guerrillas make payoffs to the cops and parade on the street as innocent as schoolgirls. It's weird here.

"But I have to say, I miss Carmelita. I didn't really love her for years, and now I do, and she worries me because she slaves so hard to please me. I'm scared she's gonna crack up. Reminds me of a wino I used to hang with in Mission Beach, California, twenty years ago. He said, 'The ones you love are the ones that stick around.' He divined the truth—winos often do—that's why they're winos."

"I'm meeting Marta and Ciros for dinner. Stay in contact. We're eating at the Holiday Inn."

"Class."

Let's hook up for breakfast tomorrow at nine at the street cafe."

"You're buying," Rudolph said.

A couple of well-thumbed paperbacks were stacked on the nightstand, and Rudolph listened to the riff-flowing jazz of Miles Davis on the radio.

"I got a letter from a pal of mine before I came south," Rudolph said. "He told me about a brother of ours from the service who died of a heart attack while teaching his son to rope a bronc at a rodeo in Wichita, Kansas. He wrote that we had one KIA, and he just knelt in stunned silence when he got the news. He knelt in stunned silence. It makes me cry. I wouldn't admit this to just anyone. Lots of death this year: my mother, a sister. But I'm here for you."

Finn gripped the wrought-iron bedstead, and said, "My father was a clarinet player for an orchestra in London. He made some records. We lived in England when I was a kid. Lately, I've been dreaming of my father. In the dream, I wake in the early morning and he's sitting in a rocker in my bedroom with his army rifle from the Korean War on his lap. He takes a cartridge round from his shirt pocket and taps it against the bolt. And, other times, he's sitting on my bed at night, the rifle and whiskey bottle in his lap, and I pretend not to see him. I hear him telling me I'm worthless, and my mother should have taken me when she lit out on a bus for Palookaville. The bed springs creak, and I know he's raising a hand to strike me. I read somewhere there's a psychiatric term for repressed childhood memories that suddenly re-emerge when you're older. They call it echo trauma. This has been happening to me for months. Many a night these memories force me awake, and I don't recognize my surroundings. I'm lost and can't find a light switch. It's as if I'm in a hallucination without escape."

Embarrassed by his frankness, Finn lowered his hands. "We all remain children, in some way, I guess."

"What are you saying?" Rudolph asked.

"No secrets."

"Intimacy breeds harmony, Eddie. We're not alone."

'Mercifully, God knows where to find our souls,' Finn thought.

"I heard that," Rudolph said. "He sure does."

"Heard what?"

"Time to bathe."

*****

Rudolph stripped and entered the bathroom. His tenor voice hummed in synch with Etta James on the radio, beneath the weak shower spray. The window, high on the mold-crusted wall, allowed tepid air into the cell. A bird swooped by the aperture. "I always wanted to fly," Rudolph said aloud.

After the shower, he lazed on the bed below the ceiling fan, luxuriating in its mellifluous waves. He recalled his home and the punkah in the den and how Carmelita's nephew, Jose, relished tugging the punkah cord, fanning Rudolph as he sat at his desk, writing letters. But José was dead now, and all that counted was getting home to his beat-up old sunshiny lady.

On the avenue, dressed in a peach-colored linen shirt and jeans, Rudolph took a jeepney to the east end and entered a dive called the Blue Monkey.

"Hey, Maganda, why are you sad?" Rudolph asked the bartender, pointing at a bottle of beer.

"My sister's sick with cholera," the girl said, placing a Heineken on a paper napkin. "Many people are sick now, after the rains and the flood."

"Shots cost seventy bucks each, I hear."

"Shots?" she asked, a note of anxiety in her voice.

"I mean the injections against cholera," Rudolph said. "The high cost is the rape of the public by the rich. Who gives a horse's ass about the farmers and families that scratch out a living? Maganda, I'd give you the money for the injection against cholera if I could spare it. Truly, I would."

She smiled in a way only a Filipina can, whose hallowed disposition raised Rudolph's morale and enhanced his belief that faith generally prevailed in dire straits. The girl flipped a page in her cartoon book. Rudolph drank another Heineken, contemplating the half-dead cockroach on the bar. Rudolph's wife's cousin, Olive, had advised him that the guerrillas walked freely in the eastern part of Cotabato City, and that there was a covert treaty of neutrality with the police. Olive had arranged a session for him with an Abu Sayyaf leader she had identified as Commander Lito.

Rudolph cocked an eye at the insect. "Did you speak, Roach-bud?" Rudolph winked. "Indeed, I know. We're all part of the same charade," Rudolph confided to the cockroach, and pushed his companion onto the napkin. He guzzled a third Heineken, sauntered into the rear room and laid a Polaroid of a famous American politician who had served in the Vietnam War on the table, in front of the short-legged man smoking a Winston cigarette. Rudolph spoke in Tagalog, explaining how Americans never abandon fellow Americans, dead or captured, in a faraway country. As he searched for an erudite phrase, the man said, "Talk Eng-lash."

Rudolph took a chair and told the man an elaborate story about twenty thousand U.S. dollars in a bag buried beneath the floorboards in a hotel room in Cotabato City, and a flimsy lock that any half-wit could defeat in seconds. But there was a catch. If a certain lever wasn't switched off before the bag was opened, the money would be spray painted, ruining the whole bundle. And even if the guy guessed the correct hotel, he would still need a week to find the room with the money. Yet, maybe the loot wasn't in the floorboards but in the ceiling or camouflaged in a couch, and to get the loot there were two goons in the room he would have to kill, who were the size of Bruno Sammartino, the wrestler.

Rudolph recognized the blank look on the rebel's face, and that he was not acquainted with Bruno Sammartino, and he said, "They're as tough as President Marcos's bodyguards and as gargantuan as Joseph Estrada."

The man clapped. Rudolph surmised it was because Estrada was a bad, portly actor and a former president, and President Marcos, a deposed dictator, had bodyguards who were known to have frolicked in torture.

"Did I forget to mention the weapons in a truck in the jungle if the Americans and the Chinese priest are set free?"

"What's the man's name with the money?" he asked.

"Finn. Eddie Finn."

"And what's your name?"

"Richard Rudolph."

Lito smiled, revealing a gold capped front tooth. "You're from the American Embassy?"

"One thousand percent."

"Who told you where to find me?"

"My cousin." Rudolph inched himself closer to the table. "See, I've got this grove of mango trees in a bad way, in fact dying, and I need to replant them. New seedlings are expensive. The quicker we get this done the sooner I head on home and tend to my grove. No one else involved. No fuckin' round table accords. We select a drop point. We swap the cash for the kids and the padre, and we're both on own jolly way."

"Twenty million peso," Lito said, "and you'll get the hostages shipped to your doorstep."

"That's the drum roll I like to hear."

And the weapons?" Lito asked, taking a match from a box.

"A bonus for you and not a peso for me."

Lito's match flamed. "But you may need help with those mangos."

"I'm beholden for all contributions, bro."

*****

Poolside at the Holiday Inn in Cotabato City, Ciros wore seaweed-colored shorts and a baseball cap. Fuentes smoked a cigar and spat at the pool's drain, missed, and the saliva slid over the concrete ledge into the water. Congresswoman Cecille Lopez, who spoke English well, wore a two-piece bathing suit and lounged in a plastic-ribbed chair. Marta sat beside her.

"The Christians in the Muslim areas in Mindanao are discouraged," Congresswoman Lopez said. "They think if the government gives the Muslims their own government, their land will be taken away. It's in their mind that they have to be able to fend off the enemy. Most of our village people in Mindanao have weapons, a rifle or pistol or machete in their house. But you can't call the Christians vigilantes because they're not organized. They'll fight for their homes and property. You have to remember there are 60,000 armed Muslims in Cotabato."

"Congresswoman Lopez, we can iron out this conflict," Ciros said with authority, his face swamped with sweat. "I can assure your communities that the Muslims won't raid their businesses or abduct their children. Isn't this what we all want?"

"Sounds too simple," Congresswoman Lopez said. "Captain Fuentes, they say you were once a professor of social science at university. Then you know this is a religious war."

"No, Mrs. Lopez, this is a war of poverty, a war against the current Manila oligarchy, an overthrow of political cronyism. The Muslims want the same things you do: food and clothing for their families, decent homes, education and the freedom of the streets."

Congresswoman Lopez tugged on her straw hat, blocking the sun from her face. "When you talk about Muslims and Christians, there really is a divide. These two groups are enemies. Muslims are warriors, and my constituents simply want a normal life."

"The people respect your conviction," Ciros said. "And with our assistance you can accomplish the crucial goals to benefit the constituents in your district. Help us negotiate a covenant with the Abu Sayyaf guerillas in Cotabato."

"What religion are you, Professor?" she asked, focusing her attention on Fuentes.

"I'm a pacifist," Fuentes replied. "The end of killing is what I want. One hundred and twenty thousand are dead in the jungles and hamlets of Mindanao. Because of this, there are too many innocent lives lost in every province. I'm embarrassed by this fact. But it motivates me to seek a resolution to the conflict in Cotabato."

"It's nearly unthinkable that this animosity can end," Lopez said, shaking her head. "I buried my nephew last week. He was nine years old. A bomb detonated near a pharmacy as he and his friends walked home from school."

Ciros crunched ice from his glass, and asked, "Will U.S. dollars provide extra incentive, Cecille?"

"If that means helping the Christians—without question, money is always highly regarded. But it won't be sufficient. The money will seduce some in my communities, but it can't eliminate the belief that death can happen on any street, planting field or market, at any time of the day. You know about the fifteen Philippine journalists who were rounded up by the Ampatuan warlord clan in Maguindanao, taken to a deforested development, shot and plowed under by bulldozers?"

"Yes," Fuentes said. "Let's stay focused. We'll make this negotiation happen, where the Abu Sayyaf relinquish their weapons. Then a rapport among Christians and Muslims in Cotabato has possibilities."

"That reality doesn't match up with the situation I face each day in my district," Lopez said.

"How much money will make your fellow Christians forget about their guns?" Ciros asked.

Congresswoman Lopez licked the sweat from her upper lip. "No outlay of money can take away their fear. Even now, three Peace Corps recruits and a priest have been kidnapped by the Abu Sayyaf from Cotabato. This makes the Christian alliance nervous."

"The kidnappings, as I've been told by the local militia, were only done to get money to improve life in Cotabato," Fuentes said. "Nothing else."

"Pardon," Marta said. "I'm from the American Embassy and here to assist you."

"Are you a Filipina?" Lopez asked her.

"Yes. Half Filipino and half American."

"And do you oversee the money?"

"People I know do."

"And if the Peace Corp recruits should die?"

"Bury that worry," Fuentes interjected. "The men holding the hostages are surrogates, under my charge."

An awkward silence ensued. It was disarming that a person would acknowledge so close a connection with the recent kidnappings and the Abu Sayyaf.

"Captain Fuentes, how do you know the Muslims won't buy weapons to kill the Christians in my district with the money the Americans give them?" Lopez asked.

"I'm the negotiator, along with Miss Marta," Fuentes said. "The ransom will be given in dollars and other amenities, such as food and medicine. My goal is to reduce violence for all Filipinos, Christian and Muslim."

"I see your willingness to help settle the disputes in Cotabato," Lopez said. "How can I help? I'll do anything for my people. But you should know, having seen peace arbitrations come and go, I remain apprehensive."

"I'll keep you informed," Marta said, "and supply you with any necessities you may find useful to subdue hostilities."

Marta draped a silk shawl over her shoulders, knowing no one in this council was reliable.

"At last, we have come to a mutual appeasement," Fuentes said. "Soon all parties will be satisfied, and we can bring a peaceful settlement to the people of Mindanao."

In the evening, Marta dined with Finn, Ciros and his girlfriend, Criselda. They ate lumpia, a fried spring roll, kare-kare, a vegetable stew, oxtail with peanut sauce, and drank San Miguel beer. Marta's belly boiled with noise, and she was sure everyone at the table could hear. The water glass left a tart tang on her tongue, and even the chocolate ice cream she stole from Finn's dish did little to cleanse her palate. Ciros talked of his wandering days in

Latin America. The cities had newfangled names, and she could not conceive why a man would tour such a country, penniless, alone, so far from one's family, without a permanent job.

Marta asked Criselda, "Why are you with such an old man?" Criselda gave a gracious smile. "Do you think the rebels can save the country?"

"They are the Lost Command," Criselda answered.

"Who are?"

"The Muslim fighters in Cotabato," Criselda said, catching Ciros's and Finn's attention. "The people call them the Lost Command because they commit atrocities in the name of God."

"Are they respected?" Marta inquired.

"Not by the Christians. And many people are afraid."

"Afraid of what?" Finn asked.

Criselda fiddled with her knife.

"She doesn't know," Ciros said, polishing off his beer.

"Muslims aren't afraid of dying," Criselda said, "or losing their heads. They plot and murder and get off without a warning. They'll steal a man's wife for two days and return her damaged. Hardly anyone dares to challenge them. Don't you see? This is a war with no victors."

Ciros confided to Finn, "We meet Captain Fuentes at ten tonight. Marta can't come. They won't bargain with a woman."

"Is there a problem?" Marta asked. "Or do you two have a revived affection for one another?"

Finn paid the tab. A fever sapped Marta's energy, and she braced her hands on the tabletop, steadied herself, and rose. On the street, the sultry night bathed her shoulders, and she told herself it was only the chill of the restaurant, the fluorescent lights and the disagreeable oxtail meat that had made her ill. Criselda took her elbow and said they were going home, and for a moment, Marta envisaged her grandmother's house in Kigali, Rwanda. She was tempted to let her mind freewheel back in time to Kigali, where she had lived for half her life. Her stomach tightened. A gale was whipping inside her, an agony she had never known before, and it was exterminating the memory of her grandmother's house until all she recalled was the color of the garden she tended as a teenager and the face of her grandmother, weathered, blacker than night, ears of a child and lips which age could not tarnish. Marta did not say a word to either man. She allowed Criselda to guide her to the other side of the street. Inside a taxi, Marta observed Finn and Ciros standing on the sidewalk, knowing that their white faces would eventually condemn them for their past transgressions.

CHAPTER 12

"Where do we meet Fuentes?" Finn asked Ciros.

"Have some discipline."

Within minutes, a car pulled to the curb. The rear window was lowered. Fuentes held a newspaper in his lap, and the husky Filipino whom Finn had seen in the casino was behind the wheel.

"Come in, Mr. Finn," Fuentes said, with a friendly wave. "But not you, Mr. Greek. You're not invited."

"I'm the lead negotiator," Ciros said.

"Only Finn," Fuentes said. "He controls the money."

"This is a mistake," Ciros warned.

"I'm the boss here." Fuentes tapped the seat.

The timeworn leather cushion sagged beneath Finn's weight, and the Mercedes Benz, with its rusted chrome, sped away.

"Elwin, off with the radio. Our friend is thinking."

On the country road, they passed closed gasoline stations, stretches of banaba trees, and barbers who cut hair and shaved customers seated on folding chairs beneath incandescent lamps. A boy sold durian and pineapples from a crate and, yards away, a make-shift structure glowed, as two girls leaned on a balcony ledge in sleeveless short-hemmed dresses. An hour later, the car entered the lot of an antiquated factory. Elwin stopped the car and flicked off the headlights. In the lot, haloed by a lantern from a nearby cement patio, two men waited, holding automatic weapons.

"What happens now?" Finn asked.

"As far as I know," Fuentes said, "the world stops spinning for you."

They walked toward the men, as Finn shelved his misgivings for this assignation. Fuentes handed him a plastic water bottle, and Finn took several swallows.

On the patio, Fuentes asked Finn, "Do you want to begin?"

"Go ahead, Captain."

Fuentes nodded to each man. "He's your boy, comrades. He'll give you money for the hostages. He understands Tagalog and English. Now, what does the Abu Sayyaf organization demand?"

The older man with feral lips said in English, "Two hundred million pesos."

"We have to be rational," Fuentes said in a tone that bespoke of a reckoning if deceit invaded the negotiation. "These are just youths helping the poor in Cotabato. They can't be blamed for being naive. We offer twenty million pesos for the Americans."

The other guerrilla, younger and jittery, leveled his rifle at Fuentes's feet. Fuentes pushed the rifle barrel at the shrouded jungle. He offered each Filipino a cigarette. They smoked, and Fuentes tucked the Marlboros in the younger man's shirt pocket.

"Their nationality is not important to us," the older man said, picking at an infected blister on his cheek. "We kidnap civilians, military soldiers, priests, teachers, laborers. They become our tools. They're pieces of barter. We behead them, too. This is our way."

"Does their nationality or profession affect the ransom?" Fuentes asked.

"You must be joking. They are cattle to us."

"These Americans are from the Peace Corps," Fuentes said.

"All human cattle are the same," the older man said. "We are democratic."

"Anything you want to add to the discussion?" Fuentes asked Finn.

"Yes. I can offer food and medicine," Finn said.

"And how about guns?" asked the older man.

"That's not feasible."

He groaned and aimed the rifle at Finn's groin.

"I think he's seen too many mafia films."

"Honestly," Fuentes replied, "he's not a movie fan. He's a farmer, so he wants to blow your balls off."

"Twenty-five million pesos, food, and medicine for the three Americans and the priest," Finn said.

Fuentes kicked at a rodent that zipped over his foot.

"Is there a problem?" Finn asked.

"They didn't know the priest was included in the transaction."

"Yes, the priest is part of the package," Finn told them. "I can offer twenty-six million pesos."

The older man said, "I think my commander with find this sum adequate. I will contact Captain Fuentes with details of time and location."

The two men headed toward a pickup truck. Finn did not hear the ignition kick over.

"You're a skillful negotiator," Fuentes said.

"And what do you want?" Finn asked.

Fuentes faced him and balled his hand. "I want your money, Mr. Finn. You have nothing else to give me."

"Why do you dislike me?"

"When I was young, I had a wife and a daughter, and a gangster killed them because I owed him two thousand pesos. I buried them both. Who kills a family for two thousand pesos? All I needed was a day. Then he'd have had the money. On a Tuesday, a week after the funeral, I broke into his home and slit his throat. But I never lost my love of God. I abhor a man like you, without faith."

"I'm glad you're still religious," Finn said.

"Last week, I sat with you in church, and you blackballed me, as though I were a leper."

"Not true."

"I was there to help pave a way to solve this crisis."

"Captain, I respect you as an officer who puts his life on the line for these children."

"Diplomatic hogwash. I remember the way you treated me at the casino. But I have a solution for you. I think you should spend time with the Abu Sayyaf and know what it's like to be their hostage. Captivity will give you an education in how far a people will go to obtain their freedom, even extremists in Mindanao."

"That can't happen. I'm an envoy from the American Embassy. I have one function, to broker these negotiations, so don't jam me up."

Fuentes's posture grew rigid. "Listen to me; history in the Philippines is constantly erased by typhoon, earthquake, drought, and disease. This country is continually rebuilding itself. That's something you foreigners will never figure out. And all the so-called benevolent deeds you do are trivial. We are barbarians in your eyes. But this is a country of heroes."

"I agree."

Fuentes inhaled through his nostrils. "Are you a hero, Mr. Finn?"

"No way. I'm here in Mindanao to aid the Peace Corps volunteers."

"So, if you lost your life, it would be part of the job."

"I'm simply a government pawn."

"You're not a pawn. You are the man with the money," Fuentes said. "And you're the one person who will decide the children's fate. This makes you an unknown quantity and despised by many."

"Men like you?" Finn asked.

"Not at all. You deserve a dividend for your conduct in these difficult circumstances."

"You're a noble man."

With his thumb, Fuentes crushed a mosquito on Finn's throat. "Tomorrow will be a happier day, American."

"And tomorrow the hostages will be freed."

"Some may be dead by then."

"Impossible."

"Does that bother you? Just fooling. Tugging your chain, so to speak. I'll call you at your hotel. Don't go far."

"Are they really dead?"

"They're in excellent health," Fuentes said. "The Lord watches over them. I have details to discuss with our two friends."

At the car, Elwin smoked a cigarette in the front seat.

"Let's hit the road," Finn said.

Elwin exhaled a thin gray spiral. "I have to inform Captain Fuentes."

"Please do, then."

Elwin flicked the burning cigarette into the darkness. "I like that. *Please do.*"

He reappeared within minutes.

"Where to, boss?"

*****

The palm trees arced eastward, and the sky thinned into a waxy ceiling. Elwin navigated on the edge of a typhoon, the car writhing in a half foot of water. Finn touched the side window, and the glass pulsated from the strong gales. The radio was silent, and neither man spoke. Traversing a knoll, the glow of Cotabato City came into view. Around the bend, a jeepney had stalled on a crude shoulder, and passengers bunched together under a rock jetty, transiently harbored from the storm. Muddy streams cascaded unhindered, adjacent to the hillside, and Finn could see hurricane lanterns atop house roofs that had been swept away in the torrent.

A half hour later Elwin dropped Finn in front of the Hotel Romeo, and sped away, hubcap deep in water. On the sidewalk, Finn sprinted, splashing in puddles. To gain a brief reprieve from the storm, he used store and restaurant awnings for protection. At the Maharajah Hotel, he waited outside room 433. The rain streamed off the eaves of the red tile shingles, doused his head and shoulders, and muffled the monsoon to a low roar. He removed his shoes and entered the room.

Criselda lay asleep on the bed. The air conditioner blew lukewarm waves. He stretched out on the mattress and when her nose grazed his cheek, she twisted away. The isolation in the dank room riled him. Then the greenness of Rwanda occupied his thoughts, infused with the odor of rotting flesh and was instantaneously washed away by thunder.

Criselda's forehead was feverish, her husky, brown skin jaundiced. He repositioned the blanket over her body. They had met during the past week, away from prying eyes at this hotel, and after making love, she had sung in a melodic voice, a tune from Samar. He had no clue to the song's meaning, but it had an alluring tempo. In the room's stillness, he had been intoxicated by her balmy scent, her almond eyes, and the shape of her lips. He had told himself to hold onto this evening because he understood how readily memory moved, without resistance, to myth.

He wiped a cloth over Criselda's forehead. Her body shivered. She mumbled in Wari. A short while later, Finn slept. He tossed restlessly, and pawed at his shirt collar, as sweat flowed from his neck and chest. In his delirium, a man breached the room's entrance. Laughter see-sawed in the gloomy light, or had a bird unintentionally flown into the room? 'It's you,' he thought in a febrile stupor, leery of the intruder. As the man checked Criselda's throat, Finn felt defenseless, as if he had been plastered to the bed.

"Take deep breaths, Eddie." He reeked of barbecue, cigarettes, and beer.

"Where am I?" Finn asked.

"Bro. It's me."

Rudolph hefted Finn to his feet and led him from the room. Dawn broke in the eastern quadrant of sky, the lower stratum a roller coaster pink swirl that verged to a fairytale blue. The storm had blown inland. "She has cholera," Rudolph said.

"I'm sick myself," Finn said.

"Sure as shit, but it's not cholera. If you had cholera, you'd be puking your guts up and burning up with fever. Where you been?"

"With Fuentes, in the jungle."

"Maybe he drugged you?"

"Fuentes? Ah, the water. He gave me a bottle to drink from."

"Come on. I'll take you to your crib."

"But Criselda?"

"We'll tell the front desk to send a doc. Her boyfriend—I mean that asshole, Ciros—may be here soon. He's a bloodhound. I'm sure he's picked up on your hideaway. I've seen cholera before and she's lucky, 'cause it's not that bad a case. No doubt she had a high fever when you arrived, but now it's fading. You saved her life. You hear me? You saved her lovely life. Now, you don't want to be seen here. Nefarious vibes, man."

"How did you know where to find me?" Finn asked, as they exited the hotel.

"I tailed you a couple of days ago. Someone has to watch your back."

After the storm, a lighter vein coursed in the morning air current, removing the tropical heat. On the footpath, food sellers' carts were set up along the street curb.

At the jeepney drop, Rudolph said, "I've set you up with the guy who'll end all your headaches. He's a main honcho of the Abu Sayyaf guerrillas, a vice chairman of political affairs, Commander Lito. Funny, isn't it, even these guerrillas give themselves titles because it's all the same festival, Manila or in the jungles. I wonder, don't these guys see the human circus? Then I have to slap myself because they see perfectly. They want what the other guy has, money and power. You hearing me?"

"I'm together," Finn said.

"You'll have to give Lito an extra twenty grand above the twenty million pesos," Rudolph said. "He's able to carry the swap out with few hitches, and you'll get your people returned, sorry-assed but upbeat for having thought they were untouchable."

"Fuentes said he could do the same thing, deliver the Peace Corp workers and the priest but for twenty-six million pesos."

"The bastard's a lunatic. Fuentes will rip you off and trike you out to the fields and carve you up like a mule. Communicate with one of the commanders rather than a mediator."

"Fuentes spoke of God," Finn said, and instantly regretted the sentence.

"Enlightenment," Rudolph said, respectfully. "It's what we all seek."

"Here comes the jeepney."

"Well, what does Fuentes know? Let him humble himself before Buddha and the graves of the military dead. Then we'll see the type of man he is."

"Let's go your way," Finn said. The chrome and red-bodied chariot jeepney came to a halt. "Fuentes knows too many people I don't trust."

"Tomorrow, I'll hook you up," Rudolph said.

"You're a saint.

"Ditto, bro."

HILLS OF COTABATO

*****

At the Abu Sayyaf compound, lightning illuminated the American girl's hut, and the remains of a roasted pig littered a pit. Fuentes side-stepped a frog, unlatched the door, and entered. The boy had been assigned to another hut.

She stood in the center of the room. Her shoulders caved inward, and he clasped her upper arms. He sniffed her hair and bit her neck. The flesh darkened. He bit her again, drawing drops of blood. The brackish flavor stoked him, and he pushed her onto her knees, doggy style. He wrenched her jeans to her ankles, yanked her shirt up so that the knobby vertebrae shone in the abrasive light of the ceiling bulb. He smeared blood from her neck over her buttocks.

"Are you afraid?" Fuentes asked.

"Never," she said, her body shivering.

He whisked her around, took the knife from his pocket and held the blade to her cheek. Her eyes dilated, and he saw the barbarity in them. He cupped her breast, and her body stiffened. The breast had the sensation of a ripe mango in his hand.

Relishing his prey, he left her on the floor, unscathed, her sex wanting. In the doorway, he spat. The spit fell just short of her. She was dogged, valiant, and the loathing he desired from her was still indisputable in the thin-lipped mouth.

Fuentes paced far into the compound, passing huts made of nipa and bamboo. Sentries on guard smoked Black Cat cigarettes. Hooded kerosene lanterns etched rings of light on the soil. The jungle was pungent and noisy from the coming rain. He strode with a bejeweled clarity.

Around the bend, the hut was dark, and flowers and fruit had been arrayed on an altar. His body pressed on Lito's exterior door, and he broke the rotted wooden spike. Lito's crocodile boots were

174

on a mat outside the bedroom. Fuentes seized them and, twenty yards from Lito's hut, he took out his knife and stepped on one boot's tight arch. The knife's steel lacerated the crocodile hide. He made swift triangular gashes and pitched the pieces into a kalingag bush. He was peeved by the boot's offensive odor, as if the hide had been improperly salted. Sweating, and engulfed in the act, Fuentes reckoned a physician experienced the same glee in the operating theater.

After tossing the tattered boots into the jungle, Fuentes sensed, even from this part of the compound, the American girl's anguish. 'She's mine,' he thought, 'because I have tasted her fear. Few men know of such passions, how one can devour the psychological makeup of another, and by doing so, crush them. Though she still has spirit, she is depleted by each succeeding day as a captive, and I will feed on this weakness.'

At the outer perimeter, he changed course, and when he barged into the girl's hut, she hastened away, shoving with her heels and palms crab-like on the floor until she hit the bamboo wall. She had torn off a piece of her blouse and had applied it to her throat to stop the bleeding. He saw dirt on her bare feet and dried blood on her ankles and arms where she had scratched the mosquito bites, which had plagued her for weeks.

"You can't hide," Fuentes said, giving a snort.

She sat below the window, her hair silver from the moonlight. Her mouth shut, her eyelids fluttered, and she breathed evenly, in and out of her nose. The dried blood on her arms and legs blighted her in his imagination. It was as though another agency was defiling her. Furious, he slammed the door, and in the compound, beneath a starlight canopy, he breathed the way she had, through each nostril, glaring, as she had, at the enemy that surrounded him.

*****

Finn had been oblivious when Rudolph dumped him onto the springy mattress, having lost consciousness halfway up the stairs of the Hotel Romeo. Rudolph stretched out beside him.

As Finn snored, Rudolph said, "The last time I saw Carmelita she was watching this television show in our bedroom about animals in Nigeria. From my desk, I could hear her yelling, and I went to the doorway. The program showed a tiger ripping into a zebra with all the blood and viscera. As the tiger ate muscle and organs, Carmelita said, 'Why they show this on TV?' And I told her, 'Because people like you watch this crap.'

"I was standing there naked, and she said to me, 'Do you want some chicken and rice? I can make adobo.'

"I couldn't help but feel love for my old lady, who can shoot as well as any man, sow a garden and never cared we didn't have kids, and would take care of you, Eddie, as if you were one of the family. So, I've got you covered. And now I'm gonna drink some beers and pop my last bennies. All I want to do is be with Carmelita and let all this drivel with these despicable shits go, because it ruins my karma."

By one in the afternoon, Rudolph hunkered on a bar stool on Delgado Street drinking San Miguel. A man in a floral short-sleeve shirt faced the row of alcohol bottles. He told Rudolph he was an Air Force Master Sergeant who had once been stationed in Songtan, South Korea. On the stool beside the sergeant, a Filipina had her hand on his thigh and was sipping Kool-Aid. A dilapidated fan rotated in the ceiling.

"The Koreans are solid people," the sergeant said.

"What the hell do you know?" Rudolph said. "They're a bunch of racists. I served two tours in 'Nam and I'd take one of them Vietnamese bastards over a Korean slopehead any day. They beat their women and the women bash our dicks."

"I was married to a Korean."

"Was! She busted your balls, and you got out."

"You could say so," the sergeant said, giving the girl a peck on the ear.

"Take one of those Korean vamps over to the States and they can't fit in," Rudolph said. "They want to head home to the land of kimchi. They paint their faces like witches and yell and pout."

"Emotional people, yes."

Rudolph howled. "Take all that nicety crap and eat it. I know you. You're here in the P.I. living off your retirement pension banging cherry girls, or on R&R hooking up with a Filipina friendly to bed and maybe take to Korea to keep you warm on those hellish winter nights. Well, if you did that, you'd be doing your one princely deed for your whole rueful life."

"Rueful?"

"As in, to feel sorrow. This is your chance to do merit."

"Merit?"

"You fucking with me?"

The sergeant shook his head.

Rudolph regrouped. "Merit's the charm of life which gives you an afterlife that isn't onerous. This means if you act with dignity, you won't be reincarnated as a mosquito but rather a creature of veneration, like a butterfly. Your Filipina will send money home to her parents, and you'll be saving her family from a poverty you've never known. And I tell you this from personal knowledge, it pans out most of the time, because the majority of Filipinas are angels, and the ones who are seamstresses or clerks are pure gold. There are waitresses at Pizza Hut in Zambales and Subic with masters' degrees. And the dude at the toll gate in Manila who collects your pesos probably has more college credits than you."

The bartender took the empty and gave Rudolph another beer. "Why are you here?"

"Pussy," the sergeant said.

"You creep. I just told you about the grandness of the Filipina and you call it pussy."

The sergeant hunched over the bar. "How would you rate the Philippine man?"

"Worthless beggars, most of them. Why Cotabato City?" Rudolph asked, clasping the neck of his beer bottle. "Who do you work for? D.E.A.? The National Security Bureau? Or are you truly a lowlife scumbag who doesn't know this city isn't for ex-pats?"

"I don't get ya, man."

"You're following Finn. He's a crazy guy who wouldn't know he had the clap till he was bent double. Or are you zoomin' the guerrillas, preparing to take them out?"

The sergeant hugged his girl, leaving Rudolph with a view of the man's clean-shaven neck. Rudolph got off his stool and beat the beer bottle against his thigh. Sweat beaded his bald head, trickled over his cheeks and into his beard. Double-clutching the bottle, he waited for the sergeant to make a maneuver that deserved retaliation, the slightest malevolent gesture, as the old furor swelled within.

"*Guapo*," the girl cooed. "I want to have your teeth fixed. I want to take you home and meet my mama and all my brothers and sisters."

"You're a cutie-pie. But I'm a fat man," he said jovially.

"Darling, I'm here to watch after you, and I like a man with muscles."

Rudolph let the wrath dissipate because he realized the four-foot ten-inch Filipina was babying this government man, filleting him as one would milkfish. The man had no pride, and there was blessing in that, Rudolph told himself. For Rudolph had seen pride ravage and kill too many. The conceit put one at odds with one's wife and God and country.

Rudolph paid his tab and split.

He wandered Cotabato City in the day's soaring heat, passing Campo Muslim, a string of closely built shanties and dirt roads, guarded by sentries. At a Sari-Sari store, Rudolph bought a San Miguel. He sojourned onward. Children on motorbikes whistled at him, and he gave them the bird. The rakish, slow-moving Tamontaka River, which reminded him of the Perfume River in Hue, Vietnam, stagnated at his feet. He visualized the Vietnamese wooden sampans fishing on the river or roped to wharves, where a man would wave to a nomad if he coveted a lady for ten dollars, who lounged in the rear of the tarped boat.

He swallowed from the San Miguel bottle and watched a grandmother washing clothes in a plastic tub of soapy water. Courteously, Rudolph bowed. She gave him the stink eye. Seeing a white man in this ghetto was cause for concern. Rudolph thumbed his nose at her. A naked two-year-old girl toyed with a platinum-haired plastic doll. He tramped westward, anticipating Illana Bay. In mid-afternoon, for half an hour, he watched six boys kick a soccer ball in a dusty field. Food stalls layered Federville Village Road, and Rudolph bought a bowl of sinigang soup and ate, standing near an outdoor green grocery. After the meal, he smelled weed from a one-armed man in gladiator sandals. Rudolph pursued him by way of thinning side streets with the idea of scoring an ounce. The man entered a decrepit section of town, where children on bicycles dominated the roadway. Having eroded the range between them, Rudolph loitered at a newsstand, smoking a cigarette. The man entered an aged apartment building with flaking painted brick, and Rudolph rushed to the entranceway. The door was unlocked. Inside, Rudolph caught a woman's voice, who spoke in an endearing tone to the man in the hallway. There was love in this squalor, a room where one commingled in intimate relations. It nearly soothed his fearful heart. Saviors endured even in these slums.

Attempting to quell the willies that over-rode this momentary refrain, Rudolph exited the tenement. On the corner, he slammed open a pharmacy door, as a bell tinkled his arrival.

"You can't take that in here," the pharmacist said from behind the counter.

"This is nothing," Rudolph said, lifting the beer bottle. "I just need some aspirin. I have a migraine the size of Atlantis."

"Leave the bottle outside."

"Man," Rudolph said, "you're twisting the daylight into freaky shapes."

"What's that?" the pharmacist asked.

"Just give me some aspirin," Rudolph said.

"Get out," the pharmacist said, reaching for an object underneath the counter. He laid a shotgun on the counter.

Rudolph aired out his underarms in front of the five-foot tall metal fan. Evaluating the pharmacist, a man in his seventies, he was simply defending his establishment. 'A solid citizen,' Rudolph thought, 'earning a buck.' But there was a mole in the center of his forehead, where a demon had popped his pinky, recruiting another foot soldier. Even in this southern archipelago of destitution, the devil's legions massed. The pharmacist checked the shotgun's breach.

"Yes, boss," Rudolph said, edging away from the fan. "Hi-ho Silver. I'll be on my way. Have a phenomenal day."

On the street, he bought a bottle of San Miguel from a boy who kept the beer in an Igloo cooler. The bottom of his feet hurt. He wasn't sure how many hours he'd been walking, but the sun was crimson, as if someone had lassoed a rope around her throat and carted her through the town's baking streets. A cumulus cloud had the appearance of a trident.

Rudolph hopped the fence of a churchyard. He checked the front doors; they had been locked. They're expecting me, Rudolph said to himself. How marvelous. Out of frustration, he kicked the doors with the bottom of his sneakers, leaving an imprint. Priests shouldn't bar church doors, Rudolph fumed. The admission for supplication and prayer should never be restricted.

He desperately wanted relief from the day's trek. The church's interior contained answers to secular questions he had suppressed for years. He rapped on the front door to no effect. On the building's northern wall, the windows were sealed. As he squatted to pick up a rock to hurl at the window glass, a girl gawked at him from an iron gate. A dog was leashed with a rope to her wrist.

"That's a cute pup," Rudolph said, dropping to one knee. "Does it have a name?"

"California," she said.

"Why aren't you in school?"

"It's Saturday. Father Ramirez is home now."

Rudolph scratched his beard. "Oh, I forgot the day. That can happen at my age."

"You sad?" she asked.

"Saturday, huh?" Rudolph said meekly. "I had no idea. The day of the Sabbath."

Rudolph smiled, and the girl ran off, with the dog yelping.

Sensing exhaustion, Rudolph reached into his pocket and jiggled the three remaining methamphetamine bennies in his palm that he had saved for two weeks. He sat on the church's front stoop and polished off the bennies in one fire-breath swallow, following them with a swig from the beer bottle. He had to be alert for the negotiations, and if he could judiciously engineer the upcoming twenty-four hours, bliss and prosperity awaited him.

It was a bad sign, though, that he had forgotten the day. In his head, he recalled the portent crimson sun, but discounted the warning. He gazed at the religious cross on the church steeple. It paralleled an emaciated bird against the darkening sky. To the right of the steeple, the moon was full and white and luscious, in conflict with the forged cross, and he thought himself fortunate to see this sight. There were blessings, even here.

A jeepney barreled by, raising dust. Several people wagged their chins at him, objecting to his posture. He should have gotten up. In his own way, he was making a spectacle, a dipso lounging before the chapel. The only person he desired, darling Carmelita, was hundreds of miles away, believing in his goodness. He twirled the word goodness around in his mind and tried to find its meaning. When he could not ascertain a track forward, he sought the word's connection to his own life. And that proved disconcerting. He was a man who had achieved little in terms of wealth or prestige. He was what others might view as a failure. Yet, Carmelita prized him. He threw the beer bottle to the ground, splintering the brown glass. "Damn it!" She incensed and saddened him because she understood the convoluted nature of his character when he had no clue, himself.

Before the bennies fully kicked in, he conjured up his Zambales home, his wife and nephew, Jose. He had loved the boy, but he had never told Carmelita, nor the boy. He had presumed the ire he endured at Jose's death would vanish, as would the hole in his chest that had preserved the boy's love. The ire did flee, but the hole had inflated, and an unknown provenance now occupied that cavern where love had once dwelled for the boy. With precision, he excavated the cavern and zeroed in on the thing for what it was: a ghost. A ghost was living inside him. He banged a fist against his chest.

'This is how you die,' Rudolph thought. 'You collect ghosts until they compel you to remember the grief of life, the shrieking memory of the beginning of time. And the ghosts drill the holes of memory into you. They drill so deep and so many that we remember the birthing of stone and water and sky. Yes, we think and feel young at heart. Always young at heart. But the soul is old, and when the ghosts drill the ancient fear renews. How do you battle that? How do you challenge the fear of eternity, be it eternal damnation or salvation? How do you fight that cocksucker? We are only human, and so we suffer.'

He recalled the time the boy, Jose, was smoking weed in his mango grove with a girl from the local Catholic school. Rudolph had watched her dimpled cheeks as she inhaled. The joint glowed, and when she coughed, she apologized, her voice the tenor of a song thrush. José smoked the joint to the nub. Rudolph had stood in a hidden niche. He had concluded his exercises, calisthenics, and a two-mile jog. José was saying he loved her. "*Mahal kita*," José said. He kissed the gold crucifix on her necklace and then her lips. Rudolph stayed for a few minutes, not wishing to disrupt them, expecting, perhaps, the act of love. He discreetly withdrew into the mango nest, bare-chested, wiping the sweat from his face with his t-shirt, joyfully knowing Carmelita would be preparing his iced coffee.

Rudolph strode over the San Miguel glass and into central Cotabato City, ignoring the jeepneys that whisked past him. His heart raced. The bennies had throttled in.

Near the Pulangi River, on an active street, a dapper Chevrolet Dodge Charger with black-tinted windows and white sidewall tires was parked near the old market that sold kitchen wares, shoes, housing accessories, fresh fish, newly harvested vegetables, cathode ray televisions and goldfish. Car doors opened and closed, and Rudolph heard the squeak of hard-soled shoes on the pavement. He picked up his pace and thought of the American sergeant at the bar on Delgado and that aid was close by. As he rounded the corner, he soon realized he was lost in this southern capital. He approached a liquor store with iron bars and frosted windows. He whipped his tongue around his parched lips and marched on.

At an intersection, where the municipality dwindled to an appliance and automobile repair shop, he stopped and confronted the two men, his fists cocked. It was the Abu Sayyaf guerrilla, Lito, and a soldier in military fatigue pants.

"I thought you were gonna call me, not hold me up on the street like a punk," Rudolph said.

"This way," Lito said.

"I'm not interested."

The soldier lifted his shirt and showed Rudolph his 9MM Hungary-made pistol.

"Come with me," Lito said.

"Are you deaf, man? I'm not budging."

"What's wrong with your eyeballs?" Lito asked. "They're giant size. And your face looks like a watermelon. You must be really scared."

Rudolph unclenched his hands. "This guy's a military goofball. But that shirt, Lito, makes you a Philly pimp."

"Go get the car," Lito said. Rudolph took a step. "Not you. Him."

"My error," Rudolph replied congenially.

The car rumbled up the street and idled in front of Lito.

"Be a gentleman," Rudolph said, gesturing at the door.

"Up yours."

"Proper manners are a laudable trait," Rudolph said. "Of course, there was that madcap day when Mount Pinatubo blew her top. Remember?"

"Every Filipino does."

"Quite a pageant," Rudolph said. "But even on that terrible morning, which mimicked the end of creation—the sky full of falling ash, the sun nowhere to be seen, roads clogged, churches collapsing, prayers said by the boatloads, the dead obscured by volcanic pumice, rocks, landslides, mudslides, lahars, houses snapped like twigs from the eruption, children searching for their parents, animals and people buried alive, fanatics declaiming the Book of Revelation—there was neighbor helping neighbor. Filipinos coming to the aid of Americans and vice versa. That was the most extraordinary sight I've ever seen."

"You been living in the Philippines for years?" Lito said.

"Yes."

"Do you have a Filipina wife?"

"I do."

"That clarifies it," Lito said. "Your dippy nature."

In the rear seat of the Chevrolet, the windy gusts dried the sweat in Rudolph's beard. 'It's coming,' he told himself. 'Nirvana. Just breathe. In one nostril and out the other like a sublime Buddhist.'

"Lito, without me you've got nothing."

"I know that."

"Where are we going?"

"I just want to make sure you're honest. I have a test for you."

"Money's the test, man. That's what this is all about."

"You will make a phone call, and your friend, Finn, will bring half the money."

"So, this isn't about people."

"This is about establishing a united Muslim state," Lito said.

"What billboard did you get that from?" Rudolph asked.

Ahead, a truck struggled up the hill on the two-lane road. The soldier honked the horn, wheeled into the left lane and accelerated to pass the truck. In the truck's bed, pigs were crammed, belly to belly, snout to ass.

"Do you eat pork?" Lito asked Rudolph.

"No."

"When did you stop?"

"Today. Right now. I'm a vegetarian. Take a whiff of that swine."

"The *Manila Bulletin* said those hogs are full of dioxin. The government told farmers to butcher their pigs, and to kill the cows, because families drink the milk. The dioxins in the feed causes cancer. But these pigs aren't off to be killed and limed. They're going to the slaughterhouse. People need to eat, and the poor won't know the pigs are poison."

"I read the decree."

"The government's behind this hypocrisy."

"Democracy at work," Rudolph said.

The car wheeled behind the truck as a jeepney honked and cruised by in the oncoming lane. On the second pass, the truck driver had one hand on the wheel and the other around a bottle of Red Bull, an energy drink.

Rudolph cocked his head out the window and shouted, "Jump for your lives fellas!" He tossed peso coins at the driver, "*Compadre*, let your people go!"

Exhilarated, Rudolph opened the car door; the Chevrolet slowed, strayed into the right lane behind the truck, and Rudolph leaped from the seat. His shoulder hit the asphalt and he rolled, keeping his head cradled and his forearms close to his ears. He hurdled off the road and down a bluff. Toppling over vines, ferns, orchids, and stones, his hipbone collided with a palm tree. His elbows and knees were bruised, his cheekbone hurt, possibly fractured. A gecko blinked at him, snagged a brown worm with its tongue, and clambered onto a shrub. After collecting his faculties, Rudolph scrambled up the bluff onto the road's crest. His feet tingled, and he shook his legs until the nerve endings quieted in each limb.

Below, the car had rammed the truck, its front bumper tangled against the truck's rear end. Both vehicles had skidded on the pavement, arriving at a standstill at a ninety-degree angle.

Three pigs tiptoed off the truck by virtue of a broken plank. One landed on the Chevrolet's hood, as two pistol shots from the driver's side bore into the truck's passenger door. Lito tumbled out onto the pavement. The truck driver, holding a rifle, maneuvered to the front of the truck and crouched behind a tire. In a state of eerie repose, he loaded the rifle. Stepping onto the road, Lito's soldier fired again, the inaugural round puncturing the truck's windscreen and the second the engine block.

"Nothing will happen to you, friend," the soldier shouted. "This was just a fender-bender. Show yourself."

The driver raised the rifle barrel over the truck's hood and fired, missed and reloaded. The second round tore away part of the soldier's cheek. Teetering from side-to-side, the soldier threw away the pistol, fixed his hand to the wound, as blood accumulated in his palm. Astounded at the amount of flesh, muscle and bone the bullet had taken, he framed his lips to speak, but his vocal processes had collapsed. He eased into a trot, heading south, away from the collision.

Lito hunted for the soldier's pistol. On his knees, parallel to the car's trunk, a pig blindsided him in the buttocks, and clamped Lito's ankle with its mouth. Leaning against the tire's hubcap, Lito's fisted swings ricocheted mutely off the pudgy body. The driver had walked around his truck and aimed the rifle at the assailant's slim frame. A police siren echoed off the hills, and he lowered the nose of the rifle barrel and waited, his jeans rolled to mid-calf over his boots, one arm draped on the rifle stock, his gaze even-tempered.

Rudolph shouted from the crest, "Got you, Lito, you bum!" and was in the motion of raising a clenched fist when a convulsion struck his chest. A cramp passed through his abdomen, hopped-up his left arm, and pelted the jugular vein in his neck. His cheeks quivered, and his teeth throbbed.

When the affliction abated, Rudolph looked away from the road and toward Cotabato City, lush and shimmering in the valley, and for a reason he would never fathom, he thought, 'Go home, my man, for that is your ever-loving sanctuary.'

He stamped his feet, and they were sturdy. Without hesitation, he bounded over the bluff's rubble, high-stepping chaparral and thorny scrub brush, his heart pounding, and soon found himself on Maharlika Highway, running toward the distant city.

*****

After two furious raps on Finn's hotel door, a disheveled woman with bobbed hair barged into the room.

"Welcome," Finn said.

"I'm Congresswoman Cecille Lopez, and I represent the citizens in this district."

Finn caught a whiff of cinnamon perfume.

"You're aware of me?" Lopez asked, moistening her violet-colored lips with her tongue.

"I am," said Finn.

"Well, this is what you need to do, Mr. Finn. Stay here. Someone will contact you. The person will tell you where to drop off the ransom money. You do have the ransom money for the Peace Corps volunteers and the priest?"

"Yes. But Ms. Lopez, you should know that I've already been given the message."

"From who?"

"Captain Fuentes. However, you make it sound even simpler."

"It is. Unless you're stupid."

"I want the three Americans and the priest."

"I thought there were only two Americans," Lopez said.

"No," Finn said emphatically. "There are three Americans. You've given me the message, and I thank you."

Aware of a tactical error, he asked, "Why are you doing this? You must have known Fuentes gave me the same details."

"I didn't know he'd already spoken to you," Lopez said. "I'm here to help the Christians in my province. That's my duty as their Congresswoman. Now, wait for a call."

"When will that happen?"

"I don't know."

"Are you serious?"

"You'll get a phone call and orders about the exchange. If you miss the call, the Abu Sayyaf guerrillas may give up and execute all of them. They're disreputable that way."

"I'm worried about Fuentes," Finn said.

"What are you talking about? Captain Fuentes *is* your contact. Who else is there?"

Finn purposely neglected to mention Commander Lito. Another stratagem would destabilize Lopez's already strained temperament. Inside her bag, she removed a cigarette and lit it with a spark wheel lighter, and said, "Marta told me you're a smart man who can follow orders."

"I do my best," Finn replied. "That's why the embassy sent me. But nothing is upfront in Cotabato."

"Don't you know who your friends are?" Lopez asked.

"I can't figure that one out, Congresswoman."

"You know what to do. Deliver the money. There are larger things at stake here than three Americans and a Chinese priest. There's also the security of thousands of Filipinos in Cotabato. Their lives are valuable to me. I know that's an unfair burden to place on you, but you can shoulder the responsibility. Marta vouched for you. She called you a soldier."

"That's high praise from her," Finn said.

"I wouldn't know. She's out of her element in the Philippines, even if she claims she's half-Filipino. You have to be mercenary to live in the south, and she behaves like a gullible American."

"Never count her out. She coordinated this plan. She's not someone to be fucked with."

Lopez threw her cigarette at Finn's belly. "You're not a thug," she said. "That was my understanding from Marta. Don't talk like one."

"I'll be patient," Finn said.

"I'm glad we're working from the same script."

The bureau mirror rocked when she shut the door. Critiquing his options, Finn ascended the stairs to the fifth floor and entered Rudolph's room. Rudolph lay on the bed, still as an effigy, smelling of tropical sweat and foliage. Finn stared out the window. The somber skyline of Cotabato City converged with the metallic horizon of Ilana Bay. 'They're coming at me from all sides,' Finn thought, 'but I must be composed. Bend with the wind. You listening, buddy? When in life there's only negative fate, one's inner character must endure. I'm going to get those Peace Corp workers and that Chinese priest home. That's the goal. But for you, the romance is over. No more Filipinas to love. And what am I to tell Carmelita? I thought you had all the answers.' He stepped up to Rudolph's lifeless body. His shoes were off, and on the pillow beside his nose, Jim Thompson's *The Getaway.* Finn checked Rudolph's wrist. The pulse rate was flat, and he was surprised at the hand's suppleness. He had never seen Rudolph so mellow. Yet, even in this deathly state, the room seemed unwilling to emancipate his life force.

By early evening, the maid would find Rudolph, and if he tipped off the cops, there would be an investigation with Finn as the prime suspect, and he did not have the money for a bribe. He vowed he would not abandon Rudolph. 'Can't do that to a friend,' he told himself.

As he made his way down the hallway, the decade-old paint unveiled outlines where crucifixes had once been nailed, remnants from the time the building had been a chapel. In the foyer, in a former glass bulletin board, an archaic message in push pin letters stated, Prayer Meeti g Su day; Finding God Thru the B oze.

"Rave on," Finn said aloud.

He peered up the staircase, into the gloom, and wondered if now, through the medium of sorcery, Rudolph discerned how the life puzzle operated. He deserved to know. With his head cocked, Finn anticipated a response, a wail, and a whoop from Rudolph to signal he was merrily following his passage homeward. A layer of dust encrusted the bottom edge of the bulletin board, and on the floor near his foot was a grimy lipstick canister. He picked it up, clicked the logo button, and touched the flaky wax. He dropped the canister in his pocket and believed he had found luck.

CHAPTER 13

Forced to wait in the hotel and having exhausted his provisions, Finn lived on coffee and vitamins. As the vitamins and coffee began to chew a hole in his stomach lining, he nibbled on bread stolen from the floor's trash bin. An apparition to his neighbors, he stalked the hallways in late evening. Only the low volume of the television could be heard from his room. At night, he slept on top of the bed sheet, and when he woke before dawn, he saw phantoms in Civil War cloaks with ethereal faces.

Every so often, Finn tested the telephone, lifting the receiver, the drone a reminder that he was still part of the ongoing enterprise. He thought of Rudolph, and during those times when he could not keep him at bay, Finn would speak to his friend.

"I think the Peace Corp kids and the priest are gonna make it out alive," Finn said one afternoon, sitting on the bed in his boxer shorts in the stifling heat. "Congresswoman Lopez has her shit together. But you know, whether it's a congresswoman or a working girl, they all have an alternate scheme. As you've told me, even the girls who say they love you will chisel you for a few pesos."

"Why are you shoving this on me, bro?" came Rudolph's reply. "You know the woe of poverty. It's because of her, isn't it?"

Marta was a narcotic coursing in his bloodstream. She was his co-dependent, the solace perpetuated by an ancient entanglement.

Even after the separation of years, he could not shed her from his psyche. At night, it was Marta he fabricated as his sexual partner.

The spartan room had a malodorous stench, even with the toilet door closed. And if he shut the window and drew the shutters to silence the street noise, he would be alone in the dark with Rudolph. Then there would be no relief. With a hypnotic grin, Rudolph would lure him to his death, perhaps a fraternal leap from a hotel roof, or once lost on the street in evening rush hour, Fuentes or one of his henchmen would spot him and blast a cap into his brainpan.

At mid-afternoon of the fifth day, he lay on the bed, waiting for the phone to ring. His body tingled. Desiring a reprieve from boredom, he stretched out on the floor, with the premise that the tile would adhere, metaphorically, to his spine and intensify his courage. But the ants surged in a regimented battalion around his body, and the idea of the ants infiltrating his clothing, clambering over his thighs and privates, made the situation insufferable.

He was not sure of the hour, but he was ravenous. He made his way up to the fourth floor, where he had seen a family of five Filipinos in a single room. At arbitrary intervals, he would hear singing and shouting through the ceiling, and yesterday afternoon, with the bronze-colored daylight in his room, love making was taking place on the bed in the room above his own. The box springs creaked, and the floor moaned.

At the fourth-floor trash bin, he tore open a plastic bag, hoping to recover an apple, a box of cookies, or a half-eaten chicken breast, anything to bolster his declining health.

By pure chance, he blundered upon a three-quarter-full bottle of gin in a brown bag behind the bin. He took a sniff. After a single swallow, he nearly puked. It was as though the gin had been hidden for decades in a mildewed cellar. Undaunted, he swilled several swigs on the gin bottle and took the stairs to his room. Feeling a bit woozy from the gin, and admiring his sudden euphoria, he slipped in the dim stairwell. His feet flew up in an acrobatic somersault and his buttocks landed on the cement step. Tumbling downward, he came to rest on the third floor. He had temporarily blacked out and could feel a bruise forming on his forehead. He checked his arms and legs; they were uninjured. Holding the miraculously unbroken bottle and rubbing his hand over his bottom vertebra, the muscles spasmed, as if somebody had lashed him with a nylon rope.

In the room, and standing with his back to the full-length mirror, Finn removed his shirt. The area around his kidneys was raw, and the capillaries netted in a docile configuration. He tested his groin region. The hernia he'd had for six years appeared unaffected by the tumble. He shifted laterally to test his flexibility and cringed, swallowed what gin he could muster, stripped and entered the bathroom. Savoring the shower, he drank from the loco brew. With each swallow from the bottle, his assertive nature built. He accepted the fact that Rudolph was dead. Now there was no one to consult or harangue. He absorbed this bit of news with a gulp of gin. The shower water pacified his anxiety. Fuentes was a loose cannon and deceitful, but Marta was always two jumps ahead of her opposition. In Rwanda, she had affirmed her meticulous nature. Her monthly calendar was scrupulously heeded, and in their reckless love-making, she'd tested his endurance at various locations, at times animated in her exhibitionism, as they made love on the side of the highway, behind his car, so passersby could catch a glimpse of them, Marta pinned to a tree, her legs about his waist, or Finn face-up on a park lawn and Marta astride, a voracious twinkle in her eyes.

After toweling himself dry, Finn glared at the telephone. Two days prior, he had called the front desk for soap. The connection had been surprisingly clear. He picked up the receiver, hit O and told the operator he wanted an international line. He dialed the number he had memorized but had not called in nearly five months, his ex-wife's New Mexico residence. The telephone rang. Someone answered, and he asked for his daughter by name.

A woman spoke in Spanish, her voice abrupt, "*Quien es*?"

He said his daughter's name, Melissa, and his own in a louder pitch.

"No Melissa," the woman said.

"Pardon me. This is her father."

"Melissa not home," the woman said, and the line went silent.

Finn sat on the bed and tapped O again. The operator answered, and Finn requested another international line. He dialed, misdialed, and put the receiver on the telephone's base. Determined to succeed, he lifted the receiver and punched each digit, dialing a local number, one he had retrieved from the yellow pages on the nightstand. A Filipina answered. He recited the name to the receptionist, and she transferred him.

On the third ring, a woman said, "Hello. Who is this?"

"Eddie Finn."

"Where are you?"

"My room."

"What are you still doing there?" Marta asked.

There was mirth in her voice, as though she had been observing him the last five days and was entertained by his ordeal.

"What do you mean?" he asked.

"Get hold of the money and take a taxi to my hotel. The negotiation has been finalized."

"No one called me."

"Captain Fuentes just spoke to me. I'm to deliver the money."

"What are you playing at?" Finn asked.

"I'm the woman who looks after you, and who was once your lover."

"But what are your motives?"

"We're partners. Get your shit together, Ed-dee," Marta said.

As she came to the last consonant of his name, landing on it with the same contemptible intonation as the day she had shouted at him in their Rwandan hotel room, her arm in a sling from the dead Rwandan girl's rib bone, he realized it was rage, not disapproval, in her eyes whenever she met him, and that his unforgivable actions had cemented him on the adverse side of her love.

"Come to my hotel. Captain Fuentes told me the rendezvous point. And, if you don't bungle things from here on, we'll have the Americans returned within twenty-four hours. I'm expecting you. Hurry because we have to do this without any hiccups. And bring the money."

"Yeah, sure," Finn said. "It's in the bag."

He hung up. The floorboards in the apartment overhead creaked. He kneaded his spine. As he extended his energy past the pain and the reality of Rudolph's body, still unnoticed—there had been no police in the hallways he gauged the possibility of success. He was alone. But in his mind, he confirmed the belief in the simplicity of his mission. Yet, another choice loomed before him: dump the bank account book with Fuentes and skip town with Marta. The greater he ruminated on this option, the more inviting the plan.

Draining the final drops from the gin bottle, he deliberated the consequences of such a betrayal. No one admired him. He was the American Embassy liaison, and he had been told by the American Ambassador's aide that he was expendable. His sole concern was the release of the Peace Corps volunteers. He taped the safe deposit key to the bottom of the table lamp and thoroughly examined Rudolph's knapsack. Sewn into the lining he felt a bulge, cut the stitches with a penknife, and removed ten thousand pesos. He dressed, pocketed the Mindanao Consolidated Cooperative Bank account book in his sock, laced up his boots, and exited, gingerly taking the stairs, holding onto the banister, the strain resonating in the sciatic nerve as he descended.

He managed his way beneath the slim line of building shade, and at the corner of Rufo Manara Street, he flagged a taxi.

"Holiday Inn," he said to the driver.

The cabbie replied, "Two hundred pesos," and Finn, easing into the seat, signaled for him to proceed.

*****

Marta tapped the 25th square on the calendar. "Christmas is three days away."

"The festive season," Finn said.

He was different in this room with her. 'Cautious,' Marta thought, 'and calculating,' which was a bracing characteristic for him, one she did not know how to evaluate.

"I hear the talk about the jungle," Marta said. "The rebels will kill over sneakers. Being an American has no status. They want to kill Americans. They want to kill you. You're the prize, Eddie."

"They don't want me," Finn said. "It's all about the money."

She studied him as though he needed a nightlight to keep away malignant wraiths. She asked, "What's wrong with you? You look like you've been living in the street."

He checked the several days' stubble. Cupping his hands, he blew against his palms. The pungency was another reason Marta stayed several feet from Finn. He wore the same clothes as the last time she had seen him: dirty quill pants, a floral shirt, and battered Chukka boots. But his hair was brushed behind his ears, reaching his shoulders. She acknowledged the angular shape of his face that made him look tough and lonesome, but it could not hide his exhaustion.

You're the last person in my life," Finn confessed.

"Stop your foolishness, Eddie."

"Rudolph's dead."

"That's awful news," Marta said, without moving. "Will you complete the exchange?"

"It's the thing to do."

"Where's the money?"

Marta waited as Finn's eyes took in each physical portion of her anatomy. He explored her face, the sleek cobalt arms, her long legs in chinos, the shoeless black feet, and her sculpted fingers that he'd once told her reminded him of the painter Vermeer, how each gesture in his paintings conveyed a pose of passion, restraint, resilience, or obedience. Most probably, she thought, he was listing her character traits, diligence, and a streetwise acumen, assembling her into the woman he once possessed. Marta knew this was a futile exercise, confounding the emotional calculus that dictated his actions.

"There are towels in my bathroom if you want to shower," Marta said, hoping to ensure Finn's cooperation.

"Half the money," Finn said, "is in an account under my name in the Mindanao Consolidated Cooperative Bank. The account number is my birth date, and the last digit is Mickey Mantle's uniform number. It's in my boot. The other half is in a safe deposit box," he said. "I'm going to my hotel and wash up."

"One second. Do you know a man named Commander Lito?"

"He's been in the newspapers."

"If Fuentes founders," Marta said, "Commander Lito can be our substitute to retrieve the Peace Corps patriots and the priest."

"Why him?" Finn asked.

"He's the commander at the Aby Sayyaf's Cotabato camp that's holding the hostages. This way we have an alternative strategy. See it this way—we'll be dealing with one less villain with Fuentes gone."

"Reducing evil is an astute tactic," Finn said. His hands spread outward, as if to entwine Marta, and when she remained impassive, he balled his fingers. "I'll run with your assessment of who to negotiate with."

"I'll meet you at your hotel in a couple of hours," Marta said, opening the door. "Everything is going to work out."

As Finn walked away, passing each room, his shadow rose and dipped like a gull flying low over the sea. His gait implied a man assured of his future, envisioning himself married with children and working to pay off a house mortgage. But Marta knew he would never swing into that lifestyle; he had vaulted beyond day-to-day essentials. He was an embassy roustabout, taking posts to while away time, pursuing the milestone that would revitalize his limelight. He rounded the corner and made for the street.

*****

Finn had hiked past the circular drive on the main road when the bomb detonated. The earth shuddered, and he slipped to one knee. Regaining his balance, he trotted toward the explosion. He noted the pillar of smoke against the horizon and a woman in front of a Do Not Enter sign holding her head, which leaked blood. At the corner, a crowd gathered, and in the church quadrangle, the steeple cross had plummeted into the yard and lay on its side, as if it had been launched into the grass. The explosion had ripped asunder the southern wall of the church, leaving a mammoth archway. Inside, pews were strewn with plaster, and the life-size painted statue of Jesus, which had been welded to the wall, now oscillated, gazing at a barren sky. Pulverized Bibles were scattered in the aisles, and smoke poured from blown-out windows. A woman sat on the grass, with one naked breast, and a half moon laceration where the other breast had been. Men carried bodies from the church, as if a neutral setting could revive them. The air tasted of tin from the bomb's ammonium nitrate compound.

Finn assisted, and herded women and children to the chain link fence. They leaned against his body, weeping. He told them to trust in God, thinking it would relieve their sorrow. Sitting against a fence post, a child was missing a finger, and Finn swaddled his handkerchief around her hand. Then he saw her right ankle was connected solely by its ligaments. She wailed. He used his belt as a tourniquet, tying it around her upper thigh, and rocked her in his arms. A parishioner removed his shirt and proceeded to cover the ankle.

Police cars drove into the quadrangle. Families reunited in clusters. A woman knelt, shaking back and forth, holding a child's head in her lap, her body half-clothed. With the arrival of several ambulances, Finn walked to the far side of the street. The church roof crumbled. Flames blackened the cedar beams, and hot embers rained on the dead. He walked for five minutes, then hunkered below the neon placard of a used car firm, his body quivering in the ninety-degree heat.

After the ablutions in his bathroom, Finn met Marta on Don Rufino Alonzo Street. She was in a taxi with the engine on. He slid into the rear seat, and they motored along Gonzalo Javier Road.

"Did you shower?" Marta asked.

"I did."

"You smell."

"There was a bombing at the local church on my way home. I helped out, I think. Guess the soap and water didn't wash away all the smoke."

"Are you hurt?"

"No. The police came with volunteers. They had things under control when I left."

"I'm glad," Marta said.

A crooked piston punished the taxi's gear box.

"What are you thinking?" Finn asked.

"How the day will end."

"We'll rescue the Americans."

"You're an optimist," Marta said. "Don't talk this way when we get to the rebel camp."

"What way?"

"As if you can dictate conditions. The Abu Sayyaf are in charge. I know these people. They're my people. Let me talk, Eddie."

"You always had a way with civil servants," Finn said.

They drove into the eastern hills of Kabuntalan. The countryside consisted of olive-green vegetation, interspersed with paddy fields. As they traveled further into the jungle, off the diminishing asphalt onto a dirt road, Finn lost all sense of navigation. For a time, due to the verdant tundra of palm fronds and foliage, he could see neither sky nor sun. Aloft, stratus clouds hovered low, as though they floated only yards above them, and within reach. The road constricted and grew treacherous, with muddy potholes and branches that marked up the taxi.

At a checkpoint, with a white box painted on a tree, the taxi stopped. Two men dressed in military gear leveled their rifles at the driver. One hauled Finn from the cab. Elwin smoked a cigar in the arch of a narra tree. The soldier in a San Francisco baseball cap said in English, "Pay the driver two thousand pesos."

"That's too much!" Finn exclaimed.

Marta grimaced. Finn handed over the money, and the taxi sped off. In single file, the soldier in the San Francisco baseball cap, Finn, Marta and Elwin hiked the winding trail into the jungle. The other soldier, who carried the two-way radio, had stayed behind. The pace was vigorous, and Finn massaged his left hip to reduce the stress on his muscles, as the strain was worse on that side, where his back ailed him. They made headway amid wiry vegetation with the trail shriveling until machetes were used to slice the brambles and brushwood. After jumping a rocky creek, a sentry stepped out from behind a coconut palm tree, armed with an M-14 rifle. The soldier and the sentry spoke, traded canned beer and fried squid. Finn's cigarettes, which were in his shirt pocket, were taken by the sentry. The short respite ended.

By late afternoon the crew entered the compound. A woman with a hunting knife was gutting a chicken on a flat stone, the chicken's spaded organs already being ingested by ants. Two bored soldiers sat before a fire pit, scouring rags over their rifle barrels. Finn did not recognize the country flag attached to a thatched roof, which rarely fluttered. The flag's red background, with a yellow sword in the right quadrant and a star in the middle of a full moon, was the only color in the drab camp. The air had grown heavier, and Finn's shirt was drenched with sweat. The soldier in the San Francisco baseball cap bound Finn's hands and led him toward a Quonset hut.

"Don't be nervous, Marta," Finn shouted.

"You must be joking," she called out.

Finn glanced over his shoulder. Marta grinned, drinking water from a mercenary's canteen.

*****

Inside the hut, Carlos, the soldier in the San Francisco ball cap, turned out Finn's pockets and grouped the items onto a table: butane lighter, handkerchief, leather wallet, penknife, keys with a rabbit's foot, and he eyeballed the one photograph Finn carried, of a girl with pixie bangs, a snub nose and bony legs, wearing a soccer uniform. He shoved Finn onto the stool in the middle of the three-corner room.

"Where are the Peace Corps workers, Captain?" Finn asked.

"Very near," Fuentes answered from behind a table.

Above Fuentes, a painted window had peeled, over time, allowing tracts of daylight into the room. Finn wiggled his wrists to loosen the rope.

"Stop struggling," Fuentes said. "Rope burns are a nuisance and can become infected. Then we'd have to chop off your hands. A man without hands is as good as dead."

"Except if he has a caring wife," Lito said, seated beside Fuentes.

"Even then he'd end up a street bum. Best to pop a bullet into him now," Fuentes said.

"I'd be happy to shoot him. Better than being a cripple."

"Your altruism is remarkable, comrade."

"Why are you doing this?" Finn asked. "Is this about the payment?"

"Be quiet," Fuentes said. "You annoy me."

"The money is satisfactory," Lito said. "We do this for our religion and the freedom of our people."

"He doesn't mean the ransom, Commander. He wants to know why he's tied up like a skinned rabbit. Don't be naïve, Eddie. This is done to scare you. Are you scared?" Fuentes grated his spent cigarette onto a tin plate.

"Why did you bomb the church?" Finn asked.

"Which church?" Fuentes asked, grimly.

"The one on Oblate Drive."

Fuentes could feel the coordination of events slowly unraveling.

"The priest was writing lies about us in the newspaper," Lito said. "We shut him up. All classes of people die in war. It's the consequence of revolts. These tactics will give us victory."

"There is also the money to help the cause," Fuentes said.

"And why do *you* fight?" Finn asked the young soldier at the door.

Lito nodded permission for him to respond, and Carlos said, "We fight for our civil liberties, and for our families. We fight for self-rule against a government that despises us. We fight for equality, so the poor won't live in shacks or become ill from a poor diet." The boy's lower lip contorted defiantly. "We fight those who want to kill us, and for our religious independence."

Carlos was a brave boy, and to further his education, Fuentes wished to lead him into the jungle and dunk his head in the stream fed by the Wawa River and hold him under the water. The bearcats and monkeys would gather as the boy's legs and arms thrash amidst the terraced jungle. 'To crush such faith in one's allies is worse than murdering innocents,' Fuentes thought, 'but how do you tell the boy that his convictions are passing? And that blind devotion destroys one's soul?' Fuentes viewed himself dragging Carlos from the stream, feeling the sinewy muscles against his body, sensing the boy's relief and gratitude, as he gulped air into his lungs.

"Are they all as resolute as him?" Finn asked.

"Not many are," Lito answered.

"He's dedicated."

"Yes, he'll be a topnotch commando," Lito said.

Fuentes towed his chair toward Finn. "Where's the money, my American?"

"I want to see the Peace Corps workers and the priest," Finn said.

Fuentes boxed Finn's cheek with the wide part of his hand. Finn's head jolted backward and rebounded for a second round that drew blood from his nose. Then the door opened, and Fuentes, his arm raised for another wallop, halted in mid-flight. A woman in a billowing skirt filled the lighted space. Adhering to a previous protocol, the woman carried a stool from the wall and slotted herself next to Fuentes.

With her arrival, Fuentes's ire ebbed. The woman was not old. In fact, she appealed to Fuentes. The Tagalog phrase he equated with her was most appropriate, *pangit at maganda*. She is both ugly and beautiful. In her voice, he detected bereavement, a disarming attribute that at first made him suspicious of her. She eyed Finn, peremptory, and sneered.

"Commence," Fuentes said.

She took Fuentes's right hand and tracked her forefinger along the rugged palm lines. She spoke in the Ilocano dialect of that province, one that Fuentes understood. She told him about his future. He stared at her face, inspired by her tenacious examination. He had glorious days ahead, riches and power, and his children would remain healthy. She curled his fingers. Fuentes thanked her, and with his thumb, singled out Finn. Unhappily, she relocated her stool and gazed half-heartedly at his wrists. Fuentes loosened the rope.

The fortune teller took Finn's hand, dug a nail into his palm, and spoke in English.

"You'll die at forty, maybe younger," she said. "You will not marry, and you will earn little money. And you'll end up alone. I should lie—tell you a lie—but I won't. You will be buried with strangers. But a loved one who is more memory than flesh and blood will add flowers to your grave."

Fuentes had witnessed this display with other simpletons, and when cash was scarce, her skirt was for sale, although this did not dent her prophetic skills. Her fortune-telling had the brimstone of the Old Testament. Fuentes recalled seeing her kneeling over the dead after an altercation with the Philippine military in Marawi, Mindanao. Her courage had impressed him.

With confidence, Fuentes waved his arm in concentric circles before the soldiers in the room.

"What's this thing you're doing?" Lito asked.

"Marshalling my authority," he replied, lowering the arm.

"Do you have a story?" Finn asked the woman.

"I have no story," the fortune teller said.

The woman sat with her hands in the lap of her skirt.

"Tell us," Finn said.

"Yes," Fuentes said. "Now I want to hear about you."

"I have many stories, as we all do," she said respectfully.

"Tell one," Fuentes said.

"We don't have time for this," bemoaned Lito.

"Some entertainment, comrade."

She began, "I was a girl playing in my yard when a friend of my father took me to his house to show me a music cassette. In his bedroom, he took off my clothes and had sex with me."

"I have listened to this sort of lame story many times," Lito said.

"It was my first time, and then he would come to my home when my mother was at the factory. He did this to me day after day, until it was me who would come to his house, wanting in, wanting him. If he wasn't alone, he'd say to the woman of his house, 'It's the girl, Teresa and she wants sugar for cookies.'

"One day he took me away. He deserted his grandmother, his daughter, and the woman who wasn't his wife. He was the man I loved. I was seventeen. I had my baby nine months later. When my daughter was seven months old, he boarded a bus out of town, as we slept in our shack in the Barrio Barretto. I had no education and no money. So, I became a whore to the American or German or Swiss. Sometimes they were nice and would make promises, but generally it was just short time.

"My daughter got older, and I hid my occupation from her. She attended school. When she was fifteen, she learned I was the mistress to an American lieutenant on Subic Navy Base. She was angry with me. Within weeks, she was raped and murdered. The police never discovered who committed the crime. People spoke of seeing Filipino military. They can be as ruthless as any man.

"A fisherman found my daughter's body on Baloy Long Beach. The cross I'd given her for her birthday was still around her neck. Yes, children are murdered all over the globe. And does God hear? Does Jesus? I know they are both blind and deaf and have hollow hearts. All I valued was taken from me. This was my child. And I went mad."

"Thank you for your story," Lito said.

"Tell me the entire tale," Fuentes said, patting her knee.

"I traveled north into the mountains and entered a village. The people are called the Igorot. They fed me for a week, and one evening I saw them eating the body parts of a man, a *kano* who had trekked into their community. He had been killed and broiled. I cried. I had not cried when my daughter died. Perhaps I was still mad, but when I saw the Igorot doing this, I couldn't restrain my despair.

"Seeing my tears, one of the men laughed, and another man came over. With his knife, he sliced off part of my ear. He opened his mouth and flung the ear in, chewed, and swallowed.

"I became his woman. Once, I think, I almost ate a human. The community was celebrating. There were songs and dancing and a bonfire. Before I ate from the bowl, my daughter spoke to me from the flames and said the meat in the bowl was that of a man. I know you think I lie, but I saw my daughter in the bonfire, and she spoke to me. The world is not so predictable, and the natural ways of life are still unfamiliar to most people. I dumped the bowl on the ground and watched the dogs eat the meat. There was no sadness in my heart for the meat that had been a man. I watched the flames rise as a log was added and the figure melted away.

"I should have spoken to my daughter. But what do you say to someone you know does not exist? I tried to pray, but prayers are for those walled in abandonment. A desert gale blew through my heart.

"Soon, I left the Igorot and wandered from one village to another, hustling to get by. I met many working girls. A grandmother taught me to tell fortunes. She read my palm and said I had the gift. For two years, I lived near Subic Bay and sold fortunes to American military men and their wives.

"Sometime in January, I flew to Mindanao with a Chinese businessman and his wife. His wife respected the truths I told each time I read her palm. She had a venerable soul. When they went home to La Union, I stayed in Mindanao. I didn't want to be with the foreigner. One day, I read a child's hand. She had no future or past. I don't know how to call it except that way. She was doomed. The doomed, if you don't know, have no knowledge of this fate, and are most eloquent in their sinking. There are such women. I was friends with a whore who had a heart like hers; she was a superb whore. She hanged herself one Sunday."

Fuentes cuffed her ear.

"I read this girl's palm and told her a lie about the rich man she would marry. A Russian with a mansion, I said. I followed her and her mother to church. We sat in folding chairs. After they exited, nothing happened. I expected a reaction. The voice of God, I guess. On the street, I was the same person as when I entered the church."

"Fucking Catholics," Lito said.

Her chin lifted. "I saw the girl the next day. I knew she wasn't my daughter. I bought her a soda and recognized the gulf that separated us. I finally understood the loneliness one feels losing a child."

"Finish it!" Lito shouted.

"I spent time with one last man. I did it for the money and because I wanted to be with someone. He spoke a language I didn't know, and I was thankful for that. I didn't want to have to talk to him or hear him talk or learn anything about him. From that day on, I washed my hands of love. It was over for me. I don't think you can understand this. The relief. I will die unmarried and childless, and maybe spurned by God, but I don't know that for sure. The man paid me a lot of money, and I never saw him or the girl again."

Fuentes scanned the soldiers in the room. His dominance was still visible. The woman's story had not negated his potency.

"It's over. Remove her," Lito said.

A soldier ushered her out. The hut had altered, somehow, and it was not everyone who could make space volatile. She had also taken her sex with her, but her aura had remained in the room, and Fuentes witnessed a rising irritation from his fellow Filipinos.

"I want to see the three Americans," Finn said.

"Silence!"

Fuentes seized Finn's throat to rid the fortune teller from his head. He was sickened by her mumbo-jumbo. One who speaks with such insight is a hazard to have around. She sees, truly. He had not known that before and had applauded her game and the way her legs hugged the stool, which he pictured were as smooth as satin beneath the skirt. But she was wrong about one thing. She was not love-dead, because her presence still resided in the room, and one who is as desolate as she claimed could not leave such a stamp on people. "We will finish this tonight," Fuentes said, releasing his hold.

"I'm with you," Finn coughed.

*****

Carlos took Finn outside and tied him with hemp rope to a pole under the blaze of a brutal afternoon sun. Finn plopped on the ground. He watched a raisin-colored fantail orbit the compound in decreasing rings and come to rest atop a bamboo hut. The bird fluttered its wings from the perch. Finn closed his eyes, and when he looked up, Marta approached, carrying a canteen, and wearing a straw Panama hat that shaded her face. She squatted before Finn, fed him water, moistened her hand from the canteen, and combed her fingers through his hair.

"You're a dummy," Marta said.

She poured the remaining canteen water onto his collarbone.

"Feeling refreshed?" Marta asked.

"Let's get out of here."

"Where do you think you can go?"

"We," he whispered.

Her lips pursed. "I can help you. But you must fulfill your promise."

"What promise is that?"

"The promise you told me in the plane, that you would simply give the money to me."

"I was going to," Finn said, "but you persuaded me to come. You said you needed me."

"But you broke your promise, because here you are."

She had beguiled him from the start. And her logic had flown off the rails. Yet, she was the ballast inside him, a woman who still brought elation to his waking days, which, he determined, would lead to catastrophe. Nevertheless, he was the Peace Corps volunteers' single advocate for liberation.

"How are the hostages?" Finn asked.

"I haven't seen them," she said.

"Marta, the promise for me to stay away was made before the pact that I would come to this jungle," Finn said. "The promise was spoken days before. Do you remember? You told me the Peace Corp workers and the priest would not be harmed. Like little angels. Those were your precise words."

"Yes, Eddie, but you're here now and everyone's in the shithouse."

"I can get you the money."

"Where is it?"

He informed her of the location of the bank deposit key in his hotel room in Cotabato City.

"Let the kids go, Marta."

"But you're here. And if you're here, I can't guarantee a thing."

"You just said...."

"Screw all Americans. They're the cause for countless tragedies in the Philippines. After all the years you've known me, couldn't you see my real loyalty? Couldn't you understand what I'd do to prevent another bloodbath? After Rwanda, you should feel the same. Why you don't, I can't comprehend." She drank the last of the water from the canteen. "The Philippines economy is in the toilet. The ransom money will feed and support the people. Not these maggots," she jeered, gesturing at the compound, "but the poor and homeless."

Finn shook his shoulders.

"What's wrong with you?" she asked.

"You want what?" he yelled at her.

"I want to get as much money from you as I can. Smuggle it out where it can serve the people."

"Whose side are you on?" Finn asked.

"Not yours or theirs," she said.

The dime-size scar on her cheekbone she had received as a child, from a glass jar thrown by her drunken mother, gave her a look of frailty. Her head swayed upward, and the sunshine halved her facial features. She pinched the bank book from Finn's sock, lifted her shirt, and stored it in an interior pocket.

"I'm sorry to leave you like this. You were just the money man. I can't express what you mean to me. There has been no one since you. I have loved no one else." Marta kissed his mouth. "I don't have a future," she told him. "Marry a Filipina."

As she walked on a path, her boots made imprints in the dried mud, hieroglyphics that he strained to read. He tried to hold onto her scent, and the sensation of her hands on his face. As cumulus clouds intensified in the sky, the fortune teller appeared and sat cross-legged in front of Finn.

"There's information you should know. I couldn't tell you before but now I can."

"I don't want to hear your talk," Finn said.

"She's dead," The woman said.

"Who?" Finn asked.

"The one you have not seen in years."

"Go away."

"Your wife is dead."

"I have no wife."

"The wife you once had, and now your daughter is alone."

"No. That can't be. This is a trick of Fuentes."

"I know nothing of tricks."

"Why do you care?"

"No one can hold secrets, and if I didn't tell you, you'd find out some other way, a worse way."

"Is there anything else?" Finn asked.

Her lips curved upward, imitating a painted jester.

"Go on," he said.

"They mean to kill you."

"That would be silly."

"Your money means nothing to them. The newspapers know of the kidnapping, and there is publicity. That's the rebels' scheme: to be on the air waves. Media coverage. It's worth the same as gold to them. The foundation of this insurgency is not money or even righteousness, because people don't care about that. It's a meaningless word used by politicians." She leaned closer, so that he could see her breasts in her low-neckline blouse. "One life," she said. "Ten lives. One hundred lives. That is immaterial to the Abu Sayyaf. Their purpose is to spread the Koran's Islamic legacy. Your country cannot kill all the faithful, and even those inside the hut have an understanding of this principle."

She placed her palm on his forehead. The gesture agitated Finn.

She said, "I think you shit your pants. I can wash them for you if you want."

"Get away from me," Finn bellowed.

Her masculine hands and face, burned copper from the sun, made it difficult to find the origin of her generosity to him, the news of his wife, if that was true. She stood, glowering at him, until Elwin came and shooed her away with a rap on her buttocks.

"Time for dinner," Elwin said.

He sliced off Finn's ropes, pushed him inside the hut and onto the stool.

"Okay," Lito said, seated on the table. "Let's discuss."

"Discuss what?"

Carlos poked Finn in the groin with his rifle butt, and Finn toppled off the stool onto the floor. A second blow would cause a strangulated hernia. Then it would be only a day or two until infection spread throughout his body. For once a hernia becomes strangulated, intestinal gangrene occurs. Behind the table, Fuentes held Marta on his lap, her gaze transfixed, as if peering into the future, but her body appeared off-kilter. Her spine rested against Fuentes's arm, and she seemed like a marionette, simultaneously feeble and inert. Finn imagined Fuentes's hand inside of her, encompassing her heart, managing the levers that regulated her emotions, the tenacity that had trained her to overcome life's worse obstacles. He had seen her resilience and ingenuity, time and again in Rwanda.

Fuentes knotted his fist in Marta's hair. Around her eye a purplish welt bloomed, and blood had clotted in her ear. The bank account book, warped from the jungle's oppressive humidity, lay in the middle of the table. Finn rose and limped up to Marta.

"Eddie, I'll arrange your body with hers like lovers at Jesus's chamber," Fuentes said. "And I'll bury you both in the peasants' graveyard."

'He wants money,' Finn thought. 'He doesn't care about Marta or me, the Peace Corps workers or the Chinese priest.' Finn confided in Fuentes's ear, "I have an additional one-hundred thousand U.S. dollars in a classified locale. My backup stash. It's all yours if you let her go."

Fuentes gloated by kissing Finn's cheek. In slow motion, Finn clasped Marta's neck in one hand, her wrist in his other, and drew her away from Fuentes, who relented without argument. He took Marta and sat with her on the floor in the opposite corner.

"Listen to the news, American," Fuentes said, after checking his wristwatch.

Elwin cranked on the radio.

"Lito Gregorio," the announcer said in English, "spokesman for the communist rebel's command in Mindanao, said that former first lady, Imelda Marcos, her son, Ferdinand Junior, San Miguel

Corporation chairman Eduardo Cohungeo and Philippine Airlines chairman Lucio Tanio face arrest."

Lito's recorded voice came over the radio. "The Marcos's and their cronies must face revolutionary justice because of the wealth they stole from the country and for their abuses of the people, particularly during martial law. This goes for the current administration, who will wreck this country with their propaganda. Liberty for the Philippines!"

The announcer spoke, "Military chief General José Nazaren said yesterday that both the military and the police would augment the alert because of the threats. In Cotabato province, where Lito Gregorio's group is active, provincial police chief Superintendent Jaime Karingal said yesterday that the Abu Sayyaf guerrillas had surrounded Capingpilan Central Elementary School in Midgayap. Five hundred students and seventy teachers are detained, and one journalist has been shot. The President declared that the government would not negotiate and said any talks with the insurgents will be suspended."

Elwin reduced the volume.

"Such cheerful news, don't you agree?" Fuentes saw Lito's distress. "The government and Americans will negotiate, comrade. They have no backbone. We'll free the students and teachers. It'll be seen as an honorable token. Then they'll commit to your requests. A gratifying settlement."

"Yes," said Lito. "I'll give the order. But the dead journalist?"

"A casualty of media hype. To die for a photograph, what a dimwit. I think he was French, and the French are such cowards, anyway. Now Eddie," Fuentes said in a steadfast voice, "where's the rest of the money?"

"I don't recall," Finn said.

Lito spoke to the sentry at the door, and Finn motioned Fuentes closer.

"Your money is buried under the floorboards in my hotel room."

"Ingenious," Fuentes said. With his boot toe, he nudged Marta's thigh. "She has a hardy constitution."

"She was on your side."

"Side? No one's on my side," Fuentes said. "And she deserved the interrogation. I wanted to find out about her contacts. She told me nothing. At least nothing of value." Fuentes leaned closer, his mouth within a whisker of Marta's face, and whispered. "Now, Eddie, tell me truthfully about the money. No lies."

Marta's lips parted.

"Hello," Fuentes said. "How are you today?"

"What do you want?" she asked softly.

"Thank you for telling me the location of the deposit key," Fuentes said.

"You've made your point," Finn said. "Now that we're pals again, the arrangement is simple. The money's in the bank under my name. You have the bank book. Just bribe the bank president, and he'll hand over the cash. He may even be an ally. As a result, your access to the funds will be even easier." Finn gave Marta a shy smile. "Let him have the bank account," he told her. "It's the hostages I care about."

"You thought I trusted you, bitch," Fuentes said, standing fully erect. "Like you thought I trusted that Catholic government whore, Congresswoman Lopez. And now Finn wants me to trust him, to drive into town and collect the money, as if I were buying candy for my daughter at a Sari-Sari store."

"Who are you?" Finn asked.

"A communist," Fuentes replied proudly. "Who else would I be?"

Finn should have been distraught by Marta's manipulation of the mission. But he was a less prideful man now since Rwanda and

216

able to bear the stripe of forgiveness. He moved his palm to the side of Marta's face. Her cheek was like nothing he had ever touched before.

"Your woman is ill," Fuentes said.

"She'll rebound," Finn said. "She comes from healthy stock."

"We should guillotine her," Lito said, "and add her head to our trophy case. That would send a message the American government couldn't ignore."

"Yes," Fuentes said. "It would make a persuasive picture."

The animus within Finn rose up, and he lashed out at Fuentes with his boot heel, striking him on the kneecap. Fuentes flinched and, in retaliation, he hit Finn on the top of his head, slapping at him again and again, until Finn threw an arm over his skull. With his fist, Fuentes struck Finn on the bridge of the nose, forcing him to crouch over Marta.

"Bastard!" Finn cried. "You have the money!"

Sweat streaked Fuentes face. The attack degraded, and he sucked his tongue into his mouth. Rising to his full height, he crossed the room and jerked open the door, ripping a hinge from its slot.

"Take him to the healing hut," Lito said to the soldiers in the room.

"No," Finn protested.

"Our women will take care of Marta," Lito said. "I'll get Captain Fuentes, and we'll collect the money. Prepare yourself."

Elwin picked Marta up in his arms. "She's a bag of bones," he said.

*****

As Fuentes stalked across the compound, he knew he did not need a knife to tame the Peace Corps girl. By simple manipulation, her craven behavior would emerge, as it had with the other prisoners. And the girl would plead. Surely, this time she would not defy him. Resistance wasn't an option for her. She had lost her contempt days ago.

Disobedience. The concept offended him. Soldiers peed in the bushes and lanterns lit the footpath. At her hut, he excused the guard. When the guard delayed, Fuentes directed him to withdraw his sidearm, which he did. Approving the plastic grip, he placed the pistol beneath his waistband.

Fuentes unlatched the door. The girl was asleep. He had counted on seeing her eyes, the color of faded blue ribbon. But now, in a fetal position on the floor like a comatose cheetah, he tapped the pistol, the cadence equal to his ticking heart, calm and constant. He scrawled a foot in the dirt. There was no response. Her chest pumped in a metered flow, and he wondered whether in her dreamscape, in that fanciful refuse, her pugnacious constitution still thrived.

He watched her. After fifteen minutes, she trembled. Her cheek rested on a bare arm, and her hair fell across her eyes. In the compound, voices became frantic. Action had been taken without his endorsement.

"I know you hear me. I'm in that limbo land with you. Yes, you feel me, don't you, miss? It's glorious. But sleep's a false hiatus of relief. Do not be tricked. And even when you're home, in your America, I'll be able to wander inside of you, and you'll know this from wherever you live. I am in your head. I rule, lady," he said. "Fuck you."

He booted a pebble that hit her crotch. This is how it is done, the sacrifice. He laughed aloud, recognizing the waste—the loss of cash. He knelt and traced a knuckle against the pale chin etched with spidery, violet veins.

"We're only beginning, miss."

He examined her, like a trapper gleeful over his ambushed prey. The metaphor pleased him, and he stepped outside and walked up to Lito. A bearcat loitered at a nearby hut.

"You stay here. I'll go to the bank with Finn and get the money."

"That won't happen," Lito said. "I'll take him. Your bonus will come to you."

"I've always kept my word," Fuentes said.

Lito asked, "Did you rape her?"

"That's your neighborhood, Commander."

Fuentes flapped his handkerchief in front of Lito like a matador teasing a half-blind bull.

"Don't taunt me," Lito said, taking the handkerchief and tossing it to the dirt.

"You have sex with children and talk to me as if I'm the enemy," Fuentes said. "What's wrong?"

"You're an interloper. All you care about is money. But rest easy. We'll pay you the five hundred thousand pesos for assisting with the negotiations."

Fuentes gripped the knife on his belt. Yes, to see Lito without a nose or a lip suited him. For what whore or child would screw him then?

"Go home, Lito," Fuentes said. "I'll take care of this last financial detail."

"You traitor. You'll not steal from us."

"To win this war, you have to be crafty and intelligent."

"For the insult, you won't get a peso," Lito said. "Banishment is your reward. This is Muslim country. Muslim law. Muslim doctrine. You don't know what we're capable of. Remember the Lupao, Nueva Ecija massacre in 1987. We retaliated. We aren't stooges."

"Who could think such a thing?" Fuentes said.

Lito swung at him, and Fuentes ducked, averting the roundhouse punch. On his toes, he connected with a solid jab that lifted Lito's chin and another jab that split his nose, as blood dribbled onto his lips. Seizing Lito's throat, Fuentes shoved him against a hut's roof's overhang and drummed his head against a wooden post, the head wound secreting a musty stench. The aroma aroused Fuentes's abhorrence as he jammed Lito even more aggressively into the post. Lito squirmed, his fists making feathery contact on Fuentes's kidneys. After the fourth clout on the post, Lito's spit pasted Fuentes's cheek. Stunned by the insult, Fuentes froze, and Lito lurched forward, his teeth snapping into Fuentes's ear. He elbowed Fuentes's throat, severing the earlobe. Stepping away, he spat the cartilage from his mouth. Blood sluiced down Fuentes's neck, and a roar bellowed in his head. It was the voice of God, and he was speaking in tongues.

Fuentes shouted, "You son of a bitch!"

He raised a fist, but strong arms encircled his chest from behind.

"There's your fucking ear," Lito said, pointing at the mashed earlobe.

The voice in Fuentes's head weakened. It was as though a vacuum inhabited the ear.

"That bit of flesh is all you'll get from me, Lito," Fuentes said.

"You're not indestructible. Soon, the beasts of the jungle will feed on your carcass till you are only bones."

Lito strode into the darkness. The soldier's arms shook, his body succored to Fuentes.

Fuentes had no desire to fight him, and said, "Let go, Carlos." The boy acquiesced. "Pick that up," he ordered. "Pick up my ear. Give it to me."

Fuentes held the flimsy wedge in his palm. He slumped against the boy. What magic could he conjure up to salvage the ransom?

With his hand, he enclosed the injured ear. 'You will make up, somehow, with that brainless lowlife,' Fuentes thought. 'And you'll fix this mischief. The money will come tomorrow, and then all these Muslims can die and annihilate one another for all I care.' The din inside his ear grew opaque, as the voice shriveled. God was speaking, but He was an ignorant sot who thought only of himself.

A twinge bit into the inner ear canal.

"Captain, they can sew it up at the hospital," Carlos said. "It'll take but a minute."

"Yes. We go to the hospital, and afterward, a meeting with Lito. He'll have collected himself after an hour. Together, we'll conclude that this episode was just an evening quarrel among comrades."

"When do we go to town, Captain?"

"In the morning, we'll take a ride to the bank. All three of us, like kinsmen."

Ahead, the mountains were ringed with pinkish clouds from the falling sun. To the west, a bruised darkness capped the Moro Gulf. A wind, scented with mango, chafed their faces. In the hut, somewhere behind him, Fuentes heard the girl lament, crooning a ballad, the self-stylized misery that comes to one who is alone, without help, and knows the animal within is one's only deliverance.

CHAPTER 14

Marta crawled from the center of the hut toward a darkened corner. Leaning against the shutter, Elwin smoked an Antonio Gimenez cigar. She saw the stripped band on the ground and could smell the spicy odor, and for a time, she believed she was safe. No harm could come to her now. She had confessed every aspect of her agenda. Her Rwandan grandfather periodically smoked a cigar, which choked the house with an aroma similar to church candles. Each Sunday, in Kigali, she sang in the choir. She felt invigorated with the choir, a member of a soulful solidarity. She drew contentment from the memory. Then Lito came toward her from the doorway. He approached casually, as though he would speak of a reprieve. In his hand, he gripped a thick wooden rod with the bark shaved off. The husk had been sanded and laminated with a golden nectar resin.

"She's too big for you," Elwin said.

Marta sat against the wall. She could feel the spiny bamboo knots dig into her skin. Her shirt was torn, revealing her peach-size breasts. Lito kicked her in the shins until her legs slid to the ground. She wore one green sneaker and a tattered sock on the other foot.

"The black bitch is tall," Lito said. "A new experience for me. But I'll hammer her to my size."

"No," Elwin said, flicking cigar ash. "I mean she's too big for you down there."

Lito aimed the rod at her kneecap. "Maybe I'll just split her in half."

"She'll still be too big," Elwin said. "You can't shrink a pussy."

Elwin continued to smoke the cigar, and the scent upset her stomach, and she looked for the spot where she would vomit. Before she could upheave, the first blow from Lito's rod nailed her in the jaw and loosened her teeth, enflaming the nerve roots. She lifted her gaze. The rod see-sawed to-and-fro before her like a pendulum. She touched her lips, and blood smeared her fingers.

"I'm not through, you mother fucker," Marta said.

She had nothing else to give them, but there had to be a way to bring trust forward. She conjured up fraudulent information and an oath of allegiance. But when the second flurry pummeled her temple, and she collapsed onto her side, she acknowledged that nothing and no one could protect her. Another strike. She heard the sound of a whirling wind. It landed on her ribs and stole her breath. She could see the earthen floor and spray of blood droplets from her mouth. The next strike targeted the back of her head, and a bone broke in her neck. The trauma was painless but moved her to an uncharted territory. One that frightened her. In a lucid moment, she thought someone had cut off her pants, for she could feel the damp air on her legs as the rod smacked her between the legs.

"Enough. Please." She meant to utter these words, but they were sealed inside, and so she took all of herself to an interior isle. She would reside on this private isle and let the outer body go. You can disappear this way, and they will never win. Or hear me beg.

Two hacks on her breasts. They were tearing away her womanhood. Their voices were peals of thunder. Her eyesight fled, and it was easier now to inhabit the isle. And then she sensed the isle dwindling. Soon there would be nothing left to hold onto.

Come to me. Not love or regret. They are mere fragments. Come. Embrace me. I am yours.

The isle was loose sand, and she was sinking, stretching one way and then the other without worry. Her lifeline was severed. They would bury her in an unmarked grave.

Oh Lord, she murmured to herself. Minister to my sins. I see your house with windows of narrow lights.

*****

A caribou's head on a two-foot stake appalled Finn. Its tongue lolled over calcified lips, and its glum face made the hut oppressive. The floor, sticky from blood, preserved the rot of rancid meat. The shutters were latched, and a single low-wattage bulb glowed, fueled from the generator. The luminous dials on his wristwatch read four a.m. Then a vicious cry crossed the compound. Finn sprang to the shutter and studied the yard through a fissure in the wood. What he saw spooked him. Straining to get a better view, he rotated his head forty-five degrees clockwise and spied a blonde-haired woman on the ground. An arrow had been driven into one eye and had penetrated the rear of her cranium.

"What's going on?" Finn shouted. He pounded his fist on the shutter when the door opened, the creaky hinge laughing, and Fuentes entered the hut.

"It's all over," Fuentes announced, a pistol in his hand. "You can go home. We don't need your money. We don't want anything from you. The Muslims have what they wanted all along. They have their recognition. The kidnappings are on television and in the newspapers. The rebels are victims and victors. So, keep the money. Shit on it for all they care. The Americans and the priest are doing well. That's the compromise for this media attention."

"Compromise?"

"The Abu Sayyaf made a bargain with the Philippine military and the American government. The children and teachers from Capingpilan Central Elementary School have been liberated. The episode is over."

"And her?"

"Who?" Fuentes asked, impatiently.

"The girl in the yard."

"There is no girl."

Finn pointed. "There, for Christ's sake! That girl with the arrow in her head!"

"Oh, you sacrilegious bastard, that's no girl. It's a man—some foolhardy French journalist who believed his life was worth a photograph. They trussed him up and took him that way, to the camp, so he wouldn't be dead. But he is dead. Why are you so concerned?"

"I thought it was an American."

"You bigot," Fuentes said. With the pistol, he motioned Finn to his knees. Before Finn could react, the muzzle flashed, the volley deafening, as the bullet traced over Finn's hairline.

"I want you to eat the eyes," Fuentes said.

"What? What did you say?" Finn asked in confusion.

Fuentes spoke deliberately. "Its eyes. I want you to eat the caribou's eyes."

"I'm not hungry."

"Do what I tell you."

"I can't."

Blood had darkened the bandage of Fuentes's ear. With his boot, Fuentes dragged a spoon from a stoneware plate of un-milled rice toward Finn and cocked the pistol.

"Pick it up and gouge out an eyeball," Fuentes said.

Finn took the spoon and grappled with the caribou's jaw. He swatted flies away from the head, applied tension on the spoon, and sunk the tip into the caribou's eye socket. With an abrupt twist, he scooped out the eyeball, which hung from the socket, connected by tendons. Finn snatched the eye and spellbound by the milky sphere, he jerked it free from the socket and flung it to the wall.

"You scum. I wanted to see you eat it." Fuentes hawked sputum onto the floor. "I never liked this room."

"It stinks," Finn said.

"It's not that. This is where the wounded stayed without hope of living."

Suddenly the rapid fire of automatic weapons infiltrated the compound, and Fuentes back-pedaled, latched the door, and receded into the night. Finn hurried to the shutter, peeked through a separation in the bamboo slats, as men took refuge behind trees. The hole was too obscure. Raising his leg, and with the heel of his boot, he broke a fist-size gap in the shutter. Rebel soldiers, their weapons poised for the oncoming firefight, sped by Finn's field of vision. One soldier stepped over the journalist and peered skyward, as if expecting armed helicopters. A second later, he keeled over from two rounds to the trunk. Bullets pierced the hut, and Finn lunged for the floor.

During a lull in the skirmish, he tip-toed to the shutter. Soon, mournful cries emanated from within the compound. He was unsure whether they were women, children, or men. Stray bullets continued to tear the coconut palm sheathing. In desperation, he batted the caribou from the stake with a blow to the head. After ripping out the stake, he jammed the tip into the door's hinge. The generator groaned, the bulb expired, and a sulfurous hue saturated the hut. After the third try, the lock shattered, and the door swung open. The compound appeared on high alert, as cries recurred across the compound. He scooted around two dead men in the road and sprinted into the jungle. He had traversed less than ten yards when a blunt object impacted his skull. He wobbled to his knees, nauseated, and tested the side of his head.

"I'm American," Finn said feebly.

The Philippine soldier sneered and plodded on the camp's rough-hewn tract. Finn rose to his feet and followed. The soldier angled his M16 at the tree line. Smoke enshrouded the compound, and the only enduring light was from the three-quarter moon and low-burning campfires.

Finn gestured to the soldier's pistol. The soldier balked, but when they took additional gunfire, rounds peppering the ground near their feet, he consented. Holding the pistol, Finn scanned the jungle perimeter. Overhead, breaking branches marshalled his attention. At a foliated ridge, Lito stood poised. In reflex memory, he swung his rifle toward Finn, who fired first, with the second round bending Lito into the thicket. Finn was in the process of moving toward the ridge when the soldier indicated, with two flicks of his hand, the western side of the compound. Finn obeyed. Enemy rebels came in range, and the soldier shot in an orderly sequence. A mortar exploded, spraying dirt and rocks, and the soldier sprinted along the perimeter, abandoning Finn. In the east, a vague light entered the sky, and Finn found shelter beside a hut. Bullets fractured tree bark, and Finn tasted dried wood pulp in his throat. Slowly, the gunfire diminished.

Within a half hour, the rebels, with hands atop their heads and weapons confiscated, sat in tight groups, monitored by military troops. Soldiers policed the dead.

Finn stowed the pistol beneath his shirt. Walking toward the center of the compound, he glimpsed Fuentes behind a hut, holding a rifle. Fuentes frowned when Finn trudged up to him.

"I wasn't expecting this betrayal," Fuentes said. "I should have, though. That's what you get for trusting one's government."

"First-rate point," Finn said.

"Do you still have the money, the one-hundred thousand dollars?"

"It's in Cotabato City. Marta's information was accurate."

"What does that mean?"

"If you make it out of here, you're a wealthy guy."

"You're blind to reality. The game is nearly over, but I know how to survive such folly."

Fuentes's eyes were deadpan. Finn had seen the same enmity on Rwandan Hutu soldiers returning from a ritual cleansing. At the time, Finn hadn't known they had murdered, mutilated, and raped the Tutsi village inhabitants. Torched the village to cinders. He had watched the soldiers leap from a truck in Butare. Their glazed eyes had passed over him without distinction. He knew from previous encounters to give the troops a wide berth.

"Toss the gun," Fuentes said. "I can see it. Use your head. If you try anything, then I'll just poke this rifle into your mouth and smash your teeth."

Finn rubbed his belt buckle.

"Drop the gun. See, I'm giving you a second break."

"I can't do that," Finn said. "You should run, Captain. Just book out of here. I won't say a word."

Fuentes jammed the rifle barrel against Finn's chin. Scavenger dogs barked, and Finn saw a mongrel drag away a man's arm.

"Everywhere you see, they're killing Muslims," Fuentes said. "I'll shoot you, and they'll bury your sorry ass in a mass grave. Your god will not weep for you."

"I'm an Atheist."

"An Atheist today a Catholic tomorrow."

Yes, Finn said to himself. Revisit Marta's faith.

He looked at his hip and said, "You take it."

Fuentes hurled the pistol into the grass, released the Ak-47 clip, hesitated in an interlude of reflection, and galloped toward the jungle. Finn walked through the camp, ignoring a Philippine military soldier who kick-crotched a prone street-dressed rebel while another soldier shot a fleeing man. The camp's women marched past in one procession, while the hospital staff tended to the wounded. Searching for Marta, Finn inspected nearby dwellings. With a rock, he broke a padlocked hut. In the corner, he observed an anorexic, skulking figure and two terrified eyes.

"Who goes?" Finn called.

"Is it over? Seriously, man, is it over?"

"Yes."

The boy came to his feet, his body shaking in the equatorial heat that had already silenced the insect realm.

"Thank you, man. Oh, man, thank you. They're croakin' everyone around here. Oh shit, man. I thought they were gonna off me. Shit man… oh man… this is crazy."

He was shoeless, his skin the same gauzy color as the morning light. The boy's hands reached for Finn, but Finn reversed himself, and the matchstick arms hugged his hips.

"My name's Diablo. Anthony Diablo. Call me Tony, man."

"Sounds right," Finn said, shoving off. "Someone will be here soon and take you to a truck."

Diablo tagged along as though he had not heard. In the compound, Finn drew near a soldier staring at a figure on the ground at the jungle's rim. The soldier appeared apathetic, as though the person should have had better judgment. He reset his feet and departed. The woman lay on her stomach in hardened mud. Finn recognized Marta by her lanky frame. It was not the country that had killed her. No, Finn conceded, he had killed her. He had killed her with his reckless nature and his unwillingness to commit to anything but himself.

"Yeah," the boy said. "I'll pray with you, man, like wow, man. This is the way we can heal. Let's join hands."

Finn stood on the other side of Marta, away from Diablo who, with head bowed, mumbled in a reticent voice. 'She should get up,' he told himself. 'She should rise.' It was a child's fairyland invocation, foolish and ignorant. She would not get up. Blood darkened the ground around her chest, and red ants massed in her hair.

He knelt, swept mud off the knuckles, and after inspecting her wrist, he noted the white hand's veinless exterior. The fingers were stubby, whereas Marta's fingers were lean and aristocratic. The nails had been bitten to the cuticle. He planted his hand around her shoulder-blade, and it was more difficult than he imagined, turning her over, the body unforgiving, resisting him, as if trying to hold on to a last sliver of privacy.

"Frances," Tony Diablo wept, spinning away from the Peace Corps girl.

Her nose was bruised, and a black line, thin as string, scarred her upper lip. She had been shot in the neck. Finn took shirts from a clothesline and laid them over the body. His spine ached, and he watched the nutty kid pray. At a nearby hut, Fuentes stood on the porch, handcuffed, smoking a cigarette. His ear, minus the bandage, had a distinctive elf-like appearance.

Fuentes smiled, leaving Finn with the impression the two were compatriots, linked to a predestined future of retaliation. He turned away and thought of azure seas, feeling the sensation of the waves against his body, and swimming with dolphins in the Pacific Ocean, as he had as a boy in southern California. Motionless, he underwent the same exhaustion now as then, the same fatigue, after spending hours in the Pacific, and the same lack of desire to do anything but to float on the ocean water. He wished to let his muscles sag and remain slack, but he was a marooned vessel, moored to the girl, Frances. She was not Marta. There was a cursory relief in that fact. But she carried the same gravity inside him, as though she were tugging at the chain that wedded his balls and belly, heart and head.

I'll take you home to your family, he said to himself. Some will say I royally screwed up, and your family will stare at me in their confusion and hatred and say I killed you.

In the middle of the compound, with his hands against his chest, a man in rags knelt over a dead rebel—Fuentes's hooligan, Elwin. The man's clothes were grubby, and Finn suspected he was the Chinko priest. On his feet, the bearded priest waved a disfigured arm at government soldiers. He marked the air with erratic crosses until a soldier came over and passed him his canteen. The priest sobbed. Finn could hear the shrill voice, his hand limp on the soldier's belt.

"You were the priority," Finn said, staring at the priest. "You, you son of a bitch. You were the fucking priority."

As if embarrassed by his outburst, Finn advanced two steps to the jungle's border, aware of the maze of vegetation, the birds chirping in the branches, and the fecund undergrowth. In his exhausted mind, he journeyed into the jungle's interior, using a machete on woody vines as he hiked unconcerned about snakes and crocodiles. And when he could take himself just so far, to a point he could not comprehend, the girl at his feet beckoned, as a breeze ruffled her shirt. Squatting, Finn tucked the loosened shirt into her jeans and smoothed her hair with gentle strokes. He had failed in his mission. There was nothing to say, and there was nothing to be done. This girl was dead, deader than hell, and Finn knew he would be cursed for it. He sat and stretched his legs out, as the sunlight rent him in half.

A military Jeep entered the compound. It carried four civilians: one journalist, two photojournalists, and Jacky Ciros. Digesting the battlefield, Ciros went over to Finn. He wore a t-shirt with a Peanuts cartoon logo, a Detroit Tiger ball cap, and army boots.

"This is splendid," Ciros said to Finn, ogling the compound. "They're professional. The Philippine Special Forces are the crème of the lot. They zeroed in on the rebels and perfectly executed the operation. We only had minor casualties."

"I thought there was a treaty," Finn said.

"The Philippine military were surgeons," Ciros said, flouting Finn. "The sentries were speechless by their military stealth. The taxi man, one of ours, gave me the location. Everything followed as planned. And where are the Americans and the priest? Yes, the priest. He's important. The Vatican is uneasy. They've been busting my hump about him."

"He's doing holy work. Check the infirmary."

Ciros removed his sunglasses. "Who's this?" he asked. He pulled the shirt from the girl's face. His belly bulged over his belt buckle. "What can one say? I recognize her. Such a dear. I met her before she came south for the Peace Corps." He belched, an exhaustive whistle. "Pretty."

"Who do you work for?" Finn asked.

"Our government. You should have figured that out by now."

"What happened?"

"I'm not sure what you mean."

"The goddamn agreement between the Abu Sayyaf and the Philippine government," Finn said.

"Flim-flam at its best. How can you depend on people who blow up churches and murder children?" Ciros covered the girl with the shirt. "The U.S. government can't admonish such a contract. The extremists dishonor every document they sign. They have, for years, and the Philippine government was concerned about the prisoners. The military had the assistance of the CIA. Therefore, this template was set in motion. Shit, where have you been? You know the way these southern provinces function."

"Where's Marta?" Finn asked.

"I'm not sure. But we'll find her." Ciros lit a cigarette and asked, "Who's the man on the porch?"

"Your cohort, Captain Fuentes."

"I must have a word with him and our Colonel Indaman. The Colonel led the assault. No need to hold the captain as if he were a terrorist. He has valuable information."

"Say good-bye to the fat man," Finn said to the girl.

Ciros tilted his cap up. "Not humorous, Eddie."

Finn leveled his ear next to her mouth. "She wants you to know she forgives you, Jacky. She forgives all of us."

"You're a sick puppy."

"We all need some humor to lighten our days," Finn replied.

"You shouldn't be here," Ciros said. "You take it all too damn seriously."

Nearby, Diablo was sitting, lotus-style, chanting, his eyes half-closed. A soldier approached the boy and spat within a foot of him.

Finn stepped up to Diablo and said, "Let's go."

Diablo's abscessed lips were bleeding, and Finn stroked his greasy hair to elicit a response.

"Let me help you," Finn said, earnestly.

Sagging to his knees, Finn hooked his arm around the boy's waist, his cheek against Diablo's, not caring who saw. When a soldier strutted toward the girl, Finn scowled at him until he did an about-face.

Finn said, "Take my hand, Tony. It's time."

The boy did as he was told, and Finn felt a faint pressure in his palm. As they struggled to their feet, the pressure increased, and Finn discerned Diablo's belief that he was protected and that there is such a kingdom, as is written in storybooks, where he could live and not be afraid.

* * * * *

At the Hotel Romeo, Finn checked Rudolph's room. It was vacant. Most likely, the maid had chanced upon the body. In his own room, he lit two incense candles, and for a split second he fancied his pipe and opium. A few hours' sleep would reinvigorate him. But a quiet disillusionment now occupied his mind. Perhaps it was the dead girl's shirt sleeve beckoning him, as it had at the rebel compound, which had re-adjusted his perception. One's future, he considered, can change upon a gesture.

The incense sedated his brain, and he recalled his daughter and her laughter. In his thoughts, he constructed her face, a sensation that humbled him. Then Rudolph entered this newly designed shelter of family.

"It's wise you let the hophead drugs go," Rudolph said. "It'll smoke your soul and leave you impotent. And, man, you've got to reproduce. Spread the corn. Only government nukes can emasculate you, and I say that's 50-50 now-a-days. So, live each hour, bro. Harm no one."

A double rap on the door snapped Finn from this alternate reality. Ciros and Criselda stood in the doorway, and Finn received them cordially. He recalled Rudolph's mantra as he closed the door: Harm no one.

"I'm here to tell you, don't go home," Ciros said.

"Home?"

"Wherever it is you live."

"People are after you," Criselda said.

"I've heard that threat before," Finn replied.

"I told you he was a moron," Ciros said to Criselda. "Finn, we intercepted a rebel cable saying your ass is grass. They mean to track you down. They're convinced you were behind the assault on the compound."

"That's insane."

"Greetings from schizophrenic bandits at play," Ciros said.

Criselda's hands were in her jean pockets, her face stoic. Her hair appeared brittle, as if charged with static. She had recently soaped her face and hands, the fragrance bathing the room.

"It's over, isn't it?" Finn said.

"It's never over," Ciros said. "This war has gone on for a millennium."

"I see. Will you be okay?" Finn asked.

"Tip-top," Ciros responded.

"I'm great," Criselda said.

His back ailed him, and Finn sat on the bed. There were no chairs in the room.

"What are you smirking at?" Ciros asked Finn. "Oh, never mind." Ciros went toward the door and stopped halfway. "Take this threat seriously. Criselda and I will offer a prayer for you in church."

"I'm indebted to you both," Finn said, sensing a personal isolation that no warning could pacify.

"Let's go, Cris. This lunatic doesn't get it." Seizing the doorknob, Ciros added, "I'd say this was only business, but I detest those who use that phrase. It's never just business. So, Eddie, be clever, find a new residence and location; keep an eye out."

"Thanks. I mean it."

"Sure. Cris?"

Her eyes moistened. She daubed at her nose and left with Ciros. The door closed, and a rush of hot wind entered the room. Exhaustion stole over him. There was no urgent chore that demanded his attention. Duty revolved in another galaxy. There was sleep, though, and he would let sleep overcome him and carry his infirmity to a sedate region. He saw sleep approach, ready to soothe his muscles, ganglia, and nerves, and when she was so near he could sample her breath, he cornered her with his furor. He wanted to know why he had survived the rebel camp and been given dread instead of a governable emotion; he needed to know what he could have done to save a single life, and whether all was predestined. He shook his head. His self-indulgence was deflating. He sensed sleep marshalling her army, pressing on his wayward thinking and, as his lethargy urged his wrists from his knees and his body dipped onto the bed, he knew he was undeserving to learn the answer to such a meditation.

*****

In the morning, Finn spoke with an eighteen-year-old, baby-faced police officer at the Mabini Street Station who informed him that Rudolph was at the Cotabato City Medical Center morgue. At the outpatient booth, Finn paid the tab for holding Rudolph's body, which would be driven to the airport. Finn wired Carmelita and gave her the basics. She would, in all likelihood, want to bury him in the mango orchard Rudolph cherished.

Hours later, Finn sat at the airport, gazing at the immense sky and the banana trees that bordered the tarmac. An untethered caribou had rambled close to the runway. No one spoke to him. Maybe they sensed this *kano* was hauling three dead bodies to the mainland, Rudolph and the two Peace Corps volunteers, Tommy O'Connor and Frances Harrison. Or, most likely, he wasn't right in the head. Glancing at the main doors, he hoped Marta would come striding into the vestibule. Her silence worried him. He recalled the water she had given him when he was shackled to the metal pole, and the way she had massaged the water through his hair, and the benevolence in her eyes. He had been forced to exit the terrorists' compound before finding her, and Ciros had not informed him of her whereabouts.

For certain, Fuentes would not be the one entering the airport. A hundred yards from the compound, Finn had seen Fuentes hanging by the neck from a rope, over a tree branch, his feet dangling, and the blindfold having fallen over his nose. There had been an inquisitive slant to one eye—a conspirator recognizing the end to a repugnant joke. Mourning for Fuentes speedily evaporated as the Jeep worked its way out of the jungle and onto a paved road that windowed onto grassland and low-lying hills.

He flew with the bodies of the three dead Americans to the main island of Luzon and in Manila, he leased a refrigerated truck for a scandalous price and rode with Rudolph on the northern highway. The American Embassy had the detail of shipping home the two dead Peace Corps volunteers. At San Fernando, Finn, the truck operator, Manny, and his cousin, Gilbert, rode in silence toward Olongapo. The heat simmered in wavy lines, and the fields were torched the color of roasted pecans. Traveling west, Finn anticipated the salty sea air. Behind him, the refrigerated motor whined, and he recalled that Rudolph had not spoken to him in a while. Perhaps he was simply preoccupied with other tasks.

At the beginning of the ride, he had chatted with Manny, but the rising temperature had overpowered him, and he had fallen quiet. As they scaled a hill toward San Fernando, the road grew spacious, and on the wayside, on a shanty store's outer wall, military hardware was present from the former American Navy base at Subic Bay. There were a variety of items, from potties to hubcaps and Zippo lighters, military fatigues, ashtrays made from M16 shell casings, and the centerpiece—half a jeep stapled to the wallboards.

"You like this country?" Manny asked.

"Yes, I do."

"I want to go to America, and you want to stay. But you can go or stay, and I have to drive this cargo."

"That's geo-politics for you."

"Why do you like the Philippines?"

Finn tapped the door. Tropical heat lingered on his fingertips.

"It's peaceful," he said.

Manny laughed and gunned the engine.

In late afternoon, Carmelita stood in the doorway of her home in a calico dress and sandals. A rawboned look had overtaken her once-handsome face. She smiled ever so slightly at Finn, as if he might have been lying and the telegram she had received had been a hoax. But he knew she realized the truth when she saw the casket behind him, borne by Manny and Gilbert. She pivoted one-eighty, and her ponytail danced at her belt line. With a flip of her hand, she invited Finn to follow.

Tired from the journey, Manny and Gilbert rested on the porch and Carmelita brought them bottled Cokes and two glasses topped with ice chunks. The casket rested at the side of the house, away from the sun, among the ylang-ylang flowers, yellow-green in color and streamlined like starfish. Thickets of azaleas encompassed the yard. Finn sat in a chair at the kitchen table near the doorway. A cat leaped onto the casket's walnut top, pawed the wood, and jumped off.

"What did you bury him in?" Carmelita asked, fixing a pot of coffee.

"His regular clothes," Finn replied.

Her shoulders arched, and Finn saw his mistake. Before he could reply, she said, "Sugar, *guapo*?"

He imagined she wanted Rudolph dressed in a modern suit, his beard trimmed, and his feet clad in leather Thom McAn shoes. Instead, Rudolph wore dungarees, a paisley shirt, and sneakers. But Finn had prevented an autopsy. He wouldn't let a pathologist dissect his friend. A postmortem went against Rudolph's karma principles.

"Just black," Finn said.

He knitted his fingers, unsure how to behave before Carmelita. In the kitchen, time appeared frozen. At any moment, Finn believed Rudolph would come strutting in, sweaty and bearish from picking mangos from his orchard, his arms cradling the green fruit, inhaling the food simmering on the stove. On the walls hung Carmelita's paintings, still lifes and murals, and one of Rudolph, deeply tanned, his facial features well-defined, shaven cheeks save a white goatee, his eyes a royal blue. John Coltrane's recording, *A Love Supreme,* played from a phonograph. There was a frayed San Diego Padres ball cap on the wall rack, Rudolph's red and brown sneakers toe-crimped on the door mat, and in the adjoining room, books cluttered his desk. The house seemed enormous without him.

The coffee was hot. Carmelita took the seat opposite his and said, "I know where he'd like to rest. Not very far from here."

"I'm sorry," Finn said.

"He was a crazy man."

Carmelita soaked the coffee cups in the sink, strode onto the porch, and Finn trailed behind. Carmelita oversaw the boys to the next stage of the burial process. They picked up the casket, walked past the ylang-ylang flowers, lowered the casket onto a cart, and the party advanced into the orchard. The air was thicker in the sculpted rows, and the mango trees were bare, save for the purplish buds on the branches. Furrows had been raked in the dirt.

A noise reverberated from inside the casket and Carmelita hesitated, steadying a hand on the lid. Finn had packed four San Miguel beers and a bottle of Emperador whiskey in the casket. He wanted his friend to know he was going to Wonderland with a few amenities to aid his ascent. They stopped in a fertile expanse where the ground had been hoed for new seedlings. The hole had already been dug and Finn, standing near the edge, lobbed a rock into the pit. A bird flew up, passing within a hair's breadth of his cheek.

'Omens', Finn thought, without reservation. A sign from the land of enchantment.

The two boys transported the casket from the cart to the grave. They worked two ropes beneath the casket and stretched each rope over the hole. In silence, Finn walked to the other side of the grave. Manny took hold of Finn's rope, and Gilbert gripped the other one. After a minute's contemplation, Carmelita stepped toward Finn and held her part of the rope. On Manny's count of two, they pulled, and the casket rose off the ground. Together, Finn and Carmelita took three steps to the rear, until the casket was positioned over the hole. Feeling the weight, all four let the rope slide through their hands, gradually, then more rapidly. As the rope let out, stinging their palms, the casket descended. Once the casket settled on the bottom, they tossed in the ropes. No one spoke. In the orchard, there was the rustle of someone close by.

The Philippine boys waited for Carmelita. Rudolph and Carmelita had never been officially married in the eyes of the Catholic Church, but that mattered to neither, now. She strolled away from the grave without a word. Manny gestured at the cart and the mound of dirt. Finn nodded, and each boy took one of the cart's struts and headed out of the orchard. Removing the shovel from the mound, Finn began to fill in the hole.

The heavy shovelfuls of dirt focused his concentration on the act, arresting his thoughts. Halfway done, Finn paused, and he recalled Rudolph's stories about the seedy side of San Francisco in the Mission District, in the early days, before the shore was swamped with emigrants and malls, and how the Pacific had been one protracted sweep of ultramarine, and the whales in winter could be viewed from the shore as they migrated south to Mexico. Finn remembered the anecdotes Rudolph had told of being a soldier in Vietnam during the war. And that, even when drunk, Rudolph spoke with reverence of his love for Carmelita. It was her love that on countless occasions had lifted him out of the drunk tank and melancholia and meanness, and every morning she was there beside him, asking in her own special way, for this man to make love to her.

Daylight was fading, and Finn picked up his pace. He did not know his way to the house at night. Finished, he ran the spade on the grave, smoothing the earth. Carmelita would return at a later date, he assumed, to affix a marker.

Finn stowed the shovel at the gravesite. On his way, lengthy shadows cloaked the land, and the sun was an orange rind on the horizon. A gust sifted through the orchard. Someone had remained behind. After several minutes, he heard footfalls directly behind him. Nimbly, he ducked below a tree limb as a girl approached.

"Hey," Finn called out. She halted, and he stepped onto the path. "Who are you? What are you doing here?"

She faced him, tightening her arms across her stomach. "Girlie, sir. My name's Girlie. I was a friend of Jose."

"And Mr. Rudolph?"

"I liked him."

"Is there anything you're not saying?"

She kicked a stone, and said, "I wanted to be a part of this family. I felt only warmth and kindness with José and Mr. Rudolph and Miss Carmelita. There was always sweet music in the house." She shook her head. "I thought if I came, some of the loneliness I feel would leave."

"Like magic," Finn said.

"Something like that."

"And how do you feel?"

"It didn't work," she said.

"We should hurry home."

The breath left her chest. "I like this time of day," Girlie said.

Finn looked at the leafless trees and the night descending. "I don't understand why you're here."

"I have happy memories of this place."

"Oh." Finn held a slim branch with his fingers. "I can hardly see," he said.

She went up to him and touched his arm. "I know the way."

They walked ahead and stopped where the orchard ended and the pasture to the house began. The moonshine shone brightly, and the pasture resembled a lake of white water. In the dark somewhere, birds sang and a solo light in the house was lit behind a red curtain. Finn removed his hand from hers.

The evening was windless, and he stared at the immensity of the short distance from where they stood to the house, and he believed it could take a lifetime to cross that stretch of ground and knock on the door and say the right words.

THE END

ABOUT THE AUTHOR

For thirty years, Marc Schiffman lived and worked in Japan, South Korea, and Thailand. He has traveled extensively throughout Asia, including the Philippines, Cambodia, Vietnam, Laos, Malaysia and Indonesia. He has published short stories in literary journals and magazines and has two previously published novels. Marc continues to teach for the University of Maryland Global Campus (UMGC). When asked if he could change one thing about himself he replied, "I'd give more and take less" and instead of being a writer he would be a "pilgrim/traveler/itinerant detective."

IF YOU ENJOYED THIS BOOK

Please write a review.
This is important to the author and helps to get the word out to others
Visit

PENMORE PRESS

www.penmorepress.com

All Penmore Press books are available directly through our website, amazon.com, Barnes and Noble and Nook, Sony Reader, Apple iTunes, Kobo books and via leading bookshops across the United States, Canada, the UK, Australia and Europe.

WINDMILL POINT

BY

JIM STEMPEL

Gripping historical fiction vividly brings to life two desperate weeks during the spring of 1864, when the resolution of the American Civil War was balanced on a razor's edge.

At the time, both North and South had legitimate reasons to conclude they were very near victory. Ulysses S. Grant firmly believed that Lee's Army of Northern Virginia was only one great assault away from implosion; Lee knew that the political will in the North to prosecute the war was on the verge of collapse.

Jim Stempel masterfully sets the stage for one of the most horrific battles of the Civil War, contrasting the conversations of decision-making generals with chilling accounts of how ordinary soldiers of both armies fared in the mud, the thunder, and the bloody fighting on the battlefield.

"We must destroy this army of Grant's before he gets to the James River. If he gets there it will become a siege, and then it will be a mere question of time." – General Lee.

PENMORE PRESS
www.penmorepress.com

Better To Die

BY

Steve Smith

1996: Sergeant Nick Adair defends British Army border post "Hotel 55" from being overrun by the IRA, but the only witnesses to his bravery tell a different tale, with themselves as heroes and Adair castigated as a coward.

2021: After a five-year stint with the French Foreign Legion, Jack Adair is determined to have a career as a Sandhurst officer, preferably in his father's old regiment, the King's Royal Rangers. But the KRR considers itself elite, professionally and socially, with scant room for a rough diamond like Adair. Cadet Vyvyan Phillips is more the thing: younger son of General Philips, the decorated hero of the Hotel 55 incident. The General's reputation shines so brightly, it blinds everyone but Jack to Vyvyan's incompetence.

There is far more to the murky events connected to Hotel 55 but over time they have been either suppressed or ignored. The rivalry between Adair and Phillips extends beyond the confines of training and field command. Both take a keen interest in fellow officer Gemma Page, of Intel Corps. And then the battalion deploys to Gaziantep.

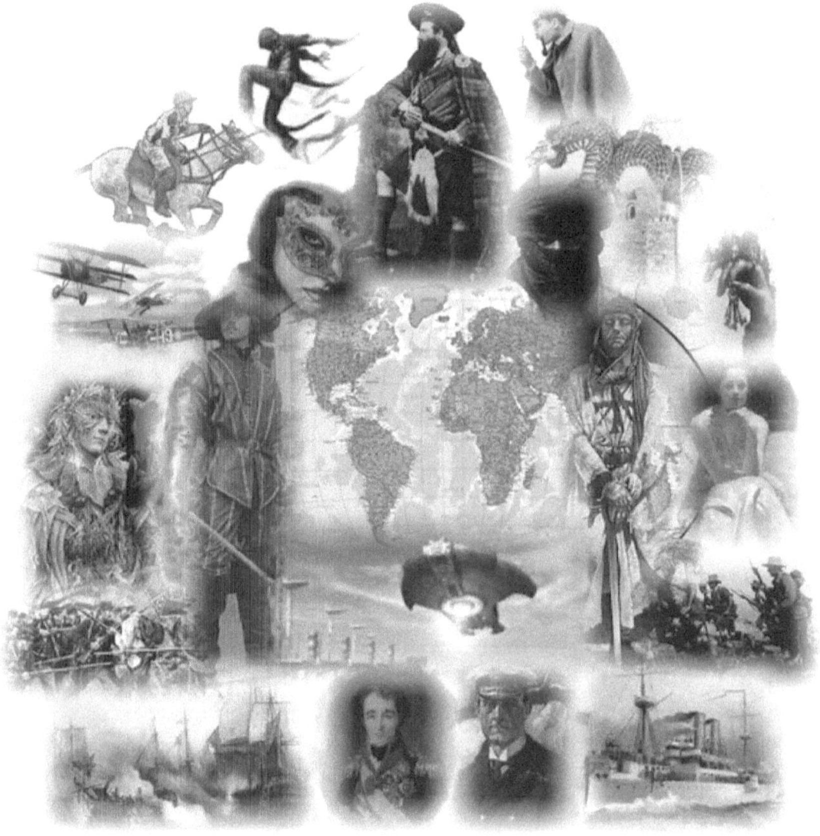

Penmore Press

Challenging, Intriguing, Adventurous, Historical and Imaginative

www.penmorepress.com